THE Corpse WITH THE Pearly Smile

CATHY ACE

FOUR TAILS PUBLISHING LTD.

PRAISE FOR THE CAIT MORGAN MYSTERIES

"…Ace is, well, an ace when it comes to plot and description."
– *The Globe and Mail*

"…a sparkling, well-plotted and quite devious mystery in the cozy tradition…" – *Hamilton Spectator*

"…If all of this suggests the school of Agatha Christie, it's no doubt what Cathy Ace intended. She is, as it fortunately happens, more than adept at the Christie thing." – *Toronto Star*

"Cait unravels the…mystery using her eidetic memory and her powers of deduction, which are worthy of Hercule Poirot."
– *The Jury Box, Ellery Queen Mystery Magazine*

"This author always takes us on an adventure. She always makes us think. She always brings the setting to life. For those reasons this is one of my favorite series."
– *Escape With Dollycas Into A Good Book*

"…touches of Christie or Marsh but with a bouquet of Kinsey Millhone." – *The Globe and Mail*

"…a testament to an author who knows how to tell a story and deliver it with great aplomb." – *Dru's Musings*

"…perfect for those that love travel, food, and/or murder (reading it, not committing it)." – *BOLO Books*

"In the finest tradition of Agatha Christie…Ace brings us the closed-room drama, with a dollop of romantic suspense and historical intrigue." – *Library Journal*

For the man who held my hand as we
watched our first Tahitian sunset

Floating

I dragged myself out of bed with my eyes still half-closed, then pulled open the floor-to-ceiling glass doors that led to our private deck. Squinting, I could see that the post-dawn haze was still blurring the shape of the island of Moorea just twenty miles away, across the turquoise sea. Our over-water bungalow was protected from the ocean's gentle swell by a coral reef, which enclosed a crystalline lagoon, and the air was full of the scent of the fragrant *tiaré* shrubs, so typical of Tahiti, that flourished in pots on our deck.

I stretched, then wandered back to luxuriate on my fluffy pillows again, wondering if I could cope with yet another day in paradise. I told myself I'd manage…somehow. I gazed at the print of Gaugin's *Pastorales Tahitiennes* on the wall. I didn't particularly care for the depiction of a red body of water beneath a green sky, with Tahitian women shown beside a blossom tree, but I liked the fact there was a dog in the foreground. I told myself it wouldn't be long before I'd be ruffling Marty's fur, in our own home, back in Canada.

Bud lay beside me, snoring gently, and I turned my head so I could watch my husband's profile; his tanned face was beatific, his hands clenched like otter paws above the coverlet, and his eyelids fluttered gently. I felt momentarily overwhelmed by the knowledge that he was safe beside me; the medics in Australia had assured us that he was almost back to his usual level of health. However, they'd advised against him being in a big metal tube thirty-odd thousand feet in the air for a while yet, so we'd cruised from Sydney to Tahiti's capital of Papeete, and were due to embark on the second leg of our trip back to Vancouver on another ship which was arriving in five days' time.

The Legrand Resort had been our temporary home for the past three weeks, thanks to Bud discovering that an old colleague from his early RCMP days had taken the leap from running a bed and breakfast in Montreal in his retirement, to opening up a boutique luxury resort in French Polynesia. We'd been only too happy to accept his offer to be his 'test guest' guinea pigs while we killed some time between sailings. But now the day was approaching when we'd have to say goodbye to Henri Legrand himself, his lovely wife Fleur, and their oh so wonderful resort manager Mahana, whose smile and laughter seemed to carry her through the multitude of tasks she had to undertake every day, while all the time living up to the Tahitian meaning of her name: "sun". She glowed despite the challenges she faced, and her joyous disposition infected all those around her. Indeed, the people we'd got to know at the resort – the staff who were preparing for the opening – had begun to feel like our extended family; we'd had such a wonderful time with them all.

I got out of bed again, rinsed myself off in the shower – mindful of not allowing body lotion and deodorant to get into the sea – then wriggled into my swimsuit. Never having learned to swim, I'd initially found the idea of staying in a bungalow balanced on spindly-looking legs over a lagoon to be quite alarming. However, knowing that the water beneath us was just a few feet deep had allayed my fears, though I'd stuck to using the infinity pool to bob about in rather than braving the lagoon when we'd first arrived. With some persuasion from Bud, I'd gradually trained myself to not feel too unnerved by the sand that shifted beneath my feet, nor the tiny fish that sparkled in the sunlight in what amounted to a natural swimming pool. Unfortunately, some of them liked to nibble at me, which was a horrific feeling, so I'd learned to bat them away with a strong swishing of my hand. Finally, I'd become accustomed to clambering down the little ladder attached to our deck to take a dip in the clear, protected waters every morning. I like to wade, and bounce, and I've even developed the confidence to float about on my back a bit, relishing the feeling of buoyancy.

I allowed myself a few moments to study the way the clouds were sitting atop the now visible peak of Mount Rotui on Moorea, then dunked myself under as far as my shoulders and pushed around the corner of our bungalow toward the view of the open sea beyond the protective coral reef. I was heading for a spot where I could float free and just *be*…when someone bumped into me.

Go away, this is my time alone, was what I thought; "Oops, sorry", was what I said…of course.

As I turned to properly apologize to whomever was invading what I'd come to think of as "my space", I lost my footing and sank beneath the surface, which sent me into an immediate panic. I launched my body up out of the water as though I'd been under there, gasping for air, for an age – only to get an even bigger shock: I hadn't been bumped into by a person at all…well, I had, but this one was face down, and completely motionless.

In my head, *Someone's mucking about* became *This person's in serious trouble…or worse* within half a second, and I did the one thing I always abhor when I see it happen on the screen – I screamed my head off. In my defense, I was calling for help.

All my decades'-old Girl Guide training kicked in; I struggled to turn the body onto its back, and lifted its head. It was a young man. I held up his chin with one hand, hooked my other under his armpit, then pulled as hard as I could toward the shore. As I tried to stop my feet slipping on the sand beneath them, I forced my own weight – and that of what I was increasingly certain was a dead body – through the surprising resistance of the glittering water, hoping someone would hear my cries.

Sinking

By the time I reached the white, sandy beach, a familiar figure was running toward me. Mahana's pale blue *pareo* and flowing dark hair fluttered as she covered the distance between us. Every part of me was vibrating with the effects of adrenaline, so I gladly accepted her help pulling the young man's body out of the water. She's some years younger than me – probably in her mid-forties – but lithe and fit, so she really did do more of the heavy lifting than I could manage.

A shocked: "He's dead," were the first words out of Mahana's lips.

"We should try to revive him," I replied, but his staring eyes told me she was right. I just didn't want her to be. I relented with a resigned: "Yes. He is."

Mahana whispered something in French, crossed herself, then she spoke quietly in what I recognized as the local Tahitian tongue. "He is on his journey now. I'll make some calls," she added somberly, moving away.

"Cait? Cait! What's happened?" Bud shouted to me as he cantered along the wooden walkway that led from our bungalow to the beach. I could see that his tanned legs were glistening below his floral boardshorts and his hair gleamed white in the sun. Even at a distance I could tell he'd pulled on his favorite powder-blue linen shirt over a wet body; I reckoned he must have got out of the shower when he heard my cries for help.

I stood and yelled back, "No need to run…I'm fine." I didn't add, "He's dead," because I didn't want to say the words aloud.

As I looked down at the corpse beside me, I could see that the young Polynesian man must have been vibrant in life: his musculature was well developed, his shoulder-length black hair lay in a halo on the sand, and he had what would have been a handsome face, were it not for the dreadful, dead eyes. I turned away. I've seen too many bodies in my life to need to focus on another, and this time…well, I didn't need to hunt for clues: the man had clearly drowned, and quite recently, by the looks of it, because there were almost no signs of predation on the body.

Before Bud could reach me, Mahana was beside me again. "His mother will be devastated," she whispered.

"You know him?" I was surprised.

"I was in school with her. Roimata Teriimana. She used to call him Little Vai. He was her pride and joy. Her only child. He was her…prince." Mahana's voice caught in her throat.

"You and his mother are close?"

She spoke quietly. "As children, yes. Even as young women, in college. But Roimata loved a man I…didn't like. We lost touch, so I did not know Vaiarii as a child – though Roimata and I have connected again, recently. Vaiarii tried to be a good son. But sometimes sons don't understand that all their mother really wants is their love and understanding, not…other things. She has had a bad year; so much sadness in her life. But she seems to be starting to find hope again. Now? This will be very hard for her. I hope this will not break her. But who can say? Roimata is a strong woman, and she can certainly rely upon the community. We all support each other as we can when life is difficult, which it often is. Families have been on this small island for many, many generations. We're all connected, somehow. Entangled. Never to escape our common fate, you might say."

Knowing that Tahiti was such a small island – only twenty-five kilometers at its widest point, and basically round, with most of the habitable land being around the coastal fringe – I could understand how the folks who lived here might well all know of each other, even if they didn't actually know each other. But I was particularly struck by Mahana's strange description of entanglement.

When Bud joined us, he looked down at the body, then hugged me close. He whispered, "Too far gone for help." It wasn't a question, but I agreed anyway. He turned to Mahana. "Authorities alerted?" She nodded at her phone. He added, "Could you take Cait to get a hot, sweet drink, please, Mahana? I'll stay here."

"I'll need to tell Henri, of course," Mahana spoke quietly. "Come…I'll make tea for you, Cait. It will help with the shock. We should grab some towels on the way. You look cold."

I was dripping wet, and Mahana was right, I was feeling weirdly chilly, given that the air was already warm. Towels and hot tea sounded like an excellent idea. I forced a smile, and replied, "Thanks, I could do with both."

I kissed Bud, and we both assured each other we were just fine – me after finding a dead man, and him after moving faster than he had done in several weeks. I joined Mahana, and we made our way past the infinity pool that bounded part of the lagoon, then across the massive deck which adjoined the open-air bar, and the large restaurant beside it. Everywhere was deserted: Bud and I were the resort's only "trial guests", but Henri and Fleur Legrand were so close to opening up that the entire place looked welcoming, with jolly blue-and-white-striped umbrellas standing to attention beside lounge chairs, and tables and chairs ready to accept those who fancied a drink during the day, or before dinner. Even the lights decorating the bar and its entrance were illuminated.

As we approached the main building, Mahana muttered, "Those lights shouldn't be on. That's a waste of electricity." She typed a note on her phone as she marched to the bank of switches behind the bar and flicked one, which I thought showed an unusual ability to compartmentalize, given the tragic circumstances. She continued, "Who knows how this might affect the opening. Who'll want to swim in a place where a man has died? That's not a good thing to do. Though maybe the tourists won't care."

The sharpness in Mahana's tone took me aback, but I didn't feel the time was right to comment. I wondered what the belief system of the dead man might have been, and realized that my understanding of Polynesian traditions surrounding death and the afterlife didn't go much further than knowing that their ancient beliefs were essentially animist – with all living things being imbued with a spiritual or god-like aspect – and that those who had died were considered to continue their existence on another plane, undertaking a journey that was largely dictated by how they'd acted in life. However, I wondered if the dead man had been brought up as a staunch Catholic or Protestant, both religions having sent enough missionaries to the islands to convert the entire population back in the 1800s. I had no clue, so decided to not say anything at all.

As I waited for my tea, sitting on one of the bar's typically French rattan chairs, with their blue-and-white woven pattern, I mused upon how I'd spent the past few weeks largely immersed in the delights of luxuriating at the resort; while Bud and I had toured the entire island a few times, we'd mainly dabbled in the "attractions", rather than bothering to do a deeper, more meaningful, dive into the local indigenous history – an oversight I promised myself I'd attend to as soon as possible. Tahiti had made an enduring impression upon me, that much was true, but largely – initially – because I'd been taken aback by how utterly French the island had felt. Yes, there was an exotic air about the place – as in the fact that the Notre Dame cathedral was a bright yellow – but I hadn't expected to see the French patisseries, cafés, restaurants, and…well, everything being written in French, and mainly hearing French being spoken, which just goes to show how ill-prepared Bud and I had been for our "visit".

At that moment, however, I was glad to swaddle myself in two massive beach towels as Mahana busied herself behind the bar, eventually producing a pot of tea in what she called "The British Style". Henri had explained to Bud and me that he was aiming to make the resort appeal to the French, Brits, Aussies, New Zealanders, Canadians, and Americans – rich ones, of course, and with no children or minors allowed – and had therefore ensured that every element of the catering had been developed to satisfy the differing, and no doubt demanding, needs of each culture.

As I sipped the tea, it tasted like the best I'd ever had – which is saying a lot for a Welshwoman whose late mother had prided herself on the fact that the teapot in the house was always warm, and the kettle always ready to boil.

"Have one of these." Mahana held a plate toward me.

"Good grief, Eloise must be up at a ridiculous hour for these to be fresh at this time of the morning." I knew that the resort's chef, Eloise Tremblay-Martin, was hard-working; I'd become used to seeing her tall, willowy figure dashing about when she left her kitchen – which wasn't often. She seemed to be forever in a rush, with her face always a bit pink beneath her severely shorn chestnut hair, which I'd imagined was as short as it was for practical reasons; sitting in the shady bar was warm enough, I dreaded to think how hot a working kitchen could get.

Mahana replied with a surprising smile. "Eloise isn't in the kitchen yet; she preps these at night so Fleur herself can cook them each morning for those of us who need a very early breakfast. Once they're ready, Fleur pops them into a warming drawer so they're there for all the staff to take, as they want. It's Fleur's special gift to us…to get up early to bake them. We all love Eloise's *pain au chocolat*, though Fleur teases us by insisting upon always calling them *chocolatines*, which I am sure you know is the Canadian name for them."

I suspected that both pastries on the plate had been meant for Mahana herself, so replied, "Thanks, they look good. I'll take one, but only if you'll have the other."

We sat in silence, eating and drinking, and gazing pointedly toward the sea…rather than at the beach. The warm, rich, flaky pastry lifted my spirits as well as my glucose levels to such an extent that I was feeling much more my usual self by the time I'd finished it, along with a second cup of sugary tea.

"Thanks for this, Mahana, it was thoughtful of you."

Mahana smiled again, and, as always, her smile was accompanied by a joyous little chuckle. "It is my pleasure. This was a difficult start to the day for you. I am so terribly sorry for…everything." I suspected she was thinking of the young life that had been cut short, rather than me. My suspicion was confirmed when she added, "Roimata has had such a difficult life. This will devastate her."

Mahana's tone suggested she was speaking as much to herself as to me, and – for once – I didn't want to pry; a woman's child was dead, and that would be a tremendous blow for anyone, whatever their life had been like up to the seismic moment when they received the news. The terrible anguish that inevitably follows in the wake of a sudden death overwhelmed me for a moment.

Mahana checked her phone. "Where can Henri be? He hasn't replied to my texts."

When Henri Legrand himself rushed into the bar from the kitchen beyond moments later, his expression immediately informed me that Mahana's message about the tragedy had reached him; his watery blue eyes were bulging, and his face was glowing red above his large, broad-shouldered body. Upon first meeting Bud's old colleague, I'd thought that his choice of a Van Dyke beard, topped by a mustache with curled, waxed points, represented an enormous commitment to his daily personal grooming; now, the parts of his face not covered by his neatly trimmed snowy beard were stubbly, and his equally snowy mustache was completely droopy. I suspected that Mahana's texts had reached him before he'd had time for his morning ablutions.

He gushed, "I was on my way back from Papeete when I got your texts, Mahana. Is that him? The Teriimana boy? With Bud on the beach, over there?"

Mahana nodded. "Yes. It is Vaiarii Teriimana."

Mahana's French accent always sounded somewhat different to Henri's: his was thick Québécois, hers, Polynesian. Bud and I had struggled a bit when we'd arrived, but everyone who'd been hired to work at the resort could speak English, and Henri encouraged them all to do so when we were around, so they'd be well-practised by the time the real guests arrived. That said, when they chatted among themselves it was usually in their unique mixture of different French dialects, with Bud's own west-coast Canadian French blending in quite well. Everyone had mentioned how "charming" my Welsh-accented French was. I was pretty sure that "charming" was code for "difficult to understand", but we all managed.

Henri's shoulders sagged. "You're sure it's him? Really *him*?"

Given his focus on the dead man's identity, I suspected that Henri must have been acquainted with Vaiarii Teriimana in life, too.

I said, "I'm sorry you've both lost someone you know."

"I only met him once. That was enough," snapped Henri with a dismissive wave of his hand. "This'll be the end of us, before we've even opened. Everyone on the island – the entire archipelago – will know about this within hours, and it'll get around the world just as fast. I don't have to tell you how dangerous, and damaging, the effect of bad press can be, do I, Cait?"

I nodded, but didn't add anything. The topic of how the British tabloids had hounded me out of the UK more than a decade earlier, after I'd been arrested on suspicion of killing my ex-boyfriend Angus, had come up in one of the many conversations Bud and I had with Henri and Fleur over our shared dinners. However, it wasn't something I particularly wanted to discuss in front of Mahana…or anyone else, for that matter. Yes, it's the sort of thing that almost inevitably gets mentioned when I meet folks who would have seen all those front-page headlines…or who might have at least heard about them. However, I don't bring it up when there's an outside chance that the people I'm with know nothing about it. Even though I was completely cleared of any wrongdoing, it's not a part of my past I care to dwell upon.

That said, and despite the fact that I more than keenly understood Henri's observation about the utterly caustic potential effects of press coverage, I was still confused. I asked, "Why would this man being found dead at your resort make news around the world?"

Henri spoke despondently. "He's the guy with those fabulous teeth. On all the posters. The face of Ducasse Pearls here, and around the world. Has been for a few years. His girlfriend – his fiancée now – is the daughter of the company's owner. One of those so-called 'influencers'…you can't avoid her online. Got an opinion about everything, that one. But him? Drowned? Here? He was a famous pearl diver back when he was a teenager, for goodness' sake. How on earth did he manage to *drown*? And in *my* lagoon, of all places."

I cobbled all this information together in my head: I'd seen the posters for Ducasse Pearls – a large, well-established supplier whose advertising it was almost impossible to avoid on Tahiti – and there was indeed a young man on all of them. I recalled the face that had beamed at from me from billboards, the sides of buses, and display cards in jewelry store windows, and I could see the resemblance between the pearly smile I'd become familiar with over the past few weeks, and the face of the corpse. So the dead man was a model. And he'd once been a pearl diver, suggesting he'd have been a strong swimmer, with remarkable lung capacity. Which meant that the question of how such a person might have drowned, and particularly in a shallow body of water characterized by its serene beauty, was indeed an interesting one. And he was also globally famous? And engaged to one of those "influencers"? I could see how that might give Henri a few nightmares; businesses could be adversely affected so easily, especially when a tragic death was involved.

Of course I felt sorry for the young man himself, and for those he'd left behind, but my heart went out to the poor Legrands: Henri and Fleur hadn't just put every penny they'd owned and could borrow into this venture, they'd also put their sweat, and possibly even a part of their souls, into it, too. I knew Bud would be anxious to console his old friend and comrade, though suspected he had no idea that the identity of the corpse over which he was currently standing guard had the potential to prove so lethal for Henri's business plans.

I stood, finally not feeling wobbly at all. "I'm just going to pop back to our bungalow to put on some proper clothes," I said.

Henri's expression told me he was so distracted that my words hadn't reached his consciousness.

Mahana said, "Good idea, Cait. Obviously, we've no idea how the day's going to progress – but the police might want to talk to you about how you found him."

"You found him?" Henri was suddenly very close to me, breathing hard.

I nodded. "I was taking my usual early morning dip, and I…just bumped into him."

Henri's tone was unusually curt when he barked, "Didn't you see him before you got into the water?"

I sometimes curse my eidetic memory, but – often – it can be helpful. I employed it at that moment to recreate exactly what had happened earlier on. As I recalled my every move – and the sights, sounds, and smells that had surrounded me, as well as everything my body had been feeling – I realized something that hadn't occurred to me before…but decided to give the matter some more thought before I mentioned it.

I said, "No, I didn't see him before I got into the water, but I was looking at the horizon, so I dare say I was a bit distracted."

Henri sounded desperate when he said, "He must have died out at sea, then his body got washed over the coral into the lagoon. Did he look as though he'd been swimming when he died?"

"He was wearing shorts," replied Mahana, "but a lot of men wear them all the time anyway, so it's hard to say. He was shirtless, but the same goes for that."

"Could have been in a boat…fell out of it," added Henri. "I'll mention that when the police get here – they should look for a boat out there somewhere, abandoned, or adrift. Maybe he was diving, and one of those terrible stonefish got him? Those creatures are so dangerous – the deadliest fish in the seas, with such a powerful toxin in their spines. Though you'd think that someone like him would know better than to tread on one. But…you never know."

I could tell that Henri's retired-cop brain was kicking into gear, and I imagined how Bud must be thinking along similar lines to those of his old colleague as he stood on the beach, waiting. Alone.

"I'm just going to reassure Bud that I'm okay before I head off to dress," I said, "then I'll come back here, so I'm ready if I'm needed by…whomever might show up. Is that likely to take a long time, do you think?" I had no idea about how fast the police, or any medical people, might arrive at the resort, which wasn't the easiest of places to reach. True, it wasn't too far from the capital, as the crow – or the Pacific swallow – flies, but the road you had to take to reach it was poor and narrow.

The Legrands' choice of location for their resort allowed idyllic remoteness to be offered to guests because of the fact it was the only inhabited part of a spit of land that was surrounded by the sea on three sides; a particularly large river of lava had flowed down the side of the volcanic peak of Mont Orohena at the heart of the essentially-round island, then had run further out into the sea than the rest of the general sweep of the coastline.

"Who knows when anyone will arrive," replied Mahana pensively.

Henri sighed. "Nothing happens quickly here – which is usually a part of the charm."

Just as I was about to leave, Henri's wife, Fleur, arrived, and I paused while Henri explained the situation. The look of horror grew on Fleur's face as her husband spoke rapidly, then she embraced him saying, "Oh my darling – don't worry…we'll weather this, together." She turned to me and said, "I'm so sorry about this, Cait. Please apologize to Bud for us?"

I smiled as warmly as I could, given the circumstances. "Oh, don't be silly, Fleur, there's nothing to apologize for. You know Bud's faced worse, and I've…well, as part of my training as a criminal psychologist I've had to do all sorts of research involving…the deceased. I'm fine, and Bud is too, I'm sure. But I was just about to check in with him before I get dressed, so I'll be back soon."

"Thank you," said Fleur, tears welling in her eyes.

I decided to leave before shock set in for Fleur, and I ran the risk of getting caught up in another round of tea-drinking.

Worrying

Bud spotted me approaching him as soon as I left the bar, and he walked toward me, so that we met a little way away from the body – something for which I assumed he knew I'd be grateful. His eyes wrinkled with concern as he saw me gather the towels around me, and I smiled my own worry at him; I could tell he was getting a bit hot, having rushed to stand guard without a hat, or even his sunglasses.

I filled him in on the news about the identity of the dead man, then added, "Henri's clicked into cop-mode, and I'm guessing you have, too."

Bud chuckled. "You know me too well, Wife. Guys like Henri and me never revert to becoming normal civilians when we retire, I guess. And I have, in fact, been wondering how a body could wash up here. But I've realized I don't know enough about local currents and so forth to be able to get very far with that one. However, I have noted that the dead guy's knuckles have been scraped. Pre-mortem, I'd say, though I'm no expert."

I hugged my husband. "Okay, let's accept your lack of forensic expertise…but let's at least acknowledge your experience in the field throughout your career, especially as a homicide detective. I know you know the difference between knuckles that have been skinned before death, when they'd bleed and even start to bruise or scab over in a certain way, and those which have been injured after death…as a result of maybe dragging across something rough."

"Mighty kind of you, ma'am," mugged Bud, saluting me. "And I spotted that the deceased had a tattoo removed from his lower leg, and not too long ago, by the looks of it. Just in case you're interested, it was a large one, on the inner part of his calf, above his left ankle, to be exact."

"Anything else, oh Great Master of Observation?" I grinned.

"Not that I could see, initially, without moving the body…which, of course, I would never do." Bud winked at me, then whispered, "But those little wavelets have moved him just enough that I was able to spot a bit of a lump on his scalp, behind his left ear…which might reveal, upon a more detailed examination, a severe laceration – or that his head had made contact with something hard."

I gazed out toward the reef. "Coral?" I was thinking about Henri's theory about how the dead man had ended up in the lagoon.

"Or a rock…or an oar."

I chuckled wryly. "It seems you can't help but consider suspicious circumstances, Bud. Poor Vaiarii Teriimana. 'Little Vai', as Mahana referred to him. Though there's nothing little about him, is there? Got to be over six feet tall, I'd say. But…yes…I'm not sure about him having fallen out of a boat as Henri suggested, then washing up here."

"Go on, Cait – I can tell there's something you want to say." Bud hugged me closer.

I conceded, "There is, but you're not going to like it."

"I'm a big boy, Wife – out with it."

"Well, as I was recalling everything I could about this morning, I stitched together a few things that might suggest that this isn't as straightforward a death as it might seem."

Bud loosened his grip on me, pulled back a little, and started tending to my hair – which I realized was probably all over that place. As he fiddled – which was lovely – I continued, "Other than the fact that Vaiarii would have probably been an exceptionally good swimmer – given his past experience as a pearl diver – there's this lagoon itself to consider: it's small, and bounded by coral barriers, and what I realized when I was doing my recollection thing was that I'm pretty certain there wasn't a big sea last night. You know that the slapping of the water against the legs of our bungalow when the sea swells over the coral into the lagoon wakes me up; it did for the second time a few nights ago, remember? I was back and forth to the loo like nobody's business."

Bud nodded and smiled kindly. "Oh yes, I remember that only too well. I was surprised there wasn't a path worn into the wooden floor when I got up the next day." He hugged me. "You poor thing – who knew that the sound of the water against the bungalow's supports would do that to you…or to anyone, for that matter. I saw Henri roll his eyes when you gave him that bit of feedback."

I chuckled. "Yes, well, I don't think he really wants us telling him about things he's powerless to change. Anyway, I didn't hear a thing last night, so I don't believe the body could have been washed into the lagoon from the sea. Which means that Vaiarii must have drowned here, actually in the lagoon. Or…he might even have been dead before he went into the water: I'll admit I was assuming he'd drowned because of how I found him."

Bud looked deeply puzzled, then I realized he was squinting against the sun. "You're right about the coral that encircles the lagoon: usually, like now, the sea barely comes over the top of it. The idea of a corpse being pushed over it by the waves – unless there was a decent swell – is a bit of a stretch…and he'd be cut up pretty badly if that had happened, in any case. And he's clearly not. The mark I saw on his head might mean he was unconscious when he went into the lagoon…unable to save himself because he was incapacitated. Or, as you say, he might not have drowned at all – he might have already been dead when he went into the water. The medics will be able to find that out easily enough."

"So, we agree…definitely a suspicious death."

"Agreed."

"Shall we put aside the idea of a body dump for now?"

Bud nodded.

I sighed. "Okay, but that leads to a question: what was Vaiarii doing here, at the resort? *If* we assume he came here of his own free will."

Bud shrugged. "You said that both Henri and Mahana were surprised he was here, and it looked as though Fleur was too?" I nodded. "So they obviously hadn't invited him. Do you think any of the others who live here might have done that?"

I ran through the list of everyone else at the resort. "Annette or Edouard Wong? I have to say that seems unlikely: they're very much a couply-couple, aren't they? Not especially outgoing. I'll admit I feel I know Annette a bit better than Edouard because I see her several times every day…and we've nattered quite a bit when she's come in to clean our room."

"After you've spent ten minutes tidying it up before she arrives, you mean." Bud winked, and I poked out my tongue.

"Oh, come on, I don't spend that long doing it. Besides, we might be test guests, but there's no reason why we should live like slobs. Anyway, as I was saying, I see more of her than of him: she's quite a chatty type, but she's never mentioned any friends or family, so maybe not too social? And Edouard's…well, polite, always busy doing one of his handyman jobs, and ready to smile, but, to be honest I don't really know that much about him. But them inviting Vaiarii here? I'm going to say I think it unlikely. Then there's Eloise and Nadine Tremblay-Martin. Either one, or both, of them might have asked him over, I suppose; Vaiarii was a model, and we both know that Nadine teases Eloise about how she did a bit of modelling in the past."

"But Eloise is Henri's chef here now," said Bud, turning so he didn't have to squint quite as much. "And you know how she puts Nadine in her place when she brings up that modelling stuff

– says it was only for a few months, and long before they even met, let alone before they were married. Eloise says Nadine only ever mentions it because she's stupidly jealous of Eloise's old girlfriend…whatshername."

"Wanda."

Bud chuckled. "Oh yes, Wanda – the woman who promised Eloise the earth, but only ended up giving her the boot. Someone should ask them all if they invited him over, I suppose. But even if someone did, how did he get here? Is there an unusual car parked here anywhere? Or maybe an unusual boat moored at the dock? I can't see that far from here. But, no, hang on…look, Cait – we don't know anything, really. All we have are questions, so this is pointless speculation at the moment. Why don't you go and get yourself dressed…and do something with your hair, because it's drying into sandy clumps right now, which I know you hate. And – if you wouldn't mind – I could do with a hat, my sunglasses, and some sunscreen, if I'm going to be hanging about here for much longer."

I kissed Bud's deeply tanned nose and agreed that the best thing I could do was get myself sorted and bring him supplies, so I headed across the beach to the wooden walkway leading to our bungalow, and set about getting myself into a fit state to face what was likely to be an extremely unusual day.

Cleaning

Given that we were, in fact, in the South Pacific, I couldn't help but hum the tune of "I'm Gonna Wash That Man Right Out Of My Hair" as I scrubbed my scalp in the shower for several minutes. Bud was right about my relationship with sand; I hate it. Memories of gritty sandwiches, followed by my late mother literally sandpapering my feet with an old towel as I sat sideways in Dad's ancient Ford Anglia overlooking Oxwich Beach in Gower when I was a child are to blame for that, I suppose…though the coziness of the socks she'd pushed onto me immediately afterwards was one of the best feelings in the world. Yes, I'd always hated getting sandy – though the fact I'd been grappling with a corpse meant I'd hardly noticed that my entire body had been covered with the stuff earlier on.

Finally clean and dry, I pulled on the cerise version of the baggy, crinkly-cotton pants-and-top combo that had become my go-to outfits on Tahiti; I'd found them in a shop in Papeete and had bought a set in every vivid color available. I grabbed what Bud needed from around the bungalow and headed toward him on the beach. He hadn't moved, and I hoped the authorities would arrive soon: the sun was getting higher, and the temperature was climbing, too. Not good – especially where corpses are concerned.

Just as I reached the part of the walkway closest to the bar, I noticed that Mahana, Henri, and Fleur had been joined by all the other worker-residents at our not-so-humble abode. I waved and indicated I was off to see Bud, then would return, but Henri beckoned to me. As I approached, he bounded toward me, meeting me halfway.

He appeared to have regained his usual jolly-but-slightly-gruff manner. "Tell Bud to come on over for a cool drink. No use him standing there like that. The body's not going anywhere, and we've no idea how long it's going to take someone to get here."

I hesitated, then decided it was best to say what was on my mind. "Okay, thanks, I'll let him know what you suggested. But you know what he's like…he might prefer to stand guard until he no longer feels responsible for the poor bloke. I mean . . ." I didn't really want to say it, but felt I had to, "Bud might be able to keep insects and scavengers, and so forth, away from the…remains. You know?"

Henri sighed. "I see, yes. You're right. Well, he's the senior officer around here for now, let him decide." He shrugged, in his most French-Canadian manner, and we parted.

As I made my way to my husband, I considered how, during our time together, Henri and Bud had reminisced and joshed about how stellar Bud's career development had been after he'd left the RCMP in his youth. Henri had remained a Mountie, usually in rural parts of Canada, always in communities where the service fulfilled a dizzying range of functions, many being way beyond what some might consider "policing". I'd noted how the two men had taken different paths, led different lives, and held entirely different views on so many topics – something which had become clear as the days and weeks had passed. In some ways, I was glad we'd be leaving soon, because I feared that any kinship that had once existed between Bud and Henri might not survive unless they restricted their discussions to topics like the weather until we left, most other matters having shown how little the two men had in common, despite having trained in the same cohort.

I managed to slap a smile on my face as I joined Bud. He downed one of the three bottles of water I'd brought him, then slathered on sunscreen before pulling his hat onto his head and sliding on his sunglasses.

"That's better," he said. "I finally feel ready to cope with the conditions. So Henri thinks it's okay for me to abandon this guy? Not gonna happen, Cait. But I dare say you've already guessed that. I took loads of photos as soon as you left me alone with him – best I could do to preserve…well, let's not call it a crime scene for now, eh? But you know what I mean. No idea how fast things might change for the body given it was in the water, and now it's in the sun. I was thinking we should bring over one of those umbrellas to provide some shade. Do you think Henri would be up for that?"

I couldn't see why our host would object and said as much. "I could phone him to ask – or you could; you've got your phone, and I know you've got his number."

Bud chuckled. "Good thinking. I'll blame the sun being on my head for too long for not having thought of that. Give me a tick, eh?"

The conversation was brief – to the point of being almost abrupt – then Bud finished with: "Thanks, Henri. Let me know if you guys need a hand."

As he tucked his phone away, Bud mused, "Henri sounds tense. To be expected, I guess. How d'you think he's holding up, Cait?"

I shrugged. "Fleur seems to be good at putting the pieces back together again when he's falling apart – maybe she'll be able to help him get through all of…well, whatever might happen because of young Vaiarii's death."

Bud burrowed a toe into the crumbly, white sand. "Poor Henri, eh? This happening – and so close to his opening date. Of course, I'm sorry for this guy too – and whoever will miss him. But Henri? This could be…tough for him and Fleur. And I mean financially, as well as emotionally."

I'd really taken to Fleur; she was younger than me by four years, whereas Henri was older than Bud by the same margin;

they, like us, had been married for almost three years. However, in their case, they'd spent that entire time getting all the permits for, then overseeing the construction of, the Legrand Resort…which meant they'd been through some stressful times together. Unlike Bud and me, they'd been a couple for several years before they'd married, and it was a first marriage for both of them. The lovely thing about them was that they seemed incredibly well suited to each other, though they were complementary characters, rather than matching ones; Henri tended to be a bit bombastic, whereas Fleur was quietly determined. But they both had a certain grit, which I admired.

"I think Henri's emotions will follow the business impact, to be honest, Bud. He said he'd only met Vaiarii once, and clearly wasn't impressed. But even Mahana's first impulse was that this man's death could adversely impact the business. I don't think folks like to think of a tragedy having happened at the place where they're on holiday – especially if what they're after is a slice of idyllic paradise, for which they're happy to pay through the nose."

"And Henri reckons this guy's girlfriend is some sort of internet star?"

"His fiancée is an influencer. And no, before you go off on one, I don't get that whole thing, either. I mean, I recognize that I've been 'influenced' by people in the past, but only if they've got some actual expertise in whatever it is they're talking about. You know – scientists, medical professionals…even wine experts about wine, or book reviewers about books – that sort of thing. Maybe I've always been ludicrously naïve about how 'expert' those people were, but I don't think that the opinion of some Generation Whatever about the impact on menopausal skin of sleeping on a satin pillowcase is going to 'influence' my decisions. Apparently – and I only know this because I Googled her quickly while I was changing – this CeeCee Ducasse's specialisms are travel and fashion…which might just mean she gets lots of free hotel rooms and clothes. I've no idea. All I can say is that if her online 'content' is anything to go by, I'm surprised she and poor Vaiarii here could even call themselves 'boyfriend and girlfriend': she doesn't seem to be in any one place for more than two minutes. Though she made a big song and dance – and I mean that literally, I kid you not – about returning to Tahiti from Brisbane three days ago. Since then, she's been surprisingly quiet online, except to post photos of plates of food I'm convinced she doesn't actually eat; she's curvy alright, but still probably wears a size zero."

Bud's eyebrows had appeared above his sunglasses. "Now, now, Cait, consider all the progress you've made in terms of trying to be a little less judgy about people you've never met."

I laughed. "Yeah, you're right. Sorry. She might have a PhD in tourism and fashion for all I know – though I suspect she'd have mentioned that in her mini bio. She's listed the number of hotels she's stayed at, and her running total of miles flown, so you'd think she'd have at least nodded toward her academic achievements, if she had any – wouldn't you?"

"Maybe they wouldn't be of interest to her audience?"

"Influencer? Expertise? I rest my case, Your Honor."

"Here comes Henri and Edouard…and Mahana, of course," said Bud, nodding over my shoulder.

I turned to see the two men struggling with one of the large, and obviously heavy, beach umbrellas which they were carrying from the deck area, while Mahana shouted instructions. Edouard Wong – Henri's general handyman and all-round helper about the place – had hold of the base of the umbrella, which I had to believe represented the bulk of the weight, it being a wide plastic container I knew to be full of gravel. They finally reached us, and Mahana pointed to the best spot to dig the base into the sand to allow for maximum coverage of the body once the umbrella was opened. The entire process took several minutes, and the three men seemed to work well as a team, so I stood back with Mahana and we watched, as they worked.

Mahana observed, "Bud is a kind and thoughtful man," as we waited. "You are a fortunate woman."

I was surprised by the personal nature of her comment, but her cheery delivery meant I went along with it. "He is. I think that maybe the fact that we didn't get together until later in life means…well, we were both fully formed by the time we met, and started dating, so I suppose we both knew what we'd get."

Mahana nodded sagely. "It is true. Sometimes, when we are young, we think we know the person we love, but they…grow in a way we hadn't expected."

Her comment intrigued me, so I dared to ask, "Did you love someone who…grew away from you?"

Mahana didn't look at me when she replied. "I did, but I cannot blame him for preferring another woman; I never told him I loved him, so how would he know? In my mind he was perfect – in himself, and for me – but maybe I just did not know him at all. Maybe I only knew what I wanted him to be."

I said, "Unrequited love?"

She whispered, "More like a secret love, I suppose."

Poor Edouard's retching – which happened every time he looked at the remains, which he had to keep doing, just to make sure he didn't step on something he shouldn't – started to get the better of him, which got our attention. Each time he came close to throwing up, he'd apologize to Henri and Bud, then the body. By the time they were finished, Edouard looked as though he was fit to drop. Bud handed him one of his bottles of water, which Edouard accepted with gratitude.

As he sipped, he puffed, "I am so sorry that I am not good with this. Death is…yes, I know it is natural, but *this* death is not natural. A healthy young man like this should not die. Death is the relief granted to those who are sick, or who are very old and tired. It should be a blessing, not a…not this."

Henri and Bud nodded sadly, then Henri said, "Why don't you get on back to the bar, Edouard? I think a few of your duties can wait for a while – grab a drink and get some shade. And maybe Annette could do with a bit of company, eh?"

Edouard eagerly scampered off, followed by Mahana, while Henri remained with us. Then he and Bud gave one of the best displays I'd seen in a long time of two men saying absolutely nothing while using a great many words. I gathered – after about five minutes of twaddle – that they at least agreed that the tragic death of Vaiarii Teriimana wasn't likely to be good for Henri and Fleur Legrand, nor the Legrand Resort itself.

When Henri eventually fell silent, I felt able to observe, "You must have been out of here before dawn, if you were on your way back from Papeete when Mahana texted you this morning…which was still quite early."

Given how flushed Henri still was after his exertions with the beach umbrella, and the fact he had a deep tan in any case, it was hard for me to tell if he was blushing when he replied – though his whiny tone suggested he wasn't very happy about being challenged on the point.

"I have to get to the suppliers in Papeete early, if I want the best. Especially the fish – I wanted that for tonight. When we're open, everything will be delivered, but we need very little at the moment; no one's going to trek all the way over here until the quantities are significant. But I want all the guys with the good stuff to know me, and understand what I'm after. This is a small island with a surprisingly large number of high-end restaurants and a solid reputation with foodies. I need the good stuff making its way here, not the gnarly bits the well-established places, or the big chains, don't want. I need the best fish, meats, fruits, vegetables, and flowers. They all need to see that I know what I'm talking about — that I'll notice if they try to under-deliver. That's why I get there early — so they know I care. And I always show up looking a little…scruffy, so they know I'm like one of them — hardworking." Henri sounded wounded.

"No one could be in any doubt that you care, nor that you're hardworking," said Bud reassuringly. The two men did a bit of handshaking and backslapping, then Henri headed back to the main building.

From our chats about Henri, I knew that these were things about which Bud was certain, and for which he still admired his old colleague — that he truly did want to do the best possible job when it came to the entire customer experience at the resort. Indeed, Henri and Fleur had both pressed us to give them feedback on seemingly more and more petty "guest experience" points the longer we'd stayed. Bud and I had made an effort to overcome our natural desire to brush things off, or put them down to circumstances beyond anyone's control, but the Legrands had pushed us, so we'd done it. Unfortunately, eventually we felt as though we'd become the biggest nitpickers in the world, which wasn't a feeling we cared for; another reason I wasn't going to be exactly heartbroken when we finally got onto the cruise ship that would be sailing us home.

Just as I was thinking all this, Bud made a comment that led me to suspect he really could read my thoughts. "Sometimes, paradise isn't all it's cracked up to be, eh? I'll hang on here with the body until someone comes, but I reckon you could be doing more good by joining everyone at the bar and having a bit of a dig about for any interesting tidbits."

I kissed him and said, "You're not wrong, Husband," then made my way across the sand, hoping a cool drink was in my not-too-distant future.

Reflecting

The sun was still climbing as I entered the bar. To say that the gathering there was somber would have been kind. Mahana bounced off the stool she'd been perching on as soon as she saw me.

She asked hesitantly, "Iced water…or something else? Maybe a beer?"

Everyone had a beer bottle in their hand, so I didn't feel there was an expectation that I'd say no. "A *la blanche* would be great, if you've got one, Mahana. Thanks."

"Of course we do," she replied with a bright smile. "Glass, or bottle?"

"I'll take it in the glass it comes in, thanks." I glugged at the blue bottle I knew I'd forever associate with Tahiti, grateful for the refreshment. I recalled how I'd chuckled when Henri had told me he planned to stock only one brand of beer at the resort, because I'd suspected his guests might prefer a wider range, but – over the weeks – I'd realized that Tahiti's own *Hinano* brand offered a beer to suit pretty much every palate. The white beer was my favorite, and I usually took it in a glass with a slice of orange, but, on this occasion, I didn't want to sip daintily…I just wanted to let the icy bottle chill my hand while the beer itself cooled my throat; it was going to be another hot, humid day.

"It's gonna rain later, I can tell," said Henri Legrand heavily. "Start of the wet season's coming early by the looks of it, and we've got a corpse on our hands. Great way to launch this business."

Fleur was obviously trying to sound reassuring when she replied, "The really wet weather won't hit us until December, you know that my dearest, so we've got a decent six weeks ahead of us. And we agreed that offering lower prices to those who want to risk visiting during the hotter, wetter months was a good way to work on getting things perfect here before the high season. Come on, it's not all bad."

"Looks it to me," snapped her husband. I wasn't used to hearing that tone from Henri when he spoke to Fleur. He added, "That…that thing out there won't do us any favors. Vaiarii Teriimana was trouble in life, and he'll be trouble in death, you'll see."

I had to ask, "What do you mean, Henri? You said you'd only met him once."

Henri snorted. "Couldn't keep himself out of the news, could he? Always some sort of problems with him, right, Mahana?"

I felt my multipurpose right eyebrow shoot up as I looked in Mahana's direction, and hoped she'd elaborate on Henri's cryptic comment. She didn't say anything, though, so I dared a prompt. "Good-looking young men can face all sorts of challenges, I dare say. Did your friend's son get himself into a few sticky situations, Mahana?"

Eloise Tremblay-Martin burst into tears – which took me aback. Her wife, Nadine, usually bubbly and bouncy, glared at me – which confused me even more.

I spluttered, "I'm sorry…I didn't mean to cause any upset. I just meant…"

Mahana jumped in. "Don't worry, Cait, Eloise is on edge – we all are. This is very upsetting for all of us. And what Henri means is that Vaiarii was well known, and popular, but this is a small island; sometimes it's difficult to be famous in a small place. He couldn't help being so attractive. Sometimes men think…well, they can feel threatened when another man gets a great deal of…attention."

I could tell there was a lot that wasn't being said but was nevertheless clearly understood by everyone in the bar…*except me*. However, I still couldn't work out why the death of a good-looking young man would impact Eloise to the point that she was the only one in tears. Her wife was consoling her, and that left me…confused.

I was grateful when Edouard Wong explained quietly, "Vaiarii came here to do a photo shoot several weeks ago – just before you arrived, in fact – and managed to hit on Fleur, Eloise, Mahana, and my own dear wife Annette. It appeared he thought he could make suggestive comments to any woman, and had no shame at all when he flirted."

"He was just teasing, Edouard," whispered his wife. "You took it all the wrong way." Annette Wong looked at me with a dimpling smile. An attractively rounded woman in her mid-thirties whose ethnic background was a fairly common Tahitian cocktail of Polynesian, Chinese, and French, she added – quite coquettishly, "Vaiarii was stunning to look at and so full of life…oh! You know what I mean. He just teased me a bit; my Edouard got it all wrong. He's too jealous for his own good." She patted her husband's hand affectionately.

He rolled his eyes. "He upset you. He…he shouldn't have spoken to you about your brother."

Annette whispered to him, "They were chums, once…he was being polite." She explained to me, "My brother and Vaiarii used to dive together when they were young."

Edouard harrumphed.

"He had Eloise backed up against the wall outside the restaurant," snapped Nadine throatily. "He wasn't teasing her, he was…terrifying her."

"I could have taken care of myself," replied Eloise, her voice thick with tears. "You didn't need to beat him like that."

Nadine Tremblay-Martin was about my height, five-four-ish, and half my girth, though admittedly wiry; I pictured her launching herself at the living version of the man I'd dragged onto the beach. He couldn't have been an easy target for her.

"You hit him?" The words flew out of my mouth before I could stop them.

"He deserved worse," snarled Nadine, then she realized the situation and deflated a little. "Sorry," she added, not seeming to really mean it.

During our weeks at the resort, I'd come to know Nadine rather better than Eloise, because Eloise seemed to spend most of her time in the kitchen, whereas Nadine regularly used the beach and pool when she wasn't actively helping her wife as a *de facto* prep-chef and general gofer. She'd confided to me that she was making the most of the facilities while she could, because the public areas were going to be off-limits to her once paying guests arrived. Nadine had struck me as someone who didn't possess a violent bone in her body; she invariably had a smile on her face, and usually a telling quip ready to go.

During one particular afternoon on our deck, where a few beers had been consumed, I'd learned that she and Eloise had met when they'd both been working at a hotel in London – Eloise as the pastry chef, and Nadine in the spa. When Eloise got a better offer, Nadine had seen that as her cue to make up her mind about their blossoming relationship. From then on, they'd always gained employment together, with Nadine taking on any spa-related job available at, or close to, Eloise's next posting; not difficult, because she was qualified in massage, Reiki, yoga, and various other "wellness" disciplines I knew I'd never experience. Nadine was happy to help her wife in the kitchen both now, and on a part-time basis once the customers arrived, because then she'd also be hired out to give individual wellness treatments to guests in their bungalows. She often spoke of Eloise's prowess in the kitchen – praise I knew was richly deserved. She informed me they were true soul mates, and I'd seen how well suited they were in all their interactions; well-matched – each always supporting the other.

However, until that moment, I'd never seen Nadine lose her temper; now I could see a vein pulse in her neck as she recalled Vaiarii's actions toward her beloved Eloise. Her tall wife's long, lean arm reached out to pull the much shorter Nadine into her, and the couple sat sadly beside the bar tending to old wounds that had been reopened.

Meanwhile, Fleur Legrand was twirling her short, gray-blonde hair as if she wanted to pull it out; I wondered why she was so…*angry?* It seemed an odd emotion for Fleur to be displaying, even if she was focussed on the chance that the business was going to be impacted by the tragedy.

I decided that this was as good a time as any to ask, "So Vaiarii had been here before. Had one of you invited him to return?"

I watched carefully as everyone reacted to my question, and assessed their responses: Henri and Fleur Legrand both harrumphed and shrugged in their best Montrealer manner; Nadine looked at me as though I were bonkers, while Eloise didn't make eye contact with anyone, but shook her head; Mahana also shook her head, looking resigned, while Edouard and Annette Wong simply looked confused. *Nothing there to suggest anyone was lying.*

I followed up with: "So I wonder what he was doing here."

Henri said, "Must have come off a boat, out there somewhere, like I said." He waved his arm in the general direction of the sea.

"He didn't drive here?" I asked.

"Why would he drive?" Edouard asked politely. "The road's not good, and lots of people use boats to get about, as you know. There's no car in the car park that shouldn't be, but there might be a boat out at the dock, I suppose."

"More likely he fell off a boat – his own, or someone else's," said Fleur forcefully. "Or maybe he stepped on a stonefish when he was diving." I suspected that she and Henri had been discussing the matter.

"Coming off a boat somewhere would be most likely," added Mahana.

A general nodding of heads followed, and I began to suspect that the idea had been thoroughly discussed by the entire group, prior to my joining them. Which gave me pause: what else might they all have chatted through, and agreed upon?

As I sipped my beer – amazed to find that the bottle was almost empty – I allowed myself to analyze the body language being displayed by everyone in the bar: my key conclusion was that they were, in fact, operating as an actual *group* – not a collection of individuals. The sensation niggled at my core; what was it that had pulled them all together like that? Could it be as simple as a common desire for the resort to be a success, because all their livelihoods depended upon that? Or was it something more?

I plunged in with: "So was the photo shoot that took place here for the pearl advertising campaign that Vaiarii appeared in?"

Mahana took up the gauntlet I'd laid down. "Yes. We thought it would be good publicity for the resort. CeeCee Ducasse, his fiancée, reached out to me and suggested it. She put the wheels in motion. She even had her own videographer here so she could record the process for her personal online content. Which meant we got double the coverage. CeeCee has well over a million followers."

"It was a good idea," concurred Henri flatly. "We got a few bookings because of it. Because of CeeCee's online thing, I mean, not because of the new photos – I don't think they're being used yet."

"Fancy another beer, Cait?" Mahana was being attentive. "And anyone else want anything? Something to eat?"

"Good idea, but don't worry about food, Mahana," said Eloise, who seemed to have regained her normal cool composure. "Nadine and I will bring some nibbles through from the kitchen. We're none of us going to want a proper lunch, so let's snack while we wait."

I hadn't seen the video Mahana had just described within CeeCee Ducasse's online content, so I pulled out my phone as Eloise and Nadine disappeared and Mahana tended to everyone's drinks needs. I couldn't help but want to see Vaiarii Teriimana in life, and as more than a smiling face in a series of photographs.

When I found the video in question, I was surprised to see just how many people had been required to take photographs of one man and a variety of pearl jewelry and props: more than half a dozen people were flitting about setting up all sorts of contraptions on the beach just beyond the bar, while Vaiarii himself was attended to by three women who primped and prepared him for the camera. Meanwhile, CeeCee Ducasse was in and out of the video shot; she looked stunning in a white *pareo* which set off her long dark hair and tanned skin. She cooed about how critical it was that "her darling Vaiarii's" presence on film was captured perfectly, because the results would be seen around the world in what she called a "massive push" in terms of advertising presence for her family's pearl company. To my eyes, it all looked utterly chaotic, and – in the background – I could occasionally hear angry voices being raised if something wasn't quite right.

"Please, all take what you want." It was Eloise speaking, and I looked up from my phone to see that she and Nadine had laid out platters of sliced fruits and cheeses on the bar beside a basket full of crusty baguettes. There was even a plate of *Po'e* banana squares, which made my mouth water; I assumed they were from the batch Eloise had baked the previous day. It took time to prepare the mixture of tapioca flour with vanilla seeds and mashed banana, wrapped in banana leaves, and I couldn't imagine it was something she'd have bothered doing after the discovery of the body. Whenever she'd made it, I was glad she had, because I'd become quite addicted to the gooey, sweet treat during my stay at the resort.

Just as we were all giving our attention to picking out what we fancied, the sound of motor vehicles reached our ears, and I saw Henri's back stiffen. He grabbed a few slices of cheese, shoved them into his mouth, washed them down with half a bottle of beer, then said to his wife, "Here we go, then, Fleur…this is it."

I just about caught Fleur saying quietly, "Remember, Henri, this is not our fault. It's not something we want to forever be associated with the resort."

Offering

I desperately wanted to be on the scene when Henri and Fleur talked to whomever was clattering out of the vehicles in the parking lot, but I was already juggling a plate of bread and cheese, so had to make a choice: eat, or be on the spot.

My tummy rumbled at me as I surrendered my snack and announced, "I dare say they'll need to talk to the person who actually found the body," and I hightailed it out of the bar.

I spotted Mahana's concerned glance as I left, but wasn't sure what to read into it. Instead, I turned my attention to the uniformed officer striding toward Henri and Fleur, who was…impressively huge. Well over six feet tall, he looked as though he'd just walked off the rugby pitch, where he'd probably pushed the entire scrum all on his own, and flattened several opposition players, too. Greetings were exchanged, Henri flung an arm in Bud's direction, and the three set off toward my husband, leaving me to catch up.

When I did, I introduced myself to the officer, who enveloped my hand within his enormous one, and said quietly, "*Bonjour*, Madame Morgan, *ia ora na*. I am Sous-Lieutenant Puletua. But everyone, including Monsieur Henri here, calls me Sonny." His English was heavily-accented, and I did my best to not stare as I noted how his bald head – topped with a jauntily angled hat – seemed to grow directly out of his wide shoulders. His pale blue shirt strained at its buttons, and it was wet through across his massive back. He appeared to be bemused by his current situation. "I was telling Monsieur Henri that I am pleased to be able to visit this resort. I have driven past the new road as they have been making it, on my way to Tahiti Iti, where I go to Teahupo'o to watch the surfers. It is very beautiful here. But not what is on this beach, today, eh?"

I knew that Tahiti was almost two islands, not one – the smaller land mass of Tahiti Iti being reached from the larger Tahiti Nui across an isthmus. Bud and I hadn't explored Tahiti Iti at all, it being largely uninhabited, and offering a drive that didn't take you all the way around; the road stopped on both the south and north sides, meaning you had to backtrack whichever route you chose. We'd said we'd do it "one day", and now we were running out of days. As I was regretting some of our indolence, we continued walking toward Bud, who was sticking to his spot in the shade of the umbrella, beside the body.

"Monsieur Henri tells me you discovered the body this morning Madame Morgan, and that this is your husband here. He and Monsieur Henri were once police officers together, I hear. The deceased has a security detail of his own, then…whereas I have arrived alone. Except for the recovery team."

I'd seen two people in high-vis vests grappling with a complicated-looking carrying device at the rear of what clearly wasn't an ambulance, though it had a red cross on its side.

"You don't have any forensics people?" I had to ask. I was surprised.

The officer paused. "For the recovery of a drowning victim? No, that would not be usual."

"But we have no idea how the young man died." It was out of my mouth before I could stop it.

Officer Puletua didn't move. "Monsieur Henri has told me he drowned – that you found him floating in the lagoon. This is not in question – correct?"

I stared at Henri, who didn't seem to be about to reply, so I said, "That's where I found him, yes, and he was most certainly dead. But none of us know for certain that he drowned. Nor do we know – if he did – how that might have happened. He was known to be a strong swimmer, I understand."

Puletua turned his attention to Henri. "You know the man?" He sounded surprised.

Henri replied, "Yes. He is Vaiarii Teriimana. He was known by us…a little."

Puletua looked visible shaken. "Vaiarii Teriimana? No. It cannot be. He…he was at a nightclub in Papeete at three this morning. I saw him there – helped him out of there, after an…altercation, and drove him to his home myself. When did you say you found him Madame Morgan?"

"The sun had probably been up for maybe an hour, so about seven. Though I didn't look at a clock at the time."

We'd just reached Bud, so I took my chance. "Sous-Lieutenant Puletua, here, tells me that he saw our victim having a fight at a nightclub in Papeete about four hours before I hauled him out of the lagoon, Bud. Officer Puletua, this is my husband, Bud Anderson."

Puletua's hands engulfed Bud's in a warm shake before the officer said, in a friendly manner, "I am Sonny, please. Thank you for your courtesy to the deceased, Monsieur Anderson. It shows admirable respect. Now Monsieur Teriimana is my responsibility."

I could see Bud's shoulders unhunch. He was dripping with sweat and clearly needed some sort of refreshment; I mentally chastised myself for not having picked up another bottle of chilled water before I'd left the bar. *Poor Bud…you should have come first in my thoughts.*

"It sounds as though this is planned as a simple retrieval job, Bud," I noted, hoping my husband would sense my concern.

He wrinkled his eyes above his sunglasses, then removed them. "I see," he replied. "I understand why you would expect that to be the case, Sous-Lieutenant Puletua – Sonny – but…if I might just make a couple of observations…?"

The officer nodded.

Bud continued, "I haven't moved the body, of course, but couldn't help but notice a contusion on the man's head. He also has scraped knuckles – which might be explained by what you witnessed in the early hours of this morning. Now, I'm no expert, but it seems odd to me that a man with a background as a pearl diver would drown in such a shallow lagoon. However, maybe he sustained the head injury during the fight you saw…which might mean an inquiry is needed. Head injuries are tricky – they can seem harmless at first, but have repercussions later on. This could turn out to be a case of manslaughter – with the person or persons he was fighting with ultimately being held responsible for his death."

Sonny Puletua looked thoughtful. He wiped away a trail of moisture trickling down his forehead before it reached his eye. He bent down and moved Vaiarii's head to one side. "You are correct, Monsieur Anderson, there is an injury. I, also, am not an expert, however as you noted, there might be a connection between the fight he had and Monsieur Teriimana's death. But this is not a problem: the body will be handled with care and taken for examination. If it was in the water for some time, then it is likely it will have been washed of everything that might have been forensically useful. Did Monsieur Teriimana arrive by boat, Monsieur Henri?"

Henri seemed surprised to be directly addressed. "We don't know. Maybe he fell off one – out at sea. I…none of us have gone searching for a boat. Could…could you do that?"

"I mean to ask, has he moored a boat here? I have been told you have built a jetty," explained Puletua.

"Ah, I understand," replied Henri, his expression clearing. "I haven't noticed one, but I haven't been out to the dock, and there are a few little bays tucked away, around the point. Fleur and I will explore, to see what we can find."

"A good idea," replied Puletua.

He spoke to the two men in luminous orange vests who'd joined us. They put down their lifting contraption and stood back when he announced, "One moment, everyone – please clear the area. My colleagues will remove the umbrella."

Once the umbrella had been dragged away, Puletua took dozens of photographs of the body, the lagoon, and the beach. Then the two men carefully turned over the corpse, and he snapped some more.

Bud offered, "I took lots of shots when I first reached the body. I could send you those, in case you want to compare both sets."

Sonny Puletua beamed. "Most efficient, Monsieur Anderson. Thank you. Here is my email address." He snapped a card out of his shirt's breast pocket and handed it to Bud, then spoke briskly to the two men, and invited the four of us to join him in leaving the immediate vicinity.

We made our way toward the shade of the bar, at Henri's suggestion.

As we walked, the officer noted, "It will rain today."

Fleur whined, "I know there's a tendency for thunderstorms in October, but do you think the real rains will come from now on, Sonny?"

The officer grinned. "My father says not for five more weeks, and we all know he's always correct…about everything."

I asked, "Is your father a meteorologist, Sonny?"

"My father is a man who knows the ways of nature, Madame Morgan. My family came here from Samoa five generations ago, and my ancestors were well versed in natural ways before we left our island. My father is Julius Puletua the fourth. I am the fifth in the family to carry that name – hence, Sonny. But he has not passed his entire understanding of all things natural to me…though I continue to enjoy learning from him. So I agree with him – this will be a storm in its own right, not the start of the rains for the year. Never fear, Madame Fleur, your resort will open to guests with good weather – my father says so. And he sends his regards."

I didn't think it was an appropriate time to inquire about how well the Legrands knew the Puletuas, so allowed Bud to grab my hand and hold me back from the others a little, as we neared the refuge of the bar, where I could see Mahana hovering.

Bud whispered, "You know that tattoo I said the dead guy had removed?"

I nodded.

"I didn't have much else to do but try to work out what it might have been, and I reckon it was a name. Depending upon which way up he'd had it done – you know, whether he'd had the beginning of the name nearest his ankle, or his knee – it looked like three small letters, and then a letter that went both up and down – which means it must have been a lower-case, cursive 'f', I reckon." Bud paused and sighed. "I worked it out by going through all the alternatives. And, yes, I have been standing here that long. Anyway, after that were a lot of lower-case letters. So, a few lower case, an 'f', then lots of lower-case letters…or else a lot of lower-case letters, then an 'f', then a few more lower-case ones. What do you think of that?"

No specific name leaped to mind. "An ex-girlfriend, maybe?"

Bud nodded. "That's what I thought, too. But the scarring was still pretty fresh. I also used my phone while I was hanging about to check on that CeeCee Ducasse you were talking about. According to her, they've been engaged for over a year…so he took a while to decide to get another woman's name removed from his skin, if that's the case."

"I understand that's a specialized task; maybe he couldn't get it done here on the island. Or maybe he was afraid of the pain. They say that tattoo removal's a lot more painful than getting the thing done in the first place, don't they?"

Bud chuckled. "Not something I'm ever likely to find out, firsthand. But, yes, you make two good points. However, this whole situation raises a lot of questions, don't you think?"

"You're not wrong, Bud. A lot. And I really don't think we're being too sensitive to matters that don't…well, matter. In other words, I don't think this is us making something out of nothing. Anyway, let's see where Sonny's questions take us. He's an interesting bloke, don't you think?"

Bud hugged my waist as we arrived at the bar. "Interesting, polite…and massive. Those hands of his alone are quite something. Not one of the French Gendarmes, sent here from the home country, though. Tahitian grown, as he said."

"They certainly grow them big," I replied, as we both accepted cool bottles of water from Mahana and flopped onto rattan chairs beneath the fans in the shade of the bar.

Nibbling

Once we were all seated, Puletua stood beside the bar and asked for a summary of the morning's activities – as they pertained to the corpse.

"You found the body, Madame Morgan – please tell me about that…in detail. I shall record you speaking, if I may. This means my bosses can hear your words, not my interpretation of them. I hope this is acceptable to you all."

We all agreed. I recounted my discovery of the body; Mahana spoke about how she'd heard my cries, and had helped me; then Bud explained his sentry duty. Puletua seemed satisfied with the information about how the remains had been discovered, recovered, and protected prior to his arrival. He didn't ask anyone anything else, which irked me somewhat – but then I reasoned it probably wasn't his job to do that; the island had to have an investigative arm of the police service, beyond the military gendarmerie whose duties involved safety and security for the population.

He took notes of everyone's phone numbers and email addresses, then began his farewells, announcing, "I will pass this information to my superiors, and I believe an examination of the deceased will take place, in due course. Thank you for allowing me to see this corner of my island again, which I have not seen for many years. My father would bring me to this lagoon to help me develop my skills as a swimmer. Because it could only ever be reached by boat – until you had the new road built, Monsieur Henri – it was not popular with visitors, just we locals." Sonny's expression softened, then hardened again, as he added, "It was…it was a place for fathers and sons. A special place. Now I know it will be a playground for tourists. They bring much to our economy, I understand this."

"Would you and your whole family like to visit, Sonny? Under less tragic circumstances, of course. For a meal…*ma'a. Dîner en famille?*" Henri had bounced out of his chair to shake hands with the officer. "It would be our honor to host you all."

Puletua laughed throatily. "But we're fifteen, without even any cousins – and all with appetites like mine, even the children. That would be a large dinner, Henri."

Fleur added, "We'd love to have you, Sonny. We open in a week, so…before then? You understand."

Another laugh flowed from Puletua's belly, but this time I judged it was tinged with…something less truly joyous. "But of course I understand, Madame Legrand. Let me speak to my father about this. As in all things, I will be guided by his wisdom. I shall telephone you when he has thought about this kind invitation. Until the next time we meet, I take my leave. *Mauruuru roa, nana*…thank you very much, and goodbye."

With the officer's significant presence gone, the bar felt strangely empty…as, I suddenly realized, did my tummy. The spread that had been offered earlier had disappeared, so I was relieved when Henri said, "Where'd all the food go? I'm starving."

Mahana was gathering empty bottles. "The girls took it back to the kitchen; we didn't know how long you'd be. I'll ask Nadine to help me bring it out again." She scuttled off, and I could hear her calling Nadine's name before the door had swung closed. I smiled every time Mahana referred to Eloise, Nadine, and even Annette, as "girls" – which she often did – because they were all in their mid-thirties, and Mahana was only about a decade older.

"We'll need to prepare a statement about…the death," said Fleur. I knew that within the division of labor agreed by the couple, Fleur was the one who'd taken the lead when it came to the advertising and promotion for the resort, so I wasn't surprised by her observation. And it made sense; given what I'd learned about Vaiarii Teriimana, it was more than likely that the Legrands would need to be ready to answer questions from…well, whomever might ask. The press? Did newspapers really exist on Tahiti? I reasoned that, even if they'd gone the way of the dodo, there'd still be the global travel press. But would they really be interested in what had happened at one beach, on a tiny spit of land, on a little island in the middle of the Pacific Ocean? Maybe. I also suspected there might be all sorts of bloggers around the world who'd have an interest in the death of a celebrity at a photogenic, luxury resort.

Oh dear, poor Henri and Fleur…I felt awful for them. And for the Teriimana family, of course. As I caught myself thinking this, I wondered again why I felt so much worse for the Legrands than the Teriimanas – then reasoned it was because I knew the Legrands, whereas Vaiarii Teriimana's family and friends were only conceptual to me, rather than real. I gave myself a pass on that one – a normal response, psychologically speaking.

As I was mulling this point, Bud said, "I hope that food appears soon – I haven't had a bite today so far."

Focusing on my husband for a moment, I gave him a hug. "Sorry…of course, you've been out there without anything at all to eat. I've neglected my wifely duties, Husband. I should have tended to your needs more carefully."

Bud snorted and kissed me on the head just as Nadine and Mahana appeared with what were either completely fresh platters of food, or else it was the same that had been offered earlier, but now rearranged onto smaller plates. Either way, we all dived in, and the silence that ensued spoke volumes about how peckish we'd all been.

Mahana passed around drinks, with Bud taking what I felt was a well-deserved lager. Our bottles dripped ice crystals, which added to the overall effect of reviving us.

After a good five minutes or so of happy silence, Nadine reappeared from the kitchen. "Eloise was wondering what the plan would be for the rest of the day."

She addressed her query to the five of us. Bud and I looked in the general direction of Henri, Fleur, and Mahana. Henri wiped his mouth and replied, "Let's have as normal a day as we can. Fleur and I will take a walk to see if there's a strange boat moored anywhere, which I promised Puletua we'd do. I believe Mahana's going into Papeete to conduct interviews for the last of the housekeeping staff later this afternoon, correct?" Mahana nodded. "So I suggest that you and Eloise progress with dinner prep as planned. You okay with that?"

Nadine nodded and left. Fleur asked us, "Do you two have any plans for the rest of the afternoon?"

"I was hoping for a swim," said Bud, "need to freshen up, you know?"

"Thanks for doing what you did," said Fleur. "It's – sorry, *he's* – not our problem now. At least…we can do everything possible to make sure he's not. Henri, let's talk about that statement as we walk – and let's get going, in case those clouds on the mountain top roll down. If you're going into Papeete, Mahana, I'd get going now, if I were you. And take care coming back later – the road could be bad."

Mahana stood and smoothed down her *pareo*, which – surprisingly for her – was looking rumpled. "I was planning to go by boat: it's faster, and if the bad weather rolls through I won't have to worry about the road being washed out after the rain."

"It shouldn't wash out anymore," snapped Henri, "you know how they've worked on it for the past few months. It's much better now than it was."

Fleur smiled. "Better, but still not good. It's something we'll have to think about when the real rains come. We might have to arrange for more deliveries to be made by boat than we'd originally planned. And maybe even transport our guests by boat, too. Though the luggage could go by road, I dare say."

Henri had told us, in painful detail, about how building the resort had been such a challenge because everything they'd needed for construction not only had to get to the island in the first place, but then had to be delivered to the site by boat because the road that needed to be built to connect the resort to the main highway had been held up due to a problem with getting all the permissions required. We'd also learned that, when it had eventually been built, Henri then had to fight to get them to understand it wasn't fit for purpose – hence the recent upgrades. Bud and I had driven it several times, and it had terrified me on every occasion; the passing places were so narrow it seemed they'd been designed to allow two vehicles to be accommodated only if the owners of both were prepared to risk their wing mirrors, and even paint. There again, the times we'd made the trip to Papeete in a small boat had horrified me even more, which was why we'd left the resort so relatively infrequently during our three-week stay. That said, we had managed to get as far as Bora Bora on one occasion – and we'd even had drinks at the world-famous Bloody Mary's bar there. We'd ordered Bloody Marys, of course, because…well, why not? That had been another trip that had taken me way outside my comfort zone; the tiny planes used to fly the short hops between islands seem so…vulnerable. But it had been worth it because, if Tahiti was paradise, then Bora Bora was on a different plain entirely…almost unbelievably heavenly.

As Bud unfolded himself from his chair, and I stood to join him to return to our bungalow, there was a distant roll of thunder.

Fleur sighed. "Come on, my dearest, let's get going, before the storm comes."

"I hope Sonny's father was right about the rains," replied Henri, "because bad weather on top of a dead celebrity is the last thing we need."

"Oh no," said Mahana, glancing at her phone. "Word's out on social media about Vaiarii already. How did that happen? I hope Roimata doesn't find out like this. Maybe…maybe I should speak to her."

She strode out of the bar into the kitchen clutching her phone and looking horribly worried. I felt sorry for her: she had a difficult call to make.

Breathing

Bud and I sauntered back to our bungalow holding hands; I knew I felt better for having his skin against mine, and his smile told me he felt the same. As soon as we were inside our own private quarters, my husband answered my unasked question by hugging me so tight that I could hardly breathe – so I squeezed him back just as hard. We ended up giggling like two teens, then breaking apart, gasping for air.

"Good grief," said Bud, seeming to struggle to catch his breath. For a moment, I chastised myself for squeezing a man who was still recovering from a collapsed lung. Then he smiled, which relieved me, and said, "Not the day I'd expected when I woke this morning."

"Me neither. Not the body…nor the exact situation. So – now that we're on our own – what do you really think, Husband? A tragic accident, or something more…sinister?"

Bud sat on the edge of the bed and pulled off his sweat-stained shirt. "Given our track record? Guess." We shared a wry laugh. "Seriously? That lump on Vaiarii's head could have been acquired in the fight he had in the early hours, I guess. That'll be for the cops to work out. And the medics can determine the cause of death. But, for now? Honestly, I think this is more up your street than mine, Cait. I'm a procedure guy – and I won't have the chance to 'do' anything. You, on the other hand, are a criminal psychologist who specializes in profiling victims. So, even though we don't know if the guy drowned, or somehow died before he went into the water, you could work up a profile on him, like you used to do when you consulted for my homicide division, back in Vancouver. The folks here obviously knew him, and it looks as though he might have a significant digital footprint for you to take a look at, too. What do you think?"

I'd been continuing to work with a couple of groups of final year students at the University of Vancouver via video conferencing since we'd been detained in Australia, and also since we'd arrived on Tahiti. I had a session planned with a group for two p.m., local time…which I realized, with a jolt, was in half an hour.

"I've got a tutorial at two, and I can't miss that, so I'd better get ready for it, get that done, and then…well, maybe I could noodle around online, or corner Eloise or Nadine in the kitchen."

Bud chuckled, "You're a brave woman, Cait: you know what Eloise is like about being disturbed when she's working; Nadine might bark at you to keep away – she's so protective of her. Maybe try Annette Wong, instead? You're always saying how happy she is to chatter. Wow…listen to that thunder."

"I hope the internet holds up for me to get through this tutorial," I said, "but – in case it doesn't – I'm going to send some texts to the group right now, so they know what's going on at this end. And if you plan to get yourself into the lagoon for a swim, I'd go for it now, Bud, before…well, that's stupid, because if it rains on you, you'll be wet in any case, but you know what I mean. Come on – time enough to think about the late Monsieur Teriimana when we've seen to our own needs."

Two hours later I'd lost any hope of reconnecting with my group in Vancouver; we'd started well, and they'd all been apparently understanding when I'd outlined the work I wanted them to do if we got cut off. Then the connection had died, just when I was halfway through what I hoped was a well-made point about how violent interactions can often develop from non-violent beginnings, and why, therefore, training in de-escalation techniques for law enforcement professionals was critical.

With a dead laptop on my little desk, Bud and I moved to sit on the sofa at the foot of our bed, where we watched the rain bounce off the water of the lagoon and listened to it drumming onto the straw-covered, metal roof above us. It was truly awe-inspiring. The storm had, indeed, rolled down the mountainside, and had brought both thunder and lightning with it, as well as the most torrential downpour either of us had ever seen – and that's saying something for two people who live halfway up a little mountain in a rainforest on what's known as the wet west coast of Canada. The bungalow's thermostat had told us that the temperature had dropped to what felt like a chilly twenty-eight degrees Celsius, so we'd pulled the duvet off the bed to wrap around ourselves, and were snuggled together watching the fury of nature when my phone, unexpectedly, started to warble.

Surprised I even had a signal, I answered without checking the number.

"Cait, can you hear me?" I recognized Mahana's voice. She was shouting.

I shouted back, "Yes, I can. Where are you?" I assumed she was in Papeete.

"I'm stuck. The weather's too bad for me to sail back. I'm going to spend the night here. I can't get hold of Henri, or Fleur…or anyone. You're the only person who answered their phone. Can you let them know I'll be back in the morning, please?"

I was puzzled: I'd got the impression that it hadn't been Mahana's intention to return until the evening anyway, and the storm might have passed by then. I was about to say as much when the call dropped, and I was left holding a lump of plastic – with no signal at all.

"Who was that?" Bud had to speak loudly for me to hear him over the noise of the rain.

I explained.

"Well, I guess you'll just have to pass on the message…when we can get out of here, which isn't going to be any time soon, I don't think. There's a wall of water out there. The sea's gone, Moorea's gone…it's like the whole of the rest of the world has disappeared. Magnificent, eh?"

I agreed it was, and snuggled in again, watching, listening, and smelling the air which was…electric.

I must have dropped off, because the next thing I knew Bud was standing over me, dressed, and ready to…go to dinner? I was confused, and drooly. "How long was I asleep?"

"About an hour. I left you there while I got ready. You obviously needed it."

"Storms can be soothing."

"Well, this one's gone now, and Henri called to ask me to come over to the restaurant early, because he wants to talk to me. I told him about Mahana, and he said he understands – though he sounded puzzled. Anyhow, the bathroom's all yours, Wife. Just come across when you're ready."

I pushed myself upright, feeling a bit dazed. "I know I shouldn't say it, because this is all rather lovely, but I'm really looking forward to being at home, petting Marty, and having a pizza in front of the telly. I…I miss our life, Bud. This is all so…unreal. Yes, I know I should be grateful, but…"

Bud sat beside me. "If I hadn't acted without thinking in Australia, I wouldn't have gotten myself injured. We'd have been home weeks ago if it hadn't been for me not being able to fly. But you got that extra time with your sister, and now we've had this sort of break. But, yeah, I know what you mean. Only a few more days here, then a couple of weeks on a ship, and we'll be collecting Marty from Jack and Sheila, sorting out the acreage – though I know they've popped over to look in on the place while we've been gone. And yeah…pizza – with extra cheese, and pepperoni, and even mushrooms – with our feet up in front of the TV…and back to fighting a slightly overweight Labrador for space in the bed at night, right? Not long now."

I sighed. "I know you're right. So – let's make the most of our last few days here…four days, really, because the last one will be spent getting out of here and onto the ship. It's horribly humid, even this sofa feels damp…so no make-up, and something loose and cool for me tonight, I think. Maybe the tangerine two-piece – that's always jolly. Go on – find out what Henri wants, and I'll be over before you know it."

Glowing

The rain evaporating off the wooden walkway as I exited our bungalow was evidence that the sun was doing its job of drying everything out after the storm. It would drop into the sea like a stone in about half an hour, and I hoped the air would be a lot less clammy after that. Meanwhile, I realized that I'd probably wasted my time washing my hair – again, but this time without the singing – because it was already damp at the nape of my neck. I hate humidity, so walked slowly, resisting the urge to scamper to get to the relative delights of overhead fans and artificially cooled air in the restaurant which, although it was open to the elements on one side, at least allowed diners the chance to select a table as far away from the beach as possible.

When I arrived at the main complex, I could see that Bud was standing inside the bar with Henri and Fleur. Many of our evenings had begun the same way, with our hosts then dining with us, and all of us exchanging views on the food's preparation and presentation. We'd also given feedback on the service provided by Annette Wong, who was going to be the person training up the other servers who'd be coming to work at the resort, under Mahana's oversight, of course.

I felt strangely apprehensive as I greeted Bud then exchanged French cheek-kisses with Henri and Fleur. Such niceties had been noticeably lacking earlier in the day, so at least it was good to have something return to normal – though I suspected our evening would be anything but. That said, it was clear that Henri had finally made an effort regarding his appearance; his head and face were so freshly shaved that they glowed, and his mustache had been twirled into place with obvious determination. Fleur, meanwhile, looked pretty in her ensemble; she always – and I mean always – wore a sleeveless top with a high neckline above capri pants. On this occasion, the top was pale pink, and her pants were also pink, and printed with large, graphic lemons. The pastel colors showed off her deep tan and chocolatey eyes a treat. Not for the first time, I was amazed by her naturally flawless complexion. However, I pushed any jealousy I felt to one side, knowing that I too, for once – and largely because I was slathering myself with sun protection every day – had glowing skin. Well, the fact that I was sweating helped, too.

With greetings exchanged, I was dismayed when Henri immediately launched into a diatribe concerning the rash, and increasingly ridiculous, theories about Vaiarii's death that were already being bandied about online – which was, apparently, what he'd wanted to talk to Bud about, though why, I wasn't sure. What could Bud do but sympathize? *Maybe all Henri had really wanted was a friendly ear?*

I let him rant on at Bud, and gave my attention to Annette, who was on duty behind the bar. She happily presented me with my new favorite drink. We'd decided to call it an HTTPS, which Annette had thought hilarious: a Hendricks gin; two of the small cans of tonic they served at the bar; a slice of *pamplemousse*, which I preferred over the English name for grapefruit, and a fat straw. It wasn't something I'd ever have thought of preparing for myself, because I'm honestly not a big fan of grapefruit, but Annette's slight mashing of the fruit before adding the rest of the ingredients lent the drink a delightfully bitter-sweet edge that I would forever associate with Tahiti – odd, for a drink based on a gin made in Scotland.

I sighed as the now-familiar flavors soothed me, even as Henri babbled on. To be fair to him, I could quite understand why he was horrified that murder by throat-slitting, poisoning, and being bashed over the head had already been talked about in some detail online. Then he mentioned that rumors were starting to spread that another body had been found, too.

At this point, Fleur intervened with: "I've spoken to the police about that, Henri, and they've said that not only will they make the facts clear, but they'll also make sure that our words – about how there was no connection between the resort and Vaiarii – will become a part of the official statement they've promised to give tomorrow. Everything will quieten down after that: there'll be something else for people to get themselves worked up about soon enough."

I smiled at Fleur, in recognition of her attempt to help her husband come to terms with a difficult situation.

Henri sighed, "I wish I could believe that, but you know how these things go. No one wants to hear that an autopsy will be done…in time. That results will come…in time. People these days don't want to wait, they want instant…everything. By the time there's any real information it'll be too late for us, because the void will have been filled by gossip and rumor. I'm just grateful we haven't had any cancellations. Yet."

Fleur's face creased with concern as she touched her husband's arm gently. "It might not come to that, Henri. There's the old saying that all publicity is good publicity: maybe people will want to come to see where the beautiful and famous Vaiarii Teriimana was last photographed. Let's see what happens, eh?" She put down her empty wine glass – which had been almost full when I'd arrived – and kissed her husband's cheek tenderly. "Now, come along, it's a little early for our 'booking', but we need to be sure that when the guests are ready, the restaurant is ready, too…so let's go through and see how they cope. We need to keep them on their toes."

Bud left his empty beer bottle on the bar, and I took my drink with me. I'd explained a couple of weeks earlier that I couldn't cope with drinking wine with our evening meals; I prefer red to white, and it was just too warm for me to properly enjoy it. That hadn't prevented Henri from roping us into a load of tastings, however, so Bud and I had fulfilled our test-guest duties, and had swirled and sipped, then swirled and sipped some more, over many days. Henri had reached the point where he was happy with his selection of mainly French offerings, with a few good alternatives from Australia and New Zealand thrown in for good measure, and a couple from Tahiti's own vineyards. He'd even heeded my suggestion of sourcing a decent Argentinian Malbec, and had plumped for an excellent one, which I'd agreed was a good medium-bodied, medium-tannin option. But not even that held any appeal for me as I glowed my way into the blessedly cool interior of the restaurant, where I suggested we all sat as close to the air conditioner as possible.

As usual, Annette passed us the now-familiar bamboo menu-boards after we'd settled. It had been decided that the restaurant would always offer only a small range of dishes, designed by Eloise on the day, depending upon the availability of worthy ingredients. Thus, the menu was always going to be handwritten by Nadine – who had excellent writing skills, with the classic French appearance – then photocopied, and inserted into bamboo holders designed for the task, with the resort's logo burned into the back. I was surprised to see only five items listed: mango dusted with *li hing mui* for *hors d'oeuvres*; *plats principaux* of *ma'a tinito* with rice or bluefin tuna in coconut milk; cheese; pineapple sorbet.

Henri's head snapped up. "What's this? This isn't a complete menu. No *aperitif*, only two main dishes, and only one dessert."

Annette tilted her head coyly. "This is me, Annette, speaking to you, Monsieur Legrand…not a server addressing a guest. Eloise says she's had a terrible day, and hopes you'll understand. It's a one-off, she said – because of the…death."

Henri harrumphed. "Tell Eloise…just this once."

I was surprised that Henri had been so gruff with Annette and, by extension, Eloise. It had been nothing if not an unusual day, and I reckoned the entire "test" aspect could be relaxed for one evening at least. It appeared that Fleur agreed with me, because she stroked her husband's arm and whispered something into his ear that I couldn't catch, but which allowed his brow to unfurrow a little as he nodded. I hoped the rest of him relaxed soon, too, because all this tension was starting to get to me…at least, it was either that or the heat and humidity; I could feel a headache starting to niggle in my temples.

After we'd all placed our orders, Bud clearly decided that a rush of bonhomie was called for, and he did his best to engage Henri in reminiscing about a senior RCMP officer named George who'd been responsible for their training in Saskatchewan almost forty years earlier. Unfortunately, soon after the almost immediate arrival of our first course, it became clear that Henri had despised the man. "I was glad when I left that place, and he was the main reason. I calm myself with the knowledge he must be long dead by now."

Bud finished his last mouthful of mango covered with the salty plum flavoring that the Chinese had brought with them to Tahiti back in the late 1800s, when they'd come to work on the plantations. We'd grown to enjoy its flavor a great deal since our arrival, though it was always a challenge to get all the rust-colored powder off your fingers after eating it. Bud wiped at his as he said, "Nope, George isn't dead. He's in a care home just outside Regina. Approaching ninety, and as fit as a fiddle, I hear."

Henri shook his head. "Those poor people," he said, with a ghost of a smile on his face. "I bet he orders them all about like he did us."

"I dare say," replied Bud. He added thoughtfully, "But we were all so young, so clueless. We needed someone like old George to give us a wake-up call before we went off into the world to face what we did. To do…what we had to do."

Henri didn't respond directly to Bud's comment. Instead, he sipped his wine. "This should work with the flavor of the mango, but it doesn't." He sounded annoyed. He shook his head, and sighed heavily. "But I guess we'll never be putting what's essentially street food on our real menu when we open, so maybe it won't matter. I'll try both a red and a white with my main course; people never know what to chose with pork, so it's best if we can make alternative pairing suggestions, if they ask."

He called Annette across and asked her to open two bottles of wine after she'd cleared the table, which didn't take long.

As we waited for the next course, I could see that Henri's knee was bouncing, Fleur was nibbling the corner of her lip, and Bud seemed…well, off in a little world of his own. "Penny for them," I said to my distracted husband, hoping he'd snap out of it.

Bud's brow creased. "I was just thinking about something old George used to say. Remember, Henri, how he'd drum it into us that we'd eventually find ourselves in a situation where all we could do was rely on our gut? How all the training in the world couldn't prepare a recruit for every circumstance they might find themselves facing?"

"How could I forget?" Henri looked bleak. "That was one of the things I hated most about him. George always acted as though he'd seen everything, done everything…and that none of us had any idea about how the real world worked. Tried to give himself an air of authority by putting us all down."

Bud leaned forward, smiling. "But you have to admit he was right, Henri. Like I said earlier, we were all young, and some of us had lived pretty small lives. You from Montreal and me from Vancouver? City boys, us. We'd seen a bit of life. But some of those guys from tiny places out in the middle of Canada's vastness, they couldn't have imagined even what little we knew, let alone what a guy with thirty years of service under his belt had seen. So maybe George had earned the right to tell us we didn't know up from down. But that thing he said about trusting our gut? I took that to heart, and while I'd honestly say it's about more than just gut — it's about all the stuff Cait's good at understanding, as a psychologist, you know, all those cues we pick up subconsciously — I still think we *feel* it in our gut, Henri. You and I might not be cops any longer, but we've still got our instincts. Mine's telling me there's something badly off about this Teriimana guy showing up dead in the lagoon. Did you find a boat anywhere, by the way? Something he might have used to get here after he left Papeete in the small hours?"

Henri and Fleur shook their heads.

Bud sighed and sat back. "See? That's what I mean. No car. No boat. How did he get here? And how did he get into the lagoon, anyway? And…why? For all that you fancy the idea of him falling overboard out at sea and washing up here, Henri, we both know that couldn't have happened. He'd have been cut to pieces by the coral if he'd come over the reef into the lagoon, and he wasn't. And I know your main concern is about how all this might impact your business — but, surely, what we both *really* think is that we want to know what happened. We've both spent our entire careers in law enforcement, Henri, and searching out the truth is what's at the bottom of that, right?"

I noticed Fleur flash a brief glare toward her husband. *Odd.*

Henri fiddled with the base of his wine glass and didn't look at Bud as he replied. "Yeah, I want to know what happened, but don't forget that I was always the cop, Bud, while you were the detective. I kept the peace; you tracked down killers. Big difference."

I suspected Bud was inching his way toward trying to get Henri onboard to investigate the puzzling death, but I didn't want him to do that; all his talk of gut instincts and subconscious cues was niggling at me, and I felt even more sure that Henri and Fleur knew more than they were saying about the late Monsieur Teriimana. I managed a little contact with Bud's ankle beneath the table and was delighted when the door from the kitchen swung open.

"Oh look, the food's coming," I squealed. If Fleur's reaction was anything to go by, I'd probably overdone my enthusiasm by a good few degrees, but at least I'd managed to get everyone off the topic of a mysterious death, and onto the main reason for our being there: to eat, and to judge.

The *ma'a tinito* that Fleur and Henri had ordered was being served in the fanciest way I'd ever seen it presented; Bud and I had eaten it a few times on our sorties to Papeete and it had been slightly different every time, as is often the case with a dish that's become a staple in a community where cultures are blended. To be honest, if it hadn't been for the fact that the name of the dish actually translates from the Tahitian as "Chinese food", I'd never have guessed its Chinese origins, especially since the first couple of times we'd eaten it, it had been accompanied by bananas.

On this occasion, Eloise had chosen to present the layered dish of marinated, twice-cooked pork, red beans, green beans, and transparently thin slices of shallot, on a bed of pasta…and it looked, and smelled wonderful. I inhaled the fragrance of the meat, laced with the aroma of soy sauce, that was floating across the table, and could feel my saliva glands kick into overdrive.

"I thought we'd agreed this would only be served with rice, and the menu even said it would be," noted Henri. "I can't imagine there's a good reason for Eloise not using rice, as she promised us. What's going on in the kitchen, Annette?"

Annette placed the stunningly presented plates of fish in coconut milk that we'd chosen in front of me and Bud with great care, then gave her attention to her boss. "It's hard for me to say," she replied enigmatically.

"Well try," urged Henri.

Annette straightened up. "Nadine had to prepare the pasta — she's not good at rice — and plate all the food. Eloise has gone to her room. She's extremely upset about the…circumstances today."

Henri flipped his napkin onto the table and stood. "Right, this is enough." He stomped toward the kitchen, leaving Fleur open-mouthed, Bud round-eyed, and me feeling a bit embarrassed…and puzzled. Why on earth was Eloise so upset about Teriimana's death?

Drinking

The three of us sat there for a moment, then Fleur said, "Come on, let's eat up. We shouldn't let the meal go to waste, and I dare say we're all hungry. I'll let Henri lead on this – staffing is his area of responsibility."

Bud and I exchanged a furtive glance, then did our best to talk our way through the food, commenting upon presentation, the balance of ingredients, flavors, and textures. A few weeks earlier, when we'd begun our "role", Fleur had asked us to complete forms with scores for every aspect of each meal, but the entire thing had become ludicrously cumbersome, so we'd all agreed that verbal feedback would be adequate. But she always pressed us for details that Bud, especially, found it a challenge to provide. He'd often commented to me – after we were back at our bungalow – that all he cared about was the overall effect of a meal: did he enjoy it, and did it fill him up? But he'd made a real effort over the weeks to follow my lead, and he was now more than able to initiate the feedback – which was just as well, because I got a bit lost in the textures, and he had to nudge me when it was clear that more than a series of "mmms" was expected of me. I happily described that the precise way the tuna had been cut into cubes, the expert way it had been marinated with lime, then served with thinly sliced cucumber, tomatoes, onions, carrots, and ginger was giving me all the right textures, and flavors. I added that the freshly grated coconut pulp that Eloise must have used to make the coconut milk that had then been poured over the dish added the perfect final touch, and that the balance of flavors was spot on. My summation: the dish was exquisite. Fleur looked…well, not as delighted as I'd hoped, but I put that down to her being distracted by the day's events.

With our duties fulfilled, and our tummies delightfully full, we all relaxed a little – until Henri came back into the restaurant. "Eloise is shut in her bedroom, crying her eyes out. I…I don't know what to say, or do. Nadine will plate the dessert." He plopped into his chair, stabbed at his food, then added miserably, "It's cold, gelatinous, and disgusting."

Fleur stood. "That's all you've got to say, Henri? Really? What about Eloise? Did Nadine say why she's so upset?"

Henri deflated. "She said she doesn't know."

Fleur turned to us, her eyes wide with concern. "Sorry, I think I'd better step up." She left the restaurant.

I couldn't resist. "What really happened the day that Vaiarii came here to do that photo shoot, Henri?" Even if I didn't want the Legrands getting involved in any investigating Bud and I might choose to do, I still wanted to get Henri to tell us anything he knew about the dead man, and this seemed to be a good opportunity.

Henri nibbled his lip. "It was…quite a day." He pushed away his plate, and pulled the bottle of white wine from its ice bucket. He filled his glass, and took a deep draft. "Vaiarii was strutting about the place. Good-looking guy, to be fair, and used to getting a lot of attention. He kept going on about how this area had been used by the locals when he'd been a boy, and how much it had changed. I don't think he meant to be as nasty as he was, but I have to admit I got sick of it after a while. Progress can be good for a place, and we've built this resort in a way that means that nature's hardly been impacted – everything's been planned and implemented to be sustainable; I've seen to that, and it's cost a pretty penny to do it. But, putting aside his whining, even though that CeeCee of his was fawning all over him every chance she got, and the crew of women they'd brought with them were buzzing around him all the time, it still didn't seem to be…quite enough attention for him. So he flirted with Annette, and…and Fleur. To be honest, she got a bit fluttery, which is…not her usual way. But then there was the incident with Nadine and Eloise. I didn't see or hear whatever it was that set Nadine off, but we all went running when we heard him screaming…" Henri paused, then reacted to Bud's raised eyebrows. "Yes, Vaiarii screamed like a little kid. 'Not my face…not my face!' That's what grabbed everyone's attention. When I got around to the side of the restaurant, Eloise was cowering in a corner, and Nadine was jumping up and down slapping Vaiarii for all she was worth. Fleur dragged her off him, then Nadine had a bit of a go at her, too. I had to physically grab Nadine. Fleur took her to one side to try to get her to calm down. Eloise just dissolved into tears and ran off to her room. Stayed there for hours, sobbing. Like now."

I checked by asking, "So you didn't see what happened in the first place?" Henri shook his head. I pressed on. "But did you believe what Eloise and Nadine said? That Vaiarii was trying to force himself on Eloise…got her into a situation from which she couldn't easily escape?"

Henri shrugged expansively. "Given what I saw, their version explained the facts."

Bud leaned in. "And how did Vaiarii himself react to all this?" Bud was now also sipping cool white wine, so I thought I'd join in; my gin was long gone.

Henri poured me a glass, then another for himself. "The photo shoot itself was almost over by then – they'd all taken a break before Vaiarii was due to do some final stuff in the lagoon. Vaiarii brushed off the whole thing, and insisted upon getting his hair and make-up redone, then…well, then they carried on as though nothing at all had happened. I think…yeah, I reckon that CeeCee was even more attentive of him after that, but – after he'd rolled about in the water a bit, and they'd made sure he looked sandy enough and that the water was glistening on this bit of him and that bit of him, in exactly the right way, for about an hour – then they all packed up and left. Didn't stay for a meal, which was the original plan. The early departure was at CeeCee's insistence." Henri paused and chuckled darkly. "One of the main reasons I agreed to them doing the shoot here was because I hoped she'd do one of her blog things about the food. Eloise had worked hard to come up with an offering of a wide variety of small plates that would look great on camera, but everything ended up going to waste. Well, it didn't go to waste exactly, because we all ate it. Still, at least there was CeeCee's vlog, and we were going to get full credit for the location for the photography…oh, I wonder…"

Henri pulled out his phone and started scrolling. Bud and I shrugged at each other, then Henri said, "Nope, they definitely haven't begun to use those photos yet. I wonder if…I wonder if they'll ever use them, now that he's dead. Oh no…" Henri shook his head sadly and put away his phone. "I wonder if things could get any worse."

Fleur entered through the door from the kitchen looking harried. "Eloise is saying she's going to leave us, Henri – what shall we do?"

Henri almost dropped his glass. "Leave us? Now? She can't. We'll never get anyone to replace her…not with just a week to go before we open. It took us months of negotiation to get her to come here. Why on earth does she want to leave?"

Fleur grabbed the almost empty bottle of wine from the ice bucket. "Says she doesn't feel safe. That she's sure there's a murderer in the area. I told her she was talking rubbish, tried to calm her down…but she was adamant. And, of course, Nadine will follow wherever Eloise goes. So we'd lose them both."

Just as I thought the tension couldn't get any greater, we all heard the unmistakable crunching of tires coming from behind the restaurant.

Henri said hopefully, "Sounds like Mahana managed to get a ride back from Papeete, after all. She'll know what to do."

As we listened to the sound of feet on the wooden walkway getting closer, we all looked expectantly toward the open front of the restaurant. More than one person was approaching, I could tell that much, but it wasn't Mahana who appeared.

I recognized CeeCee Ducasse from her online presence, though she was much taller than I'd imagined: an almost Amazonian figure, curvaceous, with long, glossily black hair pulled up into a high ponytail, the young woman was made up as though for a red carpet appearance, and sheathed in a fitted white dress. The other person was…well, I immediately thought of a fieldmouse: the man was dun-haired, bespectacled, dressed in khaki, and a head shorter than CeeCee even before allowing for his bent posture. He scampered after her, as she strode out in four-inch wedge heels.

"CeeCee, what a surprise," said Henri.

"Show me where the love of my life died," said the young woman. Then she fell to the ground in an elegant heap.

Weeping

By the time we all reached her, CeeCee Ducasse was on her feet again and being fussed over by the unnamed man who'd entered the restaurant behind her. She swatted him away, but accepted the arm Henri offered to guide her to a chair.

Fleur passed her a glass of water, which she sipped as though it might be hydrochloric acid, then she produced a piece of gauze from a tiny purse that was dangling from her wrist and patted her dry eyes. I was torn; I wanted to tut aloud because the young woman was so obviously play-acting, but I knew she was the dead man's fiancée, so felt some sympathy toward her. I recalled how I'd had to grapple with the death of my ex-boyfriend, Angus; by the time he'd died, I hadn't even liked him, and I had to assume CeeCee had loved Vaiarii.

With Fleur and Henri fussing over her like a pair of moths around a solitary flame, I stepped back to watch as CeeCee Ducasse relaxed into her role as the absolute center of attention as though she were born to it. Which, given that her father owned one of the largest Tahitian pearl supply companies in the world, I suspected she might have been. She was certainly sporting an impressive example of what I guessed must be her father's wares: the massive, perfectly spherical, peacock-hued pearls that sat around her neck were magnificent – and probably worth a fortune. Despite the fact that pearls really aren't my cup of tea, it had been impossible to spend much time on Tahiti without learning at least a little about them, so even I was able to tell that the necklace that stood out beautifully against CeeCee's white gown and tanned skin was made of pearls that were so large that they had to be exceptionally rare, and valuable. Indeed, as I focused on them – rather than on her annoyingly quivering chin, flawless skin, and completely unspoiled eye make-up – I wondered if I might be persuaded, after all, to leave Tahiti with at least one modest pair of stud earrings, as a memento of our time on the island. Bud had kept suggesting it, but I'd pushed back, telling him that I couldn't bear the idea of spending that much money on a pair of earrings; recalling the prices I'd seen in the jewelry shops, I reckoned that CeeCee's necklace had to be worth…well, maybe hundreds of thousands of dollars, which was a concept that shocked me.

CeeCee must have noticed me staring, though she misinterpreted the reason. It seemed as though her state of desperation had been momentarily forgotten when she smiled broadly at me and said, "Yes, I am her. Would you like my autograph?"

Why on earth would I? was what I thought; "Hello, my name's Cait Morgan, but I'm fine, thanks," was what I said. I reckoned that was polite enough.

"Hello," said the miraculously recovered CeeCee. "And this is?" She dangled a set of perfectly manicured talons in Bud's general direction. It was impossible to miss the large golden pearl held in place by two arcing bands of diamonds on her other hand, which rested languidly on the table; an engagement ring truly worthy of marking the betrothal of a pearl heiress and a pearl diver.

Bud shook her fingers with vigor. "Bud Anderson," he said, waggling her arm so much that her entire upper body jiggled about.

"My husband," I said; I felt I should, because CeeCee was almost drooling.

"What an interesting couple you make," observed the young woman as she tossed her long ponytail over her shoulder.

"Old friend of mine," gushed Henri, sounding as though he felt our presence needed an explanation. "It was Cait who found Vaiarii…Vaiarii's…" He trailed off awkwardly.

CeeCee Ducasse stood; she towered over me by almost a foot. It was an intimidating feeling. She gazed at my upturned face and said, "What happened? Tell me exactly. And show me where he was. I must know…I can't stop thinking about it, and there are so many rumors swirling about online. Please Cat, for the sake of my sanity, tell me everything."

She grabbed both my hands with both of hers – which were silky soft – and pressed them against her alarmingly ample bosom. "In here, my heart is broken," she said, then she shuddered with a fake sob, and dropped my hands as though they were on fire.

I said, "It's Cait, not Cat, and – if you can manage in those heels – I'll show you where I found the body. We'll need to cross the beach though, and it's dark, so take care." I didn't trust myself to be more fulsome; CeeCee Ducasse had well and truly got under my skin – and not in a good way.

At that moment, Annette appeared from the kitchen with a tray of what I assumed was the pineapple sorbet we'd been promised for dessert. Her eyes opened wide when she saw CeeCee and her "plus one". She stammered, "Oh d-dear…extra guests." She looked at the tray, looked at all of us, then added, "Should I…?" She allowed her unasked question to hover above the glistening mounds of sweet deliciousness which, I realized, my palate was craving.

"Back to the freezer with that lot," said Fleur authoritatively. "And maybe CeeCee will join us when we return from the beach."

Our hostess glanced at the "grieving" girlfriend of the dead man with what I could tell was a glint of opportunistic hope, though the idea that even CeeCee would bother to take photographs of a sorbet, or share the same with her adoring followers, when she was at the resort to enquire about where her late fiancé's corpse had been found struck me as unlikely.

The young influencer's reply of an enigmatic, "We'll see," made me doubt my initial reaction.

As Annette headed back to the kitchen, the rest of us trooped off toward the beach. The lights from the bar allowed us to at least cross the wide deck without too much of a problem, then we reached the beach and I was glad I was wearing flats, though CeeCee didn't even break stride as she marched ahead of me into the darkness, with the simpering man – who she still hadn't seen fit to introduce to Bud and myself – shining the flashlight app from his phone at the sand so she could see where she was going. However, her head was held so high that I could tell she wasn't looking at where she was putting her feet, which I found fascinating.

CeeCee waited at the edge of the lagoon until we all caught up.

I explained, "I sort of bobbed and walked through the lagoon from our bungalow – we're in the farthest one out there, on the left – and your fiancé was…floating somewhere in the middle. I…bumped into him, then turned him over – hoping he might still be alive. I managed to bring him back to the shore, holding his chin above the water. Mahana helped me pull him onto the beach, but…but it was clear that he was…beyond our ability to revive him." I added a quiet, "I'm so sorry," out of respect for the dead man.

"Why was he here?" CeeCee's voice carried on the night air.

"None of us know," was our host's pointed reply.

"He said he'd had a terrible time here when we came to do our photo shoot," said CeeCee, almost angrily, "so I can't imagine why he'd have wanted to come back."

"Indeed," said Fleur. "That's what we all thought."

CeeCee asked, "And no one saw him here last evening?"

I realized she hadn't heard about her late fiancé's run-in with the law.

"We know he was in Papeete at about three in the morning," offered Henri. "At a club. Got into some sort of trouble there. The cops were called. Took him home."

"He wasn't at a club in Papeete last night," snapped CeeCee. She turned to the man who was shining his flashlight across the lagoon. "There's only one it's worth going to at the moment, and we'd have seen him there, wouldn't we, Troy?"

Ah, Troy.

Finally, CeeCee turned to me and Bud and said, "Troy's my right-hand man, aren't you, Troy? My stylist, my cameraman, my editor…and he's so good with a witty turn of phrase when it comes to writing my posts. I don't know what I'd do without him."

I'm still wondering what you do, was what I thought; "Worth more than a Troy ounce, then," was what I said. When everyone including Bud looked puzzled, I decided I wouldn't bother mentioning that the Troy ounce is still used to weigh precious metals: pithy witticisms only work if you don't have to explain them, it seems.

With my non-joke having fallen flat, Troy himself decided to speak; I'd wondered if he could. "CeeCee's been in a dreadful state since she heard the news, and she insisted we came here to find out what we could. No one will tell her anything, not even though her father phoned the police. Everything depends on the autopsy, they said, didn't they, CeeCee? At least her father's influence means that will take place quickly, which is a blessing. They might know something by tomorrow afternoon, they said, didn't they, CeeCee?"

Troy appeared to be in his forties, and I spotted his New Zealand accent quite easily – my sister having taken great delight in pointing out all the New Zealanders holidaying in Sydney when we'd recently spent time there together. Despite the fact we siblings still both have our Welsh accents, it seemed that the

Aussie habit of giggling whenever a New Zealander mentioned "fish and chips" was something my sister had picked up from her Australian husband. I'd ended up having to point out to her how annoying it was, which didn't go down too well. Still, we'd kissed and made up, as sisters do.

CeeCee nodded at Troy – "imperiously" was a word that came to my mind – then managed to surprise me by saying, "Now I have to learn to live without Vaiarii. I have no idea how I'll manage, do I, Troy?"

Troy reached up to pat CeeCee on her shoulder, which she rolled away from his fingers.

Her next, almost cheery, statement of: "Let's start back," was what threw me most; Bud and I managed an eyeroll at that one, then we all headed back toward the restaurant. As we reached the deck, I couldn't help but wonder why on earth CeeCee had made what must have been a perilous journey along the road – which might not be in good shape after the storm – just so she could stare at a lagoon, then dismiss it.

"You go on ahead," she said, finally on firmer ground, "while Troy and I create some content. Troy – get the lagoon and the beach behind me, will you? Use the night settings. I'll hold my own phone out of shot; uplighting my face should work well."

The four of us paused, and I watched with amazement as Troy scampered about, fiddled with CeeCee's necklace and hair, and the hem of her dress, then stood back and held up his phone. He pointed three fingers at the young woman, then two, then one, then pointed at CeeCee herself…who transformed.

The haughty Amazonian princess became a grief-stricken creature, who wiped away what looked like genuine tears as though she cared nothing for her elaborate make-up and was doing her best to be…brave. She spoke passionately – with the occasional sob thrown in, for good measure – of her eternal love for her lost Vaiarii, and of how he'd always made her feel better about herself, even when she was feeling low. Then she gushed about how he'd always loved the way she smiled, and how he'd adored dancing with her, holding her close. She went on for a couple more minutes, and I realized that, by the time she'd finished, I knew nothing more at all about the dead man – his life, his accomplishments, his personality even – other than the many ways in which he'd been besotted by CeeCee. The entire thing was about her, not him.

When she stopped speaking, there were a few seconds of nothing, then Troy said, "Excellent. That's it. One take, as always. Perfect, CeeCee. I'll cut in a few extra shots with the sound of the waves. It'll be good lead-in atmosphere."

CeeCee gave her right eye one final, delicate sweep, then smiled. "Thanks, Troy. I do my best, as you know. And you got the background in? I want people to see where he died – to know I took the time to come here."

"All there – the moon looked great on the lagoon…and I'll make sure I put everything about the location in the text."

CeeCee nodded kindly in our direction, as though acknowledging an audience, and patted Troy on the back.

Fleur looked agitated. "Do you really need to mention exactly where he was found? Maybe just don't name the resort?"

"Don't be silly," cooed CeeCee, "I've been posting about this since the minute I heard he was dead, so everyone knows it happened here. I even posted from the car as we came down the new road, which has almost washed out, by the way. I knew that absolutely everyone would want to see how dangerous it was for me to come here, so I made sure I got that bit in. We stopped to record some special content there. Besides, you were very keen for me to mention the Legrand name when we did the photo shoot here for Papa's pearls – this is no different."

I saw both Henri and Fleur sag as we headed back to the restaurant.

CeeCee continued unabashed, "Now, let's talk about the celebration of life I want to be held here. It'll have to be a mixture of traditional Tahitian, and a bit of the Catholic stuff thrown in for his mother – she's really very keen on all that sort of thing. Let's talk about it while we eat some dessert. I hope it's nothing too fattening – I have to watch my hips, you know. Curves are good, but wobbles aren't. And after that, you can show me where I'll be staying tonight."

Despite Henri's deep tan, I could have sworn I could see him blanch. "You want to stay? Here? Overnight?" He reached for Fleur's hand.

His wife sounded…*terrified* when she said, "We're not open for guests, yet, CeeCee. Cait and Bud are here as part of our process of preparation, but none of the other bungalows are set up yet. No linens, even. And Mahana's not here, nor do we have any real housekeeping staff at the moment."

CeeCee waved a hand. "Oh, it won't take long to arrange, I'm sure. Just some sheets, and towels, and toiletries, and so forth. Troy – you don't need anything fancy for your bungalow, do you? It's not as though we'd expect your full butler service, Fleur…though I know your website says you'll be providing it. Don't worry – I won't give you low marks for that."

I felt terribly sorry for our hosts. "Bud and I could lend a hand setting things up." It was out of my mouth before I could stop it.

From the corner of my eye I could see that Bud hadn't been quick enough to stop himself from looking surprised at my offer, and, in front of me, Fleur and Henri looked horrified. I realized, too late, that my offer of help might have been incredibly unhelpful.

"There you are," said CeeCee sounding triumphant, "while I try this dessert, your…friends…can help you."

I think I blushed.

Gathering

It was a despondent Fleur Legrand who led me and Bud across the restaurant, out through the lounge and reception area that was open to the elements on three sides, and across the car park to a collection of buildings hidden by the palms and lush plants of the gardens. I'd never been to this area of the resort before. Whitewashed breeze blocks and metal roofs didn't give the little compound the same high-end feel as our bungalows, nor the well-appointed public areas. However, an air of jollity was lent to it by a few pots of colorful flowers dotted about, and in the centre of the square created by four long, low buildings was a covered area, which protected a collection of chairs and tables, as well as a large grill.

I guessed this was where Mahana, Annette and Edouard, and Nadine and Eloise lived, and that – probably – they'd be joined there by the rest of the staff who'd have to live-in, to be able to provide the service needed by the Legrands' guests. Edouard's head popping out of one of the doors confirmed my suspicions.

His: "Everything good?" suggested he was surprised to see me and Bud there.

Fleur explained the situation. The news about CeeCee Ducasse and her assistant – whose name Fleur told us was Troy Wilson – staying overnight clearly alarmed Edouard.

"We can't have guests here, now," he exclaimed. He quickly added, "Nothing is ready."

"I know," replied Fleur testily. "Henri's entertaining them at the restaurant to give us as much time for set-up as possible – but we'll all have to pitch in. We'll put CeeCee in *Iva*, suite nine, even though it's not as big as *Ahuru*, suite ten." Fleur addressed

Bud and me, "But you're in there, and I won't ask you to move. I'll put Troy in *Va'u*, number eight, backing onto CeeCee."

It hadn't even occurred to me that we'd need to pack everything and shift ourselves to accommodate CeeCee, so my thanks to Fleur for her thoughtfulness on our part was heartfelt.

"I'll come to the stores with you," said Edouard. "All the supplies are here and ready to be used. We just have to get them there. We can use the housekeeping buggies for that."

Bud and I followed behind Edouard and Fleur as they strode out toward the only structure which had no windows, but did have massive double doors. Inside, Edouard flicked on stark LED overhead lights, which illuminated the entirety of the building. It was set up with a series of dividers, making it look rather like a stable building – except there were no animals, just piles of different types of supplies. At the far end I could see a bank of washing machines and dryers, along the right wall appeared to be consumables like cleaning supplies, toiletries, toilet rolls and so forth, while on the left were the reusable supplies such as linens, towels for the beach and the bungalows, pieces of furniture, beach umbrellas, even hammocks and a couple of spare clear-plastic kayaks. It was a strange experience – a bit like being backstage at a theater, where the artifice evaporates, and the reality sets in with a thud.

Parked to the right and left of the double doors we'd entered were a row of the buggies on large, squishy wheels I'd seen Annette use when she'd cleaned and replenished our bungalow. Annette had adorned hers with a few hand-made paper flowers, a couple of others already had sand in the deep tracks of their tires and a few dings on their edges, whereas some were still wrapped in a protective plastic sheath.

"Edouard and I know what we need to set up each bungalow, so you bring one buggy and follow me, Cait, and Bud can do the same for Edouard. I'll do the reusables, Edouard, you get all the consumables. We'll tag-team on the set-up when we get there, and I'll make the final checks."

I dutifully pushed a cart behind Fleur as she selected linens, pulled vacuum-packed pillows from high shelves, then pounced on mounds of fluffy towels, counting out the various sizes. "I'd better set everything up as though each bungalow is for a pair – as they will be when we open. I don't want CeeCee thinking we skimp on towels…she often comments about that in her vlogs."

I could understand why Fleur wanted her surprise guests to be comfortable, but had to ask, "Do you think CeeCee's going to bother vlogging about her accommodations, when she's really here because of her dead fiancé?"

Fleur paused, with two oversized bath sheets in her hands. "It might only take her thirty seconds to wave that phone of hers across a set of towels for just one person, and it could look bad for us. Oh…" She turned and shouted, "Edouard – I'll bring two atomizers for each bungalow…you bring the 'Calm' fragrance pods." Returning her attention to the buggy I was standing behind, Fleur added, "I haven't been into the empty bungalows since last week, I hope they're clean."

I tried to reassure her. "They must be, no one's been here but me and Bud."

"Ah, but it's the sea air, Cait; the salt can come inside on the breeze and build up where you'd least expect it. Edouard – grab some of those cleaning cloths while you're at it – we might need to attend to some issues when we get there. I'll take a few myself."

With surprisingly full buggies, Bud and I finally followed Edouard and Fleur out of the hidden compound, along a slatted wooden path through the garden to the rear of the restaurant, and out onto the walkway that led to the bungalows. "You do *Iva* first, Edouard," said Fleur in hushed tones, "then we'll swap. Come on, Cait – you any good at making up beds?"

I did my best with the fine linens, and – with some detailed instructions from Fleur about precisely how she wanted sheets to be tucked in, and multiple cushions positioned – we ended up with a good-looking bed, fit for a…well, "princess" was the word that came to mind when I thought of CeeCee.

"Bathroom next," said Fleur with a determined look. "Let's see if anything needs a wipe-down before we take the towels in."

When we walked into the bathroom it was clear to even my inexperienced eye that not everything was as it should be. Fleur sagged. "Damn those birds. The trouble with airing out the bungalows is that we keep the doors open, then anything can fly in…as you know only too well."

We shared a wry smile as we recalled the day Bud and I had returned from lunch to discover that a beautiful Kuhl's lorikeet, with its mainly red and green – almost Christmassy – plumage had decided it rather liked our bed…and sofa…and bathroom. It had flown around our bungalow leaving its droppings seemingly everywhere, as well as having stabbed at all the soft furnishings, leaving claw and beak marks behind. Unable to convince it that flying out again was a good idea, we'd finally managed to shut it in the bathroom, where Edouard had captured it with a small fishing net on a stick, and had returned it to the garden area, where he'd set it free.

If a bird had been flying about in this bathroom, at least it hadn't pooped all over it, but it looked as though it had been wet when it arrived, because there were watermarks on the floor and on the elaborate brass tap arrangement that allowed the free-standing bathtub to be used as a shower, when the curtain which hung from an oval brass rail above it was pulled all the way around.

"I can sort the watermarks, while you place the towels just as you want them," I offered. Having watched Annette spend long minutes arranging the towels in our bathroom just so, I knew I wasn't going to be able to meet Fleur's exacting standards, so I wiped and buffed, while Fleur herself achieved towel-placement perfection. I also gave the bath a quick going over; it looked less than perfect, and I knew that was what Fleur was aiming for. Fleur checked all the other fittings in the bathroom, flushed the toilet, wiped around the basin and its taps, then declared she was satisfied. "Onto the next one. I'll come back later to check that Edouard's done everything else just as I want it."

We repeated our duties in the second bungalow – this time without there being any watermarks for me to clean up – and I watched Fleur fold a little point at the end of the loo roll, then move the toiletries that Edouard had already positioned in the bathroom by what appeared to be millimeters…until she was satisfied. Finally, we checked back on the first bungalow where Edouard had almost finished, and she went through the same processes.

"I wish we had some floral arrangements; they're a big part of what we want guests to remember about their time here, but we've only got a few at the moment – the trial ones Henri brought from Papeete. I know…I'll fetch the large one from the reception desk for CeeCee's bungalow, and Troy can have the one that we put at the end of the bar."

I couldn't help but say, "Do you really think that's necessary?"

Fleur sighed. "Absolutely. Every detail counts. Even the smell. Despite the fact we've been keeping the bungalows aired, this one smelled a bit musty when we first came inside, didn't it? Now the atomizer's starting to have an effect. You can really notice the difference, can't you?"

To be fair, Fleur made a good point. When we'd first taken up residence, I'd almost immediately moved the atomizer in our bungalow to a different spot; it had been hidden within a small, deep bowl made from what I discovered was the unique flower stone from the island of Ua Pou in the Marquesan archipelago, so-named because of the way that minerals in the rock have formed what appear to be tiny flowers within the stone itself. The bowl was a true work of art – and hefty, too – but the atomizer it was camouflaging became a bit too much for us. In fact, after about a week, Bud and I had asked to not have our atomizers operating at all, because the aroma – while initially pleasant – had become a bit overwhelming for us, especially on the few occasions when we had the doors to the deck closed at night. Having been in the bungalow for a few weeks now, it was well aired, and probably smelled of…us. But, yes, now that Fleur mentioned it, this bungalow had smelled…no, not musty. I said, "This place smelled of decay when we came in…as though a vase of dead flowers had been in here, unattended."

"It's the sea air, Cait," said Fleur, sniffing and wafting the atomizer's fragrance about the bungalow with both hands. "It gets into the soft furnishings, and all the natural wall claddings we've used. Still, at least they mean guests don't think about the fact they're really staying in a structure that's built out of modern waterproofed and soundproofed materials…which is not the image we want, though it's necessary. Folks want to feel they're the only people on earth when they're in these bungalows; heaven forbid they'd be able to hear their neighbors, however close they might be in reality. I just hope people heed our warnings about birds and close their doors at night, so the noise of any snoring or…you know, anything else…doesn't annoy the other guests."

I mentally wished Fleur luck with that hope; Bud and I hadn't been able to resist sleeping with our doors at least half-open for most of our stay, just so we could hear the wonderful sound of the surf against the coral. However, I reckoned it would be the desire to enjoy the full effect of the air conditioning overnight that was most likely to get people to close themselves in; we'd been grateful for that on several occasions, not least of all the previous night, when the atmosphere had been especially humid.

Deciding that was something I'd save up for one of our "in depth feedback" sessions, I asked, "Are you happy with the bungalows now – except for the floral displays?" Fleur nodded. "Can I help carry over the vases?" I thought I'd better offer.

"No thanks, Cait – you and Bud join the others. Annette is probably seeing to any serving requirements, so Edouard and I will get the flowers. I'll join you as soon as I can. Thanks for your help. You know…this could be useful, in a way – you and Bud have got used to being here alone, so maybe you'll notice some differences when we have other guests. Though, of course, we don't yet have the staff we'll have when we open, so there'll still be no butler delivering breakfast to your door. CeeCee will have to understand that we're not fully staffed yet. Hang on…did I hear the tap making a noise in the bathroom?" She disappeared to check for potential drips, while I hunted down Bud and we headed toward the restaurant, where I hoped there might be a sorbet with my name on it.

Sparkling

When Bud and I entered the restaurant, it was clear that Henri was feeling desperate; the look of relief on his face when he spotted us was almost comical.

"And here they are!" Henri sounded as though he might be referring to a couple of royals, not just me and my husband.

"Here we are indeed," said Bud – rather over-dramatically, I thought.

CeeCee Ducasse's tone sounded quite aggressive, to my ear, when she observed, "Two Royal Canadian Mounted Police, all the way out here in the middle of the Pacific on our little jewel of an island? What are the odds of that?"

Henri jumped in with: "As I was telling you, CeeCee, Bud and I trained together, many years ago. Then I remained with the RCMP, but Bud joined the Vancouver Police Department, right, old friend?"

Bud took his cue. "I did. It meant I could stay in my home city and not have to take postings across the country. It was good to work in the same place for more or less my entire career…though I know a lot of the RCMP folk enjoy the variety offered by the potential to move to new communities."

I wondered how much Henri had drunk while we'd been setting up the bungalows for CeeCee and Troy when he slurred, "If you scoot from place to place fast enough, the bad stuff never catches up with you, eh Bud?"

I could tell by the shift in Bud's shoulders that he thought this comment as odd as I did. He responded with a bit of a forced chuckle. "Gotta be quicker than the baddies if you want to catch them, rather than it being the other way around, eh?"

Henri nodded, then poured the dregs of a bottle of white wine into a glass. "Care for a nightcap, CeeCee?"

I could see that the trio had polished off an entire bottle of Muscat de Beaumes-de-Venise, a wine so sweet that just the thought of it set my teeth on edge.

CeeCee cooed, "I've finished my pineapple sorbet now, Henri, so, yes, a nightcap. Though you were correct that the wine paired well with the dessert – however humble that might have been. You have an…interesting wine list."

I was taken aback – yet again – by how this young woman was apparently able to show an active interest in so many things other than her fiancé's sad demise. *Heartless? A reaction to overwhelming grief?* As a psychologist I know it's sometimes difficult to tell the difference.

"Yes, I wouldn't mind something myself, too," said Henri, rising. I noticed that he steadied himself against the edge of the table before he headed toward the kitchen. "I'll rustle up a treat for us all. Just give me five minutes."

He's escaping, was what I thought; "How are you feeling, now, CeeCee?" was what I said.

"Devastated, of course," she replied, looking anything but. "My life will never be the same. Vaiarii and I were meant to be together, you see, so now I shall always be…less than I could have been with him by my side. He was a wonderful man."

I honestly didn't know what to say, because every micro-expression on CeeCee's face – those I could read beneath her heavy make-up – was telling me she was putting on a show for us all. Then I spotted Troy fiddling with his phone; he was holding it just below the table, allowing him to shoot what would, presumably, appear to be candid shots of CeeCee sharing her grief with what I hoped would be an unseen member of the public…namely, me.

I'm not having that, was what I thought; "But, surely, if you were that distraught, you wouldn't be sitting here eating dessert and drinking wine while no one really knows how an experienced pearl diver might have managed to drown in a shallow, protected lagoon," was what I said.

CeeCee flashed a palm toward Troy's "hidden" camera and snapped, "I have to eat, and the wine was to soothe my nerves. I can get very nervy, can't I, Troy?"

Troy nodded manically. "You can. But with Vaiarii's death, you have good cause."

CeeCee sneered at her underling. "I always have good cause, Troy. I'm never *unnecessarily* nervy. As you know."

Troy stammered, "Of…of course, CeeCee." He studied his hands, which were still holding his phone in his lap. He added quietly, "You're always…just right."

I was surprised he hadn't said "perfect". Again.

Bud and I know only too well that I can acquire what we refer to as "puppies" when I teach: a student who'll follow me about, looking as though they're in awe of me all the time. It's…well, it's a bit unnerving to be honest, but sort of flattering. However, in the case of Troy, I didn't judge him to be a puppy following CeeCee about with awe in his eyes; in his case his expression spoke of utter devotion, which was odd, though my creep-o-meter wasn't jangling, which was even odder.

CeeCee's next utterly dismissive comment drew me from my thoughts. "If you've never lost someone you love, there's no way you could understand how I'm feeling."

I instantly felt anger in the pit of my stomach. Of course there was no reason why CeeCee should know that Bud's first wife, Jan, had been murdered by a gang member who thought he was shooting Bud himself, but I reached out and squeezed my husband's hand, to show him I realized how deeply hurtful the young woman's comment had been. I wondered if he'd say or do anything. He often doesn't; it's too painful for him.

On this occasion, Bud squeezed my hand back before he let it fall when he stood. He looked down at CeeCee and said, "A few years ago, my wife was killed. Murdered. I more than understand what you're feeling, and I sympathize. You'll be facing some tough times. Nights when you lie awake wondering what you could have done that might have changed things. How making different choices might have meant the person you loved wasn't where they were, when they were there. How you might have been able to save them…if only you'd done something…anything…differently. That never stops. It's a nightmare that repeats itself. Too often. But – for your sake – I hope that time helps you build some protection against the pain those destructive thoughts can cause. I hope that, as the months and years pass, you're able to counsel yourself, in those dark hours, that distressing yourself because of what might have been is…is a fruitless waste of emotion. I hope you're able – with time, and the growth of some additional layers of strength – to start again. And I hope that, one day, you're able to find the joy in another person that Cait and I have done in each other. Now, please excuse me for a moment."

Bud held his head high as he made his way toward the washrooms, and I sneaked a glance at CeeCee and her minion. Troy was looking at CeeCee with *sympathy*, while CeeCee was clearly furious. *Odd.* I suspected that Bud had stolen her limelight – in her eyes – and she was cross with him because of that.

"At least Vaiarii wasn't murdered," said Troy quietly. "That must be a terrible weight to live with."

CeeCee didn't look at him as she replied, "You never know, Troy – he might have been."

I was certain I heard an undertone of excitement in CeeCee's sly response.

Just as I was thinking this, Henri appeared through the door from the kitchen bearing a tray covered with tall glass mugs full of something milky-white and all alight with sparklers. It seemed far too celebratory for the circumstances.

As he set the tray on our table, Fleur entered the restaurant and looked puzzled. Henri announced – too loudly, "To lift spirits, and to begin the commemoration of a departed loved one, I give you our special treat – Cocosizzlers."

Fleur's initial expression told me she didn't think that Henri's beaming face was quite appropriate, but she pasted a smile on her own and joined in with making a fuss, oh-ing and ah-ing as the sparklers did their thing. When they fizzled out, they looked rather sad…and dangerously hot.

"Did you get that, Troy?" CeeCee glanced at her mousy companion, and he nodded.

"Not the best angle, but you managed to look both happy and tragic simultaneously – quite wonderful, in fact. See?" He held his phone toward the young woman who studied the screen intently.

CeeCee frowned and said, "Dump it, Troy. My chin looks bad. Henri – do that again, please."

Henri and his wife exchanged a worried glance, then Henri rallied and said, "Of course. Do you want me to come in again – with the sparklers all alight? I could replace them in the kitchen."

During the time we'd spent with Henri, he'd struck me as a professional, dedicated man, prepared to put his all into making his resort a success. Yes, he was a bit of a bombast and – as this day was proving – he could get a bit grumpy. But it made me cross to see him become a simpering jester fawning at CeeCee's feet. The power she appeared to wield over the Legrands was unnerving. And all because she'd amassed a large following of people who trusted her opinion – on what basis, I still really wasn't sure.

CeeCee didn't respond, but Henri took the tray and scuttled toward the kitchen in any case.

"I'm sure he'll only be a few moments," gushed Fleur.

Her worried eyes followed her husband as he disappeared through the swing doors. She added, "I hope you're…well, not enjoying yourself, of course, given the circumstances, but I hope we can ensure your comfort tonight, as you grieve."

"I hope so, too," replied CeeCee coolly. "Set up a better angle now, Troy."

Troy stood, then moved a few feet away from the table and crouched on his haunches. "This is excellent – the light from the sparklers will be good for your cheekbones from here," he said, squatting uncomfortably.

"Good," replied CeeCee, then she closed her eyes until Henri made his entrance again.

As he approached the table, our host once again announced the arrival of the Cocosizzlers – though less naturally on this occasion. I watched as CeeCee opened her eyes and tears fell, as if on cue. I noted the way they rolled down her velvety skin. To be fair, it was an incredible performance on her part, with just the right amount of pathos to appeal to even the most hard-hearted vlog-viewer.

Unfortunately, just as Henri set down the tray in front of her, a spark flew and hit her somewhere, leading to a gasp, and an uncontrolled physical reaction, and the entire tray somehow ended up flipping over, showering CeeCee with the contents of all the drinks, as well as the still-lit sparklers.

A howling scream left her lips as CeeCee leapt up from her seat and tried to push everything off herself, but she burned her hands as she touched the sparklers, leading to yelps of pain. Troy scampered across the floor as Fleur and I leaped up to try to help. All I could think of was putting out the sparklers, so I grabbed the jug of iced water from the table and hurled it at CeeCee.

I felt bad that I took a certain amount of satisfaction from doing what I did, but I knew that someone had to act.

The young woman shrieked with shock, but at least the water extinguished the sparklers – which had left sooty marks on the front of her dress. The cherries that had topped the drinks plopped to the floor – having done their own damage to her outfit.

Just then Bud reappeared from the washroom. "What the...?" He looked at CeeCee – who was drenched – saw me with the empty jug in my hands, and his eyebrows shot up.

"There were sparklers. They could have burned CeeCee," I explained.

"What do you mean they could have? They damn well did!" CeeCee held up her hands to prove her point.

Fleur and Henri bumped into each other as they both headed to the kitchen shouting, "First aid kit!"

I picked up a napkin to pass to CeeCee, only to have it ripped from my hand by Troy, who'd finally got up off the floor. He snapped, "I'll do it."

CeeCee stood rigidly as Troy dabbed the water from her face, then he carried on blotting her dress. It was obviously ruined...though I noticed that her make-up was still impeccable.

Fleur rushed in and dumped a small suitcase onto the table. Ripping it open she dug around, then held up a tube of salve. "This should help with any minor burns. Let me see your hands, CeeCee."

The young woman curled her fingers to cover both palms. "Are you qualified to do this?"

Fleur nodded. "Fully trained and certified first-aider. I know what I'm doing."

CeeCee grudgingly opened her hands and held them toward Fleur, who gently turned them and examined the marks we could all plainly see. "No broken skin, which is good," she noted. "This cream should work, but you might prefer to put it on yourself – it doesn't hurt as much if you do that."

CeeCee seemed taken aback by the idea she should do something for herself, and I wasn't surprised when Troy whispered, "Let me do it. You're used to me doing your make-up, and I promise to be just as gentle."

She nodded, and Troy began to apply the cream, with CeeCee wincing, as Fleur pulled a fat roll from her bag.

"Use this gauze as a covering for tonight, so you don't rub off the ointment," suggested Fleur. "I'll take another look in the morning, if you like."

Once all that was done, CeeCee stood with her mummified hands held out as though they didn't belong to her. "How shall I manage tonight?" The tone was that of a small child. "I can't do anything for myself."

I wondered what she did for herself in any case, and was just about to speak, when Bud jumped in. "Maybe Cait, or Fleur, could give you a hand to get ready for bed…it's not that late, yet, but you could do that now."

"I have nothing with me," said CeeCee flatly.

"I have lots of *pareos* here," said Fleur helpfully. "They're for the resort store…all brand new. I'll bring a selection to your bungalow. How about that?"

"Nothing hideous," said CeeCee, "and Troy will help me. He's my dresser. Come on then, show me where I'm spending the night."

The nature of the relationship between CeeCee and Troy had become even more confusing to me by the time the threesome trooped out of the restaurant; Troy was certainly being treated as a minion by CeeCee, and yet he remained calm, and solicitous, and almost paternal in his reactions to her. It was a fascinating dynamic.

"Leave this mess to me," said Henri to Bud, now sounding sober, but weary. "You and Cait head off. It's been…quite a day. You must be tired out."

"It's not that late," said Bud. "We can help."

Henri stood firm. "Not necessary. Edouard will do it with me, and Annette will be back before you know it. Thanks for giving Fleur a hand setting up those bungalows. Much appreciated. But you're guests, too…not the hired help."

Henri sounded grumpy, and I didn't fancy having to deal with the mess of slimy drinks and possibly broken glass that was strewn across the floor, but I did my best to show willing. "If you're sure…"

Henri smiled – the first genuine smile I'd seen on his face that day. "Go on, away with you both. I know that all of this is going to muck up your last few days with us – in one way or another – but I want you to be able to enjoy what you can of your remaining time here. If you fancy getting away from it all, you can take one of the cars or boats and head off to Papeete, or wherever, tomorrow. I can't imagine it's going to be anything like a normal day here – again. So see what you haven't seen of the island, and get back whenever. I'll put money on us being given some pretty detailed feedback on things around here by CeeCee while she's on the premises, so don't feel guilty…you can take a break from your test-guest duties."

Bud leaned toward his one-time colleague. "I guess she might spot a thing or two that Cait and I have missed," he half-whispered. "And maybe she'll have a few tips that could 'elevate' your entire offering."

We all managed to laugh at that, because the word that Mahana and Fleur kept using when referring to every single aspect of the resort was "elevated", and it had begun to grate on both Bud and me, especially since they couldn't describe exactly what they meant, and we'd both agreed we didn't have a clue.

Henri's laughter subsided, and he sighed, heavily. "I wish Mahana was here now, she'd handle CeeCee just right. Knows her father. He started as a small name in pearls and gradually made bigger and bigger deals, meaning he bought up the supplies from more and more of the pearl farmers until now he's the biggest in the business. Came from nothing, now he's got everything. But Mahana still treats CeeCee as though she's just the child of a friend, not the heir to a fortune."

I couldn't resist. "Has CeeCee herself got much of a head for business?"

Henri rolled his eyes. "Got her own line of expensive skin creams using local *mono'i* oil, and now a perfume…all based on the stuff she does online – so either she has, or her father's helping her on that front. Designs her own line of jewelry, too…heavy on the pearls, of course. That was how she started – modelling pearls, like the Teriimana boy. Peas in a pod, those two…except for the rich father."

I noted, "Mahana said she knew Vaiarii's mother, when they were younger. So would CeeCee's father and Vaiarii's mother also have known each other?"

Henri shrugged, in his inimitable way. "Mahana said that she first met CeeCee's father when she and Roimata were at college, and he was a 'mature student' – so he's a bit older than them, though they all spent a lot of time together, I understand. But, in any case, they all seem to know each other on this island…and, sometimes, across all the Society Islands, or even the entire archipelago of French Polynesia. There are over one hundred islands in total, and a lot of people end up on Tahiti who began life on one of the other islands; there are so many more opportunities for them here. Mainly in Papeete, of course. So, yes, they know each other. Why?"

I shrugged – less fulsomely than Henri had done. "No real reason – just trying to join up the dots in my head. Relationships here seem…complicated."

"I'd best get on," said Henri, looking at the mess on the table, and at his feet.

We exchanged our goodnights, and Bud and I headed off. On our way, we had to pass the bungalows being used by Troy and CeeCee. I could tell that Fleur was doing her best to ensure CeeCee's absolute comfort as their chatter floated on the night air.

"I had no idea voices would carry like that," whispered Bud. "Maybe our little bungalow won't seem so idyllically remote with people staying around us."

"Unless CeeCee or Troy decide to start talking to themselves – or to each other from bungalow to bungalow – we should be okay," I replied softly. "But you're right – and Fleur was too, when she said this could be a useful part of our test-guest duties; until several bungalows are occupied, we won't have a true idea of how lots of people being here will feel…and sound. It's been so absolutely quiet with us being the only guests, and that – as we've both remarked – is an integral part of the charm of the place. Given what they're going to be charging when they open, I wouldn't fancy spending that much money only to be able to overhear anything going on next door…and I wouldn't want to feel as though I had to whisper all the time, either. We'd better make notes for Henri and Fleur about how sound carries. You know – even stuff like, well…if we can hear the loos flushing at night, that sort of thing."

Bud chuckled. "Okay, I'll take the first flush-watch duty, while you get some sleep."

I play-thumped him.

Surfing

It was only just gone ten: though it had been a long, and strange, day I didn't really feel I was capable of sleep, so I got changed, then sat on top of the bedclothes and pulled out my laptop. I'd had to give in and buy a cheap-ish one in Sydney because it was the only way I could fulfill my part of the compromise I'd agreed with my university: that I'd teach the tutorials online that I was scheduled to deliver in person, rather than hand them off – yet again – to a substitute. To be fair, the laptop did everything I needed it to do, though it weighed a great deal more than my own, which I knew was gathering dust in our house where, for more than a fleeting moment, I wished I was sitting, right then.

I gave myself permission to feel homesick for a while. Bud's injuries meant we'd had to extend our time away from a planned few weeks to what was now almost two months, and would be closer to eleven weeks by the time we got back. I told myself that our beloved Marty was happy staying with Jack and Sheila White, and I reckoned he might even have lost a bit of weight by the time we got back, because Jack and Sheila's dogs love to run, and Marty enjoys it too…when he has doggie company to do it with. It seems that when we humans throw sticks, he can take them or leave them, and even if he chooses to run to pick them up, he often just saunters back with them, a big smile on his face, and that wonky ear of his making my heart melt every time I see him.

As if I was broadcasting my thoughts, Bud emerged from the bathroom and said, "I might give Jack a call, on the video. Marty might be around." My surprise must have shown, because he added, "Not now…it's too late. But maybe tomorrow morning."

I pushed my laptop aside and held out my arms. Bud snuggled in. "You're missing home?" I knew the answer.

Bud sighed until I thought all the air had come out of him. It was a great sound, because – for weeks – he'd not been able to do that properly. He said quietly, "All I want is to be in our own home, with you by my side, and Marty at my feet…or even on my lap."

I patted the bed. "We get a lot more of this real estate at night without him."

Bud chuckled. "Yeah, I know…but I don't think I'll ever complain again about him stretching out sideways until I have to hang on to the edge of the mattress. Who knew Labradors could be that wide? I even miss his snoring."

"Like you'd know," I quipped.

Bud peered up at me. "Half the time you think it's me, it's him. Honest." He winked.

"Yeah. Right. Anyway, Husband dear, I was planning on sending through a few notes about the parts of the tutorial I got shut out of today, because of the storm. The internet connection seems to be quite stable at the moment, so I'll make the most of that. Will you read, or are you going to try to get some sleep?"

Bud shook his head. "Not really sleepy. But I don't think my head's in the right place for a book. What about tomorrow? Do you want to do what Henri suggested, and get out of here? Leave all this behind and just immerse ourselves in another part of the island, before we leave?"

I closed my laptop. "We could certainly give that some thought…or we could stay here to find out what transpires."

"I know that look. What?" Bud sat up on the edge of the bed.

"We're both thinking the same thing, aren't we?"

"How so?"

"We both believe there's been a suspicious death. And we can't not look into it."

Bud's body slumped. "Bump on the head. Pearl diver. Drowned. No one knew he was here, so they say. Suspicious."

"Well..."

Bud grabbed my hand. "Why is it always us, Cait? Not why does this always happen to us, but why can't either of us allow other people to...sort it all out? We're leaving in a few days, and we're not likely to ever return, or meet any of these people ever again. What could we possibly do in a few days that the proper authorities can't? When they've got the autopsy results...when they know the cause, and time, of death, that is. For all we know, Vaiarii Teriimana was as drunk as a skunk, jumped in a boat and sailed himself here – for some reason – then somehow knocked his head on a rock, or a lump of coral, and fell into the lagoon and drowned. And that's the thing – we don't know if he drowned, or not...we're just assuming. And that might not be known for days – maybe not until after we've left. Tahiti isn't that big a place, but whoever does the autopsies must have some sort of backlog; that's true around the world, so I can't see it would be different here. Monkeys and circuses, Cait. Neither being ours, on this occasion."

I was surprised, because Bud almost sounded convincing, but I knew him well enough to spot that it was himself he was attempting to talk around, not me. He was trying to tell himself he shouldn't care about how, or why, Vaiarii Teriimana had died in "our" lagoon. But I didn't think that the Bud who was speaking would win, because the Bud he was trying to convince was far too dedicated to justice to listen. *Like me.*

"We know there's something not right about it all," I said quietly, "and we know neither of us will rest until we've done what we can for the victim. And I won't say any more than that, for now. Except this..."

Bud chuckled. "Go on, what?"

"The bump on his head...can I take a look at those photos you got of it, please? I should have taken some myself, but at least I managed some general shots."

Bud stood and walked to the table where his phone was charging. "Here you go. There are dozens of photos – those ones are early on. I'd say not contact with coral, because there didn't appear to be scratches, which you'd expect. But some force was used. Of course, I've no idea what that would have done to the skull beneath the skin. It might be fractured, I guess. What do you see?"

I found the photos of the injury – Bud had taken half a dozen from varying angles. In one of them, a wavelet had managed to wash off most of the sand, so I focused on that one. Yes, I could see what Bud meant about the general nature of the wound. I stretched the image as far as I could then held Bud's phone toward him. "Would you say that's a bruise in the hair, around that break in the skin, or is it just a shadow?"

Bud took his phone, peered, fiddled about with the image, then handed it back to me. "Honestly can't say. Could be either. Are you thinking that if it's bruising that could mean he got the injury some time before he died? Maybe at that club in Papeete?"

I nodded. "Yes. Might have even had a concussion…been confused. Sonny said he was drunk, too. Decided to do the jumping in the boat thing…came here because – well, I don't know about that. But this might have nothing to do with him dying, is what I'm saying."

"Or it could have everything to do with him dying," added Bud thoughtfully. "We've both known of situations where a head wound doesn't prove fatal immediately, but it can cause death, or at least a loss of consciousness, later on. Could be what happened; he was here for some reason, swooned or passed out, fell into the water and drowned, as a result of the earlier injury."

"The scraped knuckles? Probably got those in the fight."

"Agreed. He was well-built, no question, tall too. Likely knew how to handle himself. Unless he was one of those 'gentle giant' types."

I replied, "If what Nadine said about the way he acted toward Eloise is true, then it doesn't sound as though he was very 'gentle', Bud."

"True. In fact, that sounded…nasty. I'm surprised that CeeCee would put up with her fiancé flirting – or worse – with all and sundry. I can't imagine she knew anything about that."

I recalled how CeeCee had told us that Vaiarii had had a "terrible time" at the photo shoot at the resort. "Maybe that was his way: kowtow to the princess CeeCee, then push himself onto other women when she couldn't see him doing it?"

Bud shrugged. "Who knows? We really don't know anything about him, do we?"

I picked up my laptop. "Well, that's where I can help. I had a little look into the world of CeeCee earlier on, but I could take a deep dive into both their lives with this. They strike me as being pretty keen on putting everything about themselves online. I bet I could find out a thing or two about them out there on the interwebs."

Bud smiled. "But that's only going to be what they want people to see, isn't it?"

I pushed my reading cheats up my nose. "Not necessarily; everyone's got a camera with them, these days, Bud – and we both know how folks like to get candid shots of celebrities, maybe now more than ever. Even when I was working for your team under those temporary contracts, I did a lot of this sort of thing to help me build a picture of a victim's life. Just give me an hour or so, and I might be able to come up with something…insightful."

Bud conceded defeat. "Right – well if you're going to do that, you should sit at the desk, and I'll grab a book on the bed. You'll give yourself a bad back if you just hunch over the laptop like that, there, and you know it. But don't stick at it all night, Cait – you'll regret it in the morning."

I knew my husband was right, but the tingle at the nape of my neck told me I was looking forward to sitting in the dark bungalow, delving into the backgrounds of two young people who'd enjoyed the limelight.

Profiling

The next thing I knew…it was dawn. I'd been at the desk until about three, so at least I'd managed a little sleep. I had to go to the loo, so forced myself to let go of the sheets, and head to the bathroom. As I flushed, I realized I hadn't heard a thing all night – so, either CeeCee and Troy hadn't used their facilities, or else the bungalows really were sufficiently well insulated to not allow that sort of sound to travel, something for which I supposed I was grateful.

Bud was fast asleep on the bed; he'd dropped off while holding his book, and hadn't even got himself under the covers, and I hadn't had the heart to wake him when I'd slipped into bed beside him a few hours earlier, so I let him be, while I stretched myself out, and pondered an early morning dip in the lagoon. A bit wary, considering what had happened the day before, I decided I'd at least indulge in a float around for a few moments, so pulled on my swimsuit and clambered down into the water.

The air was cool, and the movement refreshed my aching muscles. Bud had been right – I would have given myself a painful back if I'd hunched over my laptop on the bed, but I still needed to writhe about until I felt my body regain full mobility. I didn't want to make too much noise, being right next to someone who was presumably fast asleep, so I walked through the water, away from the bungalows, until I was close to the edge of the lagoon. I did my best to not enter what I judged would be Troy's eyeline from his bed; CeeCee's bungalow had its back to ours and faced the other way.

As I skulked about, sad that I couldn't just splash and float as I wanted, I wondered why I was being so careful. Presumably other guests wouldn't do the same – they'd just fling themselves into the water however they wanted, them having paid a small fortune to have the right to do so. Would it bother me to get up in the morning, hearing and seeing someone swimming in my own private lagoon, before I'd had the chance to enjoy it, completely alone? I knew in my heart it would, then smiled as I realized that Bud and I would never be able to afford to have such an experience in "real life".

I turned my attention to the coral reef as it stretched out beyond the lagoon, disappearing into the sea beyond. The colors of the water changed across the reef, and were…well, there couldn't be words for the myriad hues of blue that I could see kaleidoscope in the first rays of sunlight.

A loud splash got my attention, and I turned to see someone's bottom arcing above the water of the lagoon. It was naked, and I panicked; I didn't fancy bumping into a nude Troy or CeeCee. Whoever it was, they'd obviously decided to swim underwater, and I watched the surface of the lagoon intently. Nothing. No one could be under water for that long…surely? I walked and bounced toward where I'd seen the person's rear end, anxiously scanning the surface. They'd been under for more than one hundred steamboats, and I hadn't even started counting when I'd first seen them. I pushed myself back toward our bungalow; I had to raise the alarm – again.

A plopping noise behind me made me spin; a head popped up, then a torso. A naked one. It was CeeCee. I wasn't surprised by the sight of the fake boobs; I'd become shockingly familiar with them during my online searches the previous night, because CeeCee had felt it necessary to take all her followers on her journey toward perfection…on camera. What did take me aback was her face; she wasn't wearing a scrap of make-up and looked like an ordinary teen. I realized that one of the things I hadn't been able to discover about her online was her age. I'd imagined her to be in her late twenties. Now I wasn't so sure.

When she spotted me, CeeCee turned away, and began to swim back to her bungalow. Given the way she'd been prepared to – quite literally – bare all to her followers, I couldn't imagine she was embarrassed because she was naked. Maybe she'd been hoping for solitude? *Like me.*

I didn't think there was any point in waving at her receding figure, so returned my attention to the sea, and watched the glimmering colors change for a little while longer. The next time I heard splashing it sounded…familiar. I turned to see Bud swimming toward me, his silver hair gleaming in the sun, his tanned skin and navy shorts clearly visible through the crystal water. When he reached me, he stood up and we held hands for a few moments, allowing ourselves to take in the beauty around us.

Bud whispered, "We'll never forget this, will we?"

"I know I won't, but – even though I have an eidetic memory – I wonder if even I'll be able to recall these exact colors; we both know that none of our photos do the sea here justice. I mean, it looks fabulous in any number of shots…but it's still not *this* fabulous."

"That's why I've stopped taking photos of it. I'd rather just enjoy the moment. Be…present."

"Like they were saying to you at your rehab appointments?"

"Yeah. You know I'm not a big one for all that sort of thing, but we do seem to rush about a lot, don't we? And there's always some sort of pressure, right? This? This is what we can think, and talk, about on a cold winter's evening, in front of the fire, snuggling with Marty. It's been great. But…"

"It's time to go home."

Bud sighed. "Death seems to follow us, doesn't it? We can't avoid it – even in paradise, can we, Cait? There's no point trying to ignore it, so let's meet it head-on: did you uncover anything about Vaiarii Teriimana online that might explain his death?"

"That's a bit of a tall order, Bud. I didn't expect to trip over an explanation of why his body was floating right here, yesterday." When I spoke, a tiny flicker passed between us as we realized our situation, then it was as if we both shook it off at the same time as each other.

"No skeletons?"

I chuckled. "Given that one expects skeletons to be well and truly hidden from sight, not really. However, there's an awful lot of stuff about the dead man online that suggests…well, let's just say he lived life to the full. So many photos of him being beautiful, in beautiful situations. However, on occasion, he came over as not only an entitled ass, but one with a fiery temper and a penchant for flinging his fists about."

Bud pushed backwards. "Oh dear." He submerged himself, but the water was so clear I could see him open his eyes while he was under, which turned my tummy; I cannot imagine why anyone would ever want to do that. Popping back up, rubbing both hands over his face and hair, he came close and said, "Go on then…tell me all about him. I suspect this is about the only place we'll get to be alone today – unless you really want to borrow one of the cars and drive off somewhere." He paused and wrinkled a smile at me. "Like that's going to happen, right? Okay then – get on with it. I'm all ears." He pulled at his ear lobes to make his point.

So we stood there, bobbing up and down, the water around our shoulders, and I told him what I'd learned about the dead man.

"Bear in mind that I've pulled this together from various interviews with Vaiarii himself, as well as those who knew him…or as it was written or spoken by the bloggers or journalists who were putting stories together about him, so I haven't been able to establish how accurate it all is, okay?" Bud nodded. "Born twenty-four years ago next week to Roimata

Teriimana and a man by the name of Pai. The father was a *Bajau Darat*…a member of a nomadic people, the *Samu*, or *Bajau*, who have lived completely at sea for the better part of a thousand years. Nowadays, some of them live in bungalows built on stilts over the water – like ours is, here. Well, the *Bajau Laut* do, though those called the *Bajau Daret* have become land-livers in the true sense of the term – they've taken up residence on land in several places, though no country will accept them as citizens. So they're still truly 'nomadic' in that sense."

Bud looked confused. "They live at sea? On boats? All the time? How?"

"Off the sea, while being on the sea. Literally. They're quite amazing. Anyway, Vaiarii was born, and the mother Roimata kept what I believe was her maiden name. I say this because, although some people in various articles referred to Pai as Roimata's 'husband', I couldn't find anything to confirm that they ever actually married. Anyway, the father 'disappeared' about ten years after Vaiarii was born. The accepted story was that Pai abandoned Vaiarii and his mother to return to his nomadic existence – that he couldn't cope with the life of a land-liver here in Tahiti. Anyway, Roimata Teriimana sounds as though she was quite determined that her son would get a good education, as she herself had received. She displeased her family by taking up with Pai, the sea-nomad, when she was at college; they'd hoped she'd put her qualifications in accountancy to good use. Instead, she ended up doing cleaning jobs so she could look after her son. The main reason given for this was because she'd 'lost her good name', so couldn't find work as an accountant, and Pai found it difficult to get work once it was known that he'd fathered Vaiarii. Before he'd met Roimata, Pai had worked as a natural pearl hunter around the islands within the archipelago where such rare and precious jewels are still to be found, but it wasn't steady work. After the boy was born, Pai worked whenever he could, but it appears the jobs were few and far between 'for someone like him', so Roimata ended up having to work two or three jobs at a time. According to what I read – and maybe this part has been varnished a little – Vaiarii did well at school, but he really excelled when it came to anything water-related which, as you might imagine – given where we are – was something he discovered at an early age. 'He swam like a fish' was a phrase bandied about by anyone who'd known him as a child. By the time he was fourteen – with his father out of the picture – Vaiarii had built a reputation for being able to remain underwater for longer than almost anyone else in these parts. Which meant that, rather than staying at school past the minimum leaving age of sixteen, as his mother had hoped he would – to get some 'proper qualifications' – he took a job with a company that works across the entire archipelago hunting for natural pearls. The one his father had worked for, years earlier, in fact. Vaiarii was an honest to goodness free-diving pearl hunter – and a very successful one, it appears – until he was about nineteen. Then there was an 'incident'."

I paused when I saw Bud's eyebrows shoot up. He said, "Okay, now we're getting somewhere."

"Not so fast, Husband…because I can't find out exactly what the nature of said 'incident' was. In every source I could find, including interviews where Vaiarii himself spoke of it, that's exactly how it's referred to, with no details. The rumors online vary: some suggest it involved a large pearl – possibly of legendary proportions, depending on which source you choose to believe; there are a few that say a fishing spear was involved – either hand-held or jet-propelled, again depending on your blogger of choice; then there's wider agreement that either a small – or possibly life-changing – injury for another free diver was at the center of it, always with the name of the victim being 'unknown'. What is definitely true, is that Vaiarii didn't dive for that employer ever again, and he moved back to Papeete to live with his mother, who was still doing menial jobs, and just about managing to keep them just above the poverty line. And that's when he was 'discovered' by CeeCee's father, Charles Ducasse."

Bud dunked under the water and reemerged, dripping and smiling. He shook the water from his hair, reminding me of Marty. "Don't stop…I'm agog."

I splashed him playfully, then pressed on. "Vaiarii had been hired to stand around looking hunky and charming at some sort of fancy cultural soiree in Papeete, wearing a *pareo*, a *lei*, and a smile. His brief was to hand out inexpensive pearl trinkets to all the females who attended. The way he told it – in many, many interviews – Charles Ducasse's daughter, CeeCee, spotted his smile across the crowded room, and told her father there and then that 'the good-looking man with the great teeth' should become the face of the family company. How factually correct that is, I don't know, because it all seems a bit too good to be one hundred percent true, if you know what I mean. However, Charles Ducasse hasn't seen fit to contradict the tale. Not that he's prone to giving the sort of interview that would allow him to do so – he prefers to talk about market share and finances. But, by way of possible verification – or not – CeeCee Ducasse herself has also told the same story many times. So that's the 'origin legend' for the now world-famous Vaiarii Teriimana."

Bud bobbed a bit more actively. "So the dead guy owed his career as a famous model to the woman who became his fiancée, and to her father, for whom he worked? That's…well, that could lead to some significant pressures. Do you happen to know how the relationship between CeeCee and Vaiarii developed? Did their love grow out of their business relationship?"

"It seems so. CeeCee 'happened to be' at all the photo shoots Vaiarii was required to do, and she 'took him under her wing', according to her vlogs. Since then, they've been 'inseparable'.

They've been engaged for about a year – which was the information you'd already dug up. Which means that the tattoo on Vaiarii's leg, if it was the name of another woman as you suggested, had been there throughout a couple of years of him and CeeCee being together. Which seems like a long time, to me. They both admit – when they're interviewed together, or apart – that they're both 'working so hard' that they're finding it difficult to fix a date for their perfect wedding. To be honest, their schedules put them in places apart from each other so often that I'm surprised they're still a couple…which confirms what I suspected from my initial overview of CeeCee's social media accounts. Also – and this is where it gets more interesting, I suppose – it seems that Vaiarii took to the high life like a duck to water. Once he started to gain recognition, he began to flex his earning and – by the sounds of it – his entitlement muscles. By the time of his death, Vaiarii Teriimana was no longer 'just' the face of Ducasse Pearls, you see…he had sponsorship and appearance deals with companies who manufacture high-end watches, shoes, clothing, and cars – just for starters – so he wanted for nothing. But there are a few claims online about him using the phrase 'Don't you know who I am?' to get himself better treated than your average washed-up pearl diver at nightspots, and the like, not just here in Tahiti, but as far afield as Brisbane, Auckland, and even in Los Angeles."

Bud smiled. "Is this where you found out about his bad temper?"

"Yes: fights, brawls, that sort of thing. Never mentioned by either him, or CeeCee, and no charges ever brought, anywhere…but I found quite a few videos of him in bars and clubs getting shirty with people, then acting the big 'I am', where chest thumping turned to fist flinging. Vaiarii had a short fuse, it seems. Though he'd managed to keep it all sufficiently under the radar that he'd hung onto all his nice sponsorship deals…until a few weeks ago. Then he lost his flash car; it seems that an alcohol-fuelled encounter with a tree was something with which the manufacturer did not want to be associated. But I dare say Vaiarii had managed to make enough money to be able to afford to purchase his own vehicles, by then. He certainly lived in a nice place: bought a small apartment building between here and Papeete. He lived on the top floor, his mother lives on the floor below him, and there are two more apartments rented out, which she manages for him. He's been a good son in that regard, it seems."

"So, no known record? No known 'enemies' either?"

"It would appear that the entire world loved him. Except, maybe, for those with whom he had a passing physical disagreement, or, possibly, the unknown fellow diver involved in an 'incident' some years ago. There was talk online about several of the top international model agencies being interested in him for work other than that which he does for CeeCee's family's company; a career in Paris, Milan or New York might well have been on the horizon for him. 'An exotic look, with a smile to melt hearts,' said one agency scout. Though…that might have been a problem."

Bud chuckled, "I love the way you take me down a particular route when you're telling me about someone, then you like to turn a corner and surprise me. I'm about to turn a corner, aren't I?"

I half-splashed my husband. "You're right, as always. Well, as almost-always, in any case. I did manage to find a clip of Vaiarii when it really looked as though he didn't know he was being filmed. However, I couldn't find anything he'd ever said 'formally' about the matter. Maybe he couldn't be seen to have any controversial opinions – or, maybe, any opinions at all – I don't know. Anyway, there was this one video of him sitting in a restaurant with two men without heads – well, obviously they had heads, but they weren't in the shot, so I have no idea who they were. Vaiarii is talking passionately about how ridiculous it is that he's always being told by all the folks who use him to promote their products that it's so wonderful that he 'looks different', but then he gets treated poorly when he's out and about on his own just because of those very same looks. He goes on about how no one seems to care about what he's like on the inside – how they'd treat him differently if only they knew that."

Bud dunked his head under the water, and reemerged. "Racism…off island? Or something he's experienced here? I guess there's got to be a…tension when you're picked out of a crowd, and make a good living, because you're 'different'…but then being 'different' can, too often, bring its own challenges."

"Indeed. Sadly, there are those the world over who judge, and then choose to 'punish', people they see only in terms of how they differ from themselves…differ from their idea of what's normal, or right, or good. The dreadful thing is, of course, that it's a concept that has to be taught, and learned…we're not born with a sense of 'being different' – you only have to watch young children play together to see that. But, once it's been taught and learned, it's something that's exploited by those who want to whip up the insecurities that can be felt by humans. The clip I saw of Vaiarii talking about how he didn't understand why he was lauded for his looks when he modeled, yet couldn't get served at a club when people saw him as 'just a member of an ethnic minority', was posted about five months ago. Maybe something specific happened back then? The person who put it online didn't say where it had been filmed, though I could tell it was Los Angeles because I could see the art deco tower of the Title Guarantee and Trust building in the background."

"How long ago did he start being a brawler? Was that new, or had that been a thing for a while? Is this a pattern, Cait? Maybe a reason for someone wanting to do him harm?"

"The bar brawls? They all happened within the past five to six months or so. Before that? Model citizen, as far as the online record is concerned. And the brawls weren't all off island, some were here…so maybe they didn't all arise from possible racial tension. To be honest, Bud, while I understand the theory of 'other', psychologically speaking, and have spoken about it to students in great detail because of the way that 'otherness' can play a role in what becomes criminal activity – hate crimes, for example – it's not something I can easily relate to. Not in the way that someone who belongs to a visible ethnic minority can, in any case. Of course, as soon as I'd open my mouth in the UK and my Welsh accent came out, then I'd be judged immediately. Oh, and I'm a woman, so there's that. But…to be judged by your skin color, or the shape of your nose or eyes? I'm white, Bud, so how on earth would I know how that feels?"

Bud nodded. "I understand. We never will know how it feels, you're right. But…are you saying he was reacting to racism here on Tahiti, too?"

"I'm not, because I don't *know* anything. Maybe it wasn't just racism…though it can't ever be 'just' when it comes to that. Maybe he'd really enjoyed the celebrity for a while, but now it was starting to…grate? Diminish him? Those comments about people not caring about the inner man? You see, the big picture might be…well, 'big' isn't the right word, but it's…"

Bud nudged me. "Go on, my fingers are getting wrinkly."

I checked my own – they were too. "Okay – look…there's an area of psychology all about self-determination; basically, it considers what we need, as humans, to allow us to develop a sense of self, as created by internal and external factors. An individual's sense of self-worth is impacted significantly by how those around them react to them. And if people are constantly focusing on how a person looks – as opposed to what they truly think, or what they are capable of doing – then the individual's sense of self can become tied to that element. For example, if you're always being negatively judged because of how you look, you might try to camouflage that in some way to be more readily accepted. Or else, you might choose to show off your difference with pride…or even as an act of visible rebellion. Equally, if a person finds they're only ever praised because of how they look, they might gradually come to truly believe that they're only worth anything to the world because of that one part of themself, and become totally focussed on their looks alone, sometimes to the point of obsession. Alternatively, those judged by parts of society to be 'just a pretty face' might choose to fight against that view, leading them to say or do things that aim to get the world to reconsider their value…see the 'inner person'. In Vaiarii's case, maybe, to see him as more than *just* a model. That can result in individuals who initially become known mainly for their looks, or voice, or acting ability, let's say, choosing to use their fame and celebrity to speak up on behalf of…well, any cause they might hold dear. Which can be good. Of course, sometimes, they can do that and yet still feel undervalued, and it can become a destructive force. It might, in Vaiarii's case, have shown itself in his temper…or in other ways."

Bud nodded thoughtfully. "I get it. And you're right. It's gotta be a challenge when you're judged merely by how you look all the time. I know how that can go one way, or another. But, Cait, we've been told he was trying to force himself on Eloise…who's *married* to *Nadine.* So – what do you think that was all about? Tied up with his sense of self-worth again?"

I shook my head. "If you recall, Edouard said that Vaiarii 'hit on' all the women during that photo shoot – he didn't just…nope, I don't mean, that. It's never 'just' when a man threatening a woman is concerned. And that's not an academic observation, Bud – you know what I went through with

Angus…when he'd shift from abusing me verbally to physical threats, and worse. No, what I mean is that Vaiarii didn't focus his so-called 'flirtatious' attention solely on Eloise – he spread it around. Though Eloise was the only one he physically attacked…so, that's quite something. And yet…"

"Go on."

"I couldn't find anything at all online about him being anything other than – basically – charming toward women. And there was a ton of coverage about him being in what was touted as a 'fabulous relationship' with CeeCee Ducasse, including a gazillion pictures of them making googly eyes at each other. I needed a sick bag after seeing some of those. Yuk. PDA? FTMPDATY."

Bud imitated the emoji for "What are you talking about?".

I explained, "PDA is an abbreviation for Public Display of Affection. My version? Far Too Many Public Displays of Affection Thank You."

Bud looked glum. "And now he's dead."

"Indeed."

"And he likely died in our lagoon. When he was – quite literally – an expert at holding his breath. How did he manage that, by the way…the diving thing? That's quite something, isn't it? Not that I know much about it, to be honest, but I've always imagined that those divers who stay under for ages have to train at it for years. And trust me when I tell you that in the past couple of months I've learned more than I thought I'd ever need to know about the way our lungs work. But you say he was exceptionally good at an unusually young age. Any idea why?"

"In the same way that his skin color, facial features, and general looks would come from his genes, I believe genetics might also have played a role there, too. I found some research that shows that the *Bajau* people – who've been deep-sea divers for over a thousand years – have developed larger than average spleens, and even have a genetic mutation affecting their thyroid which changes the way their bodies react to situations of acute oxygen depletion. Some of their divers say they can be underwater for up to thirteen minutes, and it's common for them to get down to about seventy meters, which is astonishing. I've got to admit that I got lost in a bit of a rabbit hole with that research – it was fascinating to read." I spotted a mini eyeroll from Bud. "Briefly – for those of you in the cheap seats, Husband dear – with a father who was a *Bajau Daret*, it might be that Vaiarii inherited the genetic trait that the *Bajau* people have developed and was therefore physically capable of doing what his father's people have an ability to. Which begs the question…"

"If he could be underwater for that long…how did he manage to drown? *If* he was conscious?"

"Exactly."

Thinking

Having showered and dressed, Bud and I ambled across to the restaurant for breakfast. Our habit had become to graze on fruit through the day, so we always tried for a heartier start, but even that only really meant eggs, because I'd found out after about a week that I just couldn't cope with lots of French pastries every morning…well, I could, but I knew I shouldn't. But the eggs? Oh my word, there was no question that Eloise had earned her double diploma from *Le Cordon Bleu* in Paris: her eggs were consistently creamy, full of butter, and served beside a mound of glistening mushrooms, grown to order on the island by a man of Chinese heritage whose family had all but cornered the mushroom market on Tahiti for the past thirty years, apparently.

As I drank my rich coffee, and enjoyed my velvety, yielding eggs, and flavorsome mushrooms, I realized how used we'd become to chatting with Mahana as we began each day. I hoped she'd get back to the resort soon, because I wanted to ask her so many questions about the Teriimana family. However, I knew I'd have to be patient even when she did return, because she'd be eager to catch up with all the duties that had slipped past her since she'd left the previous afternoon.

CeeCee wafted into the restaurant wrapped in a full-length canary-yellow *pareo* printed with blue lorikeets – Tahiti's famous, but now endangered, birds – her phone slung around her like a cross-body bag on a long strand of what I chose to believe were fake Tahitian golden pearls…though I suspected they might be real. Gone was the youthful face I'd spotted in the lagoon, and there was that mask of make-up again – ageing her, making her look so…not mature, but hard. *Such a shame.*

I tutted at myself as I had the thought: CeeCee had every right to present herself to the world in whatever manner she chose…though I did find it interesting that she'd brought her entire make-up kit with her, but no spare clothes. Had she'd really meant to stay over? If so – why no clothes? Had the incident with the drinks and the sparklers had stopped her going back to Papeete? If so, why the make-up? But no – her plan to stay was something she'd brought up when we were at the lagoon. *Odd.* At least I could see that now her hands were no longer bound with gauze; she had a few sticking plasters on her, and she didn't look too happy about that, but – there again – she didn't look too happy about anything.

Following her pseudo-ethereal entrance, the heiress stood in the middle of the restaurant looking lost, so I said, "Please feel free to join us…though Bud and I have almost finished. The eggs are very good, if that's your sort of thing." I did my best to be jolly…but not so jolly that it would be inappropriate for the situation.

CeeCee whined, "Have you seen Troy? He's not at his bungalow, and I texted him, but he didn't reply. I had to do all this on my own." She vaguely waved her hands in front of her face, but I couldn't be sure if she meant she'd had to put on her own sticking plasters or apply her own make-up. Since neither task seemed particularly onerous to me, I felt bemused that she seemed so slighted.

"Haven't seen him yet," said Bud. "Is he an early riser? Might he have gone for a swim?"

CeeCee snapped, "A swim? In the lagoon? Where my darling Vaiarii died? He wouldn't do that."

"But you did. I saw you." It was out of my mouth before I could stop it.

CeeCee said nothing; her glare spoke volumes.

Henri bustled in. "Ah there you are, CeeCee, I thought I heard you. May I offer you something for breakfast?"

"I want to see Troy. Do you know where he is?"

Henri beamed. "I do. He came for coffee a couple of hours ago – took some fruit, too. Fleur offered some pastries, but he declined. He wasn't here for long. Said he wanted to get out to take some shots of the early sun on the sea, and some of the lagoon from beyond the reef, too, so I told him he could take one of our boats." He looked at his watch. "He said he wouldn't be long. I guess he'll be back soon. While you wait for him, can I bring you something to eat? Fruit? Pastries? Eggs? Something else?"

CeeCee raised a perfectly plucked eyebrow and said, "*Pain au chocolat*, coffee – black and strong."

I'm surprised you didn't ask for two peeled grapes and a cup of herbal tea, was what I thought; "Why not join us, while you wait for Troy?" was what I said.

CeeCee sauntered toward us and waited for Henri to pull out a chair for her. Bud courteously lifted his rear end out of his seat as she took hers, then we both got back to finishing our food while CeeCee looked at the *cafetière* on our table with an air of helplessness. Since there wasn't an extra cup, neither Bud nor I could do anything about serving her, but we didn't have to wait for more than a moment before Annette appeared with all the crockery CeeCee could possibly need, as well as fresh coffee, which Bud politely poured.

As I stirred my refilled cup, I pondered why CeeCee hadn't acknowledged that she'd been in the lagoon that morning; she must have known I'd seen her, after all, so I decided to ask, knowing that sometimes it's the best thing to do.

"Did you enjoy your swim earlier on?" I smiled pleasantly and waited for a reply.

Languid spoon-tapping was followed by a dreamy: "I wanted to commune with the place where my lover last lived. My future happiness was so close…it was almost mine. But now…now he's gone. All I have are memories."

CeeCee was back to playing her part of the bereaved fiancée. I dared to ask, "And how did that go for you?"

CeeCee's eyes flashed toward mine, and I noticed that one of her false eyelashes had been applied crookedly. "I'd thought I'd be alone."

I said, "So did I. Bud and I have been the only guests here for weeks, so we've got used to it, I suppose. It was a very different experience for us to share the resort with extra guests last night. How were your accommodations, by the way? Comfy?"

I wanted to pepper CeeCee with questions about her dead partner, but didn't think that approach would get an insightful response, so decided to try to ease her into at least being courteous toward me, even if it was unlikely that she'd ever truly take me into her confidence.

CeeCee sucked her spoon. "It's a bit mid, isn't it? Like glamping. I think the resort will appeal to people who need the essentials, and like the idea of a little bit of pampering, too. It should find its niche."

I was staggered: from my point of view, Bud and I had been living in the lap of luxury for weeks, with more creature comforts than we'd ever imagined existed being catered for, and the location being paradisical. What more could this young woman possibly expect?

Bud looked puzzled. "Did you say it's 'mid'? What's 'mid'?"

CeeCee's brow didn't furrow – *I wondered if it could* – but she nibbled her lip. "Sort of okay, but not really exciting."

I explained. "It's a current expression, used a lot online. Think 'beige' and you won't be far off…sort of serviceable, not awful, but bland."

Bud gave me a look that suggested he got it, but wasn't impressed, then said, "The butlers don't arrive until next week – so I dare say that will elevate the entire experience."

I silently applauded him for speaking up on behalf of Henri and Fleur – and for managing to sneak in Mahana's favorite description of the resort's aims.

CeeCee rolled her silken shoulders. "That should help, but there are only the basics here to be delivered, after all."

I had to ask, "What's not available that you'd want, CeeCee?"

She waved a sticking-plaster dotted hand at me. "There are no real spa facilities for a start; offering the services of one wellness consultant to visit your bungalow doesn't suggest a high-end experience. I know the website talks a lot about the quality of the *mono'i* oil they use here, but they don't make their own. Which I'd say is a bit of a black mark against them, to be honest. I'd have thought they'd have been able to rustle up a few batches of the stuff for themselves. I know that quite a lot of people don't like the part of the process that calls for using the abdomens of hermit crabs to get the oil to ferment quickly, but a bit of patience means you can leave that step out. That would be an edge for them, but they've chosen to ally themselves with an artisanal producer instead. I happen to know that their oil is excellent, but…it's not the resort's own. See? *Mid.* And the service-call stations on the beach are too far apart."

Dotted along the beach were a series of stout poles, topped with little palm-frond roofs, where a guest could enjoy a bit of shade, and press a buzzer to speak to a butler to request…well, whatever service they wanted – from a bottle of chilled champagne, to the delivery of one of the resort's intriguing clear-plastic kayaks, which allowed for fish-watching as you paddled. Each station had a color code and a collection of numbered flags, so you just told the butler which color and number flag you were going to stick into the sand, so they knew where to deliver your drinks, or your kayak…or a bucket of fried chicken with all the fixings, for all I knew. Five-minute service was the promise. I'd been blown away by them.

"Those stations are positioned literally every twenty feet, CeeCee. How close together would you expect them to be?" I probably sounded snappish, but, honestly, what did she expect?

She whined, "The sand can get very hot underfoot, and walking on it can be exhausting."

I looked at her arms, which could only be the way they were if she went to the gym on a frequent basis, and wondered – not for the first time in my life – why on earth people bothered paying huge sums to work out when all they had to do was put in a bit of proper manual effort in the real world, like walking a few dozen steps across a beach, for example. Then I reminded myself of the levels of service the young heiress was probably used to, and told myself off; I didn't walk in her shoes, and would never understand her view of life.

CeeCee played with her spoon again, and I did my best to contain my fascination with her talon-like nails. I had no idea how the pads of her fingers would even reach the screen of her cellphone on a day-to-day basis.

Luckily for me, just as Annette bustled in with a basket of *pain au chocolat* pastries, I had the chance to watch exactly how CeeCee managed to use her cellphone, because she pulled it toward her face and began tapping on it with her thumbs…well, with the sides of her thumbs, to be precise. As someone who's never been able to do the thumb-typing thing I could see how it worked, despite the length of her false nails. It was an absorbing sight…and she was fast.

"Trying to reach Troy?" I enquired, as I eyed the basket in front of us.

Might I manage just one sweet treat?

"He always replies to my texts immediately." CeeCee stared at her phone with a pout.

"If he's out and about in a boat, maybe he has no signal." Bud was being delightfully practical.

CeeCee blinked her acknowledgement of his comment then reached for a pastry, which she ripped apart with complete disregard for where the flakes might fall, which seemed to be around, rather than onto, her plate.

Having shredded the entire thing, she put the tiniest piece onto her tongue, then nibbled. I grabbed a pastry, and stuck it straight into my mouth, ripping off about half of it at once…which I immediately regretted. I think I heard Bud tut aloud as he also took one of the glistening pillows and pulled it into thirds, eating it nicely…without distributing crumbs everywhere.

I could feel my throat drying up as I chewed, so took a slurp of coffee, which was hotter than I'd expected. Of course, then I started to choke…which wasn't pretty. Bud rushed to help me; I stood up and did my best to contain everything within a large linen napkin, my eyes filled up until they were streaming and – eventually – I'd recovered sufficiently to be able to sit down again, sip some water, and regain some sort of composure.

CeeCee seemed completely untouched by my distress which – even though it had been self-inflicted – had been unpleasant. I allowed myself a moment or two to cool down, and even had the wherewithal to notice that CeeCee had pushed away her plate with at least three quarters of her pastry still on it – albeit in a million pieces.

Just as I felt able to sip coffee rather than water, Mahana entered the restaurant from the kitchen. She greeted us with her usual sunny smile.

"My apologies for having been away for so long. It's a pleasure to see you, CeeCee, though I know it's under tragic circumstances. How are you, my dear?" She bent down to hug CeeCee whose long, strong arms enveloped Mahana's small body as she returned the gesture. They exchanged kisses.

"Auntie Mahana, have you seen Auntie Roimata?"

Mahana patted CeeCee's arm. "I have, my little one. I was with her last night. She'll be here in a while. She had some duties to attend to before she could leave Papeete, so I came back by boat, and she'll be driving herself."

I hadn't expected that the dynamic between CeeCee and Mahana would be so…familial.

Mahana must have noticed my bloodshot eyes and misinterpreted them. "Are you still upset about yesterday morning, Cait? It must have been a terrible shock for you."

I knew that Bud and I hadn't mentioned our more than passing familiarity with dead bodies – though everyone who worked at the resort knew about Henri and Bud's shared past with the RCMP. I didn't think it was the right time to mention to Mahana that I hadn't been more than temporarily overwhelmed by finding a corpse.

I weighed my response. "It was upsetting, of course, but the death has impacted people who knew and loved Vaiarii so much more deeply, in ways I cannot imagine. You grew up with his mother, Mahana, and CeeCee, of course, is now grieving for a life she's lost, along with her fiancé." I hoped I'd hit the right note.

Mahana once again put her arm around CeeCee's well-worked-out shoulders. "Poor CeeCee. Is your father on Tahiti at the moment, or is he away on business?"

CeeCee spoke quietly, like a child. "He's on Bora Bora. Flying back this morning. Said he'd come here to meet me."

Mahana stood upright and smoothed down her *pareo*. "Charles is coming here? Today?"

CeeCee nodded. "Yes, it's wonderful. Everyone who truly loved Vaiarii will be in one place, together, so we can celebrate his life, here, where he died."

Mahana announced, "I'd better let Henri and Fleur know. And the kitchen. They'll need to make plans for lunch." She turned at the sound of the kitchen door. "Ah, Henri, there you are. We need to talk about some unexpected arrivals." She walked toward him. "And – before I forget – the red skiff wasn't tied up where it should be. Has someone been using it? I shifted it to its correct position after I'd sailed in. No damage done, but you need to have a word with everyone about making sure all the boats are properly positioned when they're moored."

Henri allowed himself to be steered back toward the kitchen by his manager as he replied, "The red boat? It's the one I told Troy to use earlier on; he said he didn't need a boat with an engine, and that's the best of the skiffs. Maybe he's back, and he didn't know we have specific spots for each boat. Thanks for sorting that out, Mahana. Now, you wanted to tell me about…"

CeeCee called after the pair, "What do you two mean? Are you saying that the boat Troy used is back? I haven't seen him. Has anyone seen him since he sailed off?" CeeCee leaped out of her seat. "Where's Troy? Oh no…first Vaiarii dies, then I get badly injured –" she held up her hands, limply – "and now Troy's disappeared. What's happening to me?"

I felt like pointing out that the world didn't, in fact, revolve around Miss CeeCee Ducasse, but her wailing, and the horrified looks on the faces of Henri and Mahana, suggested that wasn't the right thing to do.

Searching

At Henri's urging, CeeCee texted Troy again, then phoned him – still with no response – then he himself called Edouard and Annette, as well as Fleur, and we were joined by both Eloise and Nadine from the kitchen. With all of us gathered in the restaurant, Henri explained the situation, and came up with a plan for who should check which part of the resort in an attempt to locate the missing man.

As he was speaking, I couldn't help but note two things: first, that Bud was allowing our host to take the lead, which made me love him even more; second, that Henri was falling back on his training as a police officer. His tone was calm and commanding; his instructions were concise and clear; he paired up people who would work well together, and put those of us who might not be fully aware of the way the entire resort was laid out with those who did.

Bud went with Fleur and Nadine to check the beach, the dock, and the bays beyond the resort proper; Edouard and Annette were given the job of hunting through the four buildings which housed the staff and supplies; Henri and Eloise would attend to the rest of the main building – including the two guest suites below Henri and Fleur's own living quarters – before they covered the gardens; Mahana, CeeCee, and I were tasked with entering all ten of the guest bungalows. We decided it made most sense to start at the bungalow where Troy had spent the night.

"Troy, are you in here?" The door which gave access from the wooden walkway was ajar as we approached, and CeeCee was already through it as she shouted.

When I entered, I could see that Troy had done battle with his bedding through the night. As I recalled how painstakingly

Fleur and I had tucked, smoothed, and primped his linens the previous evening, I thought, *Being a housekeeper in a hotel must be soul-destroying*. A backpack appeared to have regurgitated its entire contents across the sofa at the foot of the bed, and I could hear water gurgling in the bathroom. I wasn't the only one who'd noticed it, and all three of us turned toward the sound. The door to the bathroom was half-open, and Mahana pushed past CeeCee as she dashed forward, loudly announcing her intention to enter, then threw it wide. The showerhead above the bathtub was dribbling. Mahana turned the controls to stop the flow. The rest of the bathroom looked as though a pod of dolphins had been through the place, there was so much water on the floor, especially around the bathtub itself.

"The shower curtain doesn't work properly," said CeeCee flatly. She added, "It doesn't in mine, either."

I couldn't understand what she meant – all you had to do was pull the curtain all the way around the hoop above the bath and make sure it actually fell inside the tub; ours worked perfectly well…though it was true that you had to pay attention to where the bottom of the curtain was before you turned on the water.

"He's certainly been here," observed Mahana.

CeeCee sniped, "Of course he has. He spent the night here. And Henri and Fleur saw him earlier on. That's not why we're here; we're checking to see if he's come back from being out in that boat – and he hasn't. So let's check all the other bungalows. Mine first, because he might have gone there."

I exchanged a slightly helpless look with Mahana, who I could tell felt uncomfortable about leaving Troy's bungalow, and especially his bathroom, in such a state, but we headed to CeeCee's bungalow…where we were faced with a different type of chaos.

"Oh, *ma petite*, I'm so sorry," said Mahana as we entered CeeCee's room.

CeeCee said, "What for? Why? Is he here?" She stared around the bedroom. "What's the matter?"

Mahana shuffled. "Nothing. I just thought…"

She shut up, but I knew exactly what she was thinking: Mahana had suspected that someone had ransacked the place. To start with, a few of the Gaugin prints on the walls were askew; the room was covered with *pareos* that had been unwrapped, unfolded, then discarded; piles of pillows had been tossed about; a cube-shaped box, with a handle on top and containing rows of little drawers, sat on the desk with necklaces pouring out of it, and other jewelry scattered about it in mounds; it also looked as though someone had emptied the entire supply of make-up for a theatrical troupe onto the floor in front of the glass doors leading to the deck…which were both wide open.

"I like to have everything where I can see it," said CeeCee. Her expression suggested her comment provided a sufficient explanation of the scene, but she added – more sheepishly, "I find it easier to make decisions that way."

Turning her back on the mess, Mahana strode into the bathroom, with me at her shoulder. If I'd thought Troy's was a disaster, this made his look pristine.

I didn't comment, but I could see Mahana's brow furrow as she glanced around. "Not here. Onto the next one."

"I don't see why he'd be there, but let's check our place next," I said.

We closed the doors leading to CeeCee's deck, then made sure the door to the walkway locked properly behind us.

I was pleased that Bud and I always kept our bungalow tidy, and we were in and out of the place in two minutes; there was no sign of Troy, of course, so we continued the hunting process through the next few bungalows, working our way closer to the main buildings, with Mahana leading the way, and our young companion becoming visibly bored by the entire process.

As we checked our sixth bungalow, CeeCee whined, "Bathrooms look so utterly sterile when they're lacking in any décor. And these are all so terribly gloomy. Why did they make the walls so dark? If these tiles were all white, or even a pale gray – not this horrid green color – they'd be much more welcoming."

"The aim is to reflect the colors of nature around us inside the bungalows," replied Mahana. "That's why the interior designer chose the natural grass cloth and bamboo for the walls, the greens and blues for the upholstery, and the green tile for the bathrooms."

CeeCee pouted. "Well, whatever color the bathrooms are, I need to use one, and I'm not using any of these, so I'll go back to my own and I'll catch up with you. Don't wait – you carry on without me."

We did as CeeCee had suggested. As we continued our search, Mahana had a bit of a grumble about the state of CeeCee's bungalow, and commented upon the young influencer's apparent dislike of the décor. "CeeCee needs to understand that the entire resort is not properly appointed yet. There'll be a lot of potted plants being delivered soon." At the thought, she paused, pulled out her phone and began to stab at it. "Oh, no, that's right…they're all being delivered today. I'd forgotten that. By five this afternoon, they said. And they'll all need to be checked over, and positioned…ah well, let's find Troy first, shall we? Onto the last bungalow, then we'll head back to the restaurant, to see how everyone else fared."

CeeCee rejoined us at the end of the walkway. I knew that proximity to all the facilities would appeal to some, but Bud and I had been delighted to be farthest away from all the action. Our temporary home felt truly remote, whereas this final bungalow seemed to be…well, "just" part of the resort was hardly fair, but it didn't feel as though it offered a great deal of privacy.

As in the case of Troy's bungalow, the back door of *Hoê*, bungalow number one, was ajar. Mahana hadn't passed comment when this had been the case at Troy's place, but now she strode forward, and sounded concerned when she said, "There's absolutely no reason for this door to be open."

She pushed the door slowly. Inside, the curtains were closed across the massive glass doors, so the whole room was dark, and the aroma of the place was…different. I felt an unpleasant tingle at the back of my neck.

I grabbed Mahana. "Stop."

Mahana swung to look at me, and the fear in her eyes was obvious; I suspected that she, too, had smelled blood, and death, before. But it seemed that CeeCee was oblivious: she shoved past us both and marched into the room, crossed to the curtains and flung them open.

I imagined her scream before I heard it, because – from our vantage point at the door – both Mahana and I saw the body before CeeCee turned to face the bed. Then she let rip.

Falling

We'd managed to gather CeeCee into our arms and bundle her out of the bungalow before we were joined by Bud and Fleur, who – I assumed – had heard CeeCee's screams. CeeCee's entire body had turned to rubber, but, between all of us, we managed to get her away from the bungalow, into the bar, and onto a seat. By the time the rest of our group had joined us, CeeCee was actually shedding real tears, sipping cool water, and Bud and I were head-to-head beside the bar, with me filling him in.

I explained, "Troy, in swimming trunks, curled up on the mattress in the empty bungalow nearest this building. Blood. Badly bashed head. To be honest, it smelled as though he'd been in there for some time, not just the few hours – at most – that it could have been if Henri saw him this morning."

Bud whispered, "What do you mean by 'if' Henri saw him this morning? You think he lied? Didn't see Troy at all? He said that Fleur saw him too."

"Look, I get it…it's hot, humid, and the conditions are ripe for…sorry – bad choice of word. You should go and take a proper look for yourself…no, *we* should go. Come on – let's not hang about. Bring some napkins; we don't want to touch anything."

I made a grab for a handful of linens and Bud had to scamper to catch up with me. A little out of breath by the time we reached the bungalow, he said, "No, Cait – if what you say is correct, this is a crime scene. We can't…"

But I wasn't having any of it. I pushed open the door with my elbow and immediately started taking photographs of the room, and the body. A groaning noise came from the corpse. We both froze. I turned to Bud and said, "The body expelling air?"

He shrugged. "It happens."

I steeled myself, and dared one step inside, having checked the floor before I tread on it – this despite knowing that CeeCee had already traipsed right across the room, and Mahana and I had all but carried her out across it, too. As I transferred the weight onto my front foot I noticed the corpse's leg twitch, which freaked me out a bit. I know that can happen, but…even so…not pleasant. Then there was another groan.

A switch flicked in my brain. "He's not dead," I gasped.

Bud and I were at the bedside in a flash, and – yes – Troy's eyelids were fluttering.

I shouted, "Troy, this is Cait. Bud and I are here. Try to stay still. You've got a nasty headwound. We'll get help."

A question immediately occurred to me: did I want to stay with Troy to discover if he could tell me what had happened to him, or did I want to see everyone's face when I told them he wasn't dead?

I looked at Bud and hissed, "Fleur's first aid kit, and calling an ambulance – I'll do that. You stay with him. Try to get him to tell you what happened." Bud nodded and I shot out of the bungalow.

As I ran into the bar, I was grateful that everyone was clustered around CeeCee – that would make it a little easier for me to judge reactions. "Heads up, folks." Everyone looked at me.

Good. Now focus, Cait. Clarity will be key. And you've got to be fast…Troy needs first aid as quickly as possible.

I announced, "Troy's not dead," and cast my eyes across the faces in front of me.

Surprise? Yes, Henri. Puzzlement? Yes, Mahana, for one. Fright, or terror, or dread? Yes. Nadine and Eloise look truly horrified. Amazement – Annette and Edouard. CeeCee and Fleur look relieved – a normal reaction.

Mahana snapped, "What do you mean? He's *alive*? We…we saw him. He was obviously dead. The body…the blood."

I nodded. "I know what we saw, but he's not dead. Bud's with him, and checking him over — but there's no question that he needs proper medical attention. Fleur — you're a first-aider, right? Grab your box of tricks and come with me. Henri — get an ambulance here as soon as you can. Head trauma was all that I saw, but there could be other issues — tell them they need to be fast."

As I waited while Fleur ran to the kitchen, where I assumed she kept her first aid kit, I continued to study the body language of the people in the bar. Nothing leaped out at me as being especially jarring, given the circumstances, but there was something off about CeeCee…*what was it? Anxiety?*

Fleur flung herself through the kitchen doors and rushed past her husband, who was on the phone. "I'll do my best," she said, sounding terrified, "I only hope the little I was trained to do is enough…until proper help reaches us."

Mahana had been fussing over CeeCee, but now the young woman pushed her away. CeeCee announced, "I'll come to help, Fleur."

I couldn't imagine how on earth CeeCee would be able to contribute something useful to the situation with Troy, so snapped, "I really think it's best if we keep the number of people milling about in there to a minimum."

"But I want to see Troy." CeeCee wailed like a child.

Mahana patted her arm as though she were six years old. "Come on, CeeCee, Cait's right — you might get in the way. We'll stay here. Let me make you some tea, for the shock."

I thanked Mahana with a smile, then Fleur and I raced out of the building, and were both at Troy's side in moments.

He was now in the proper recovery position, and Bud reported, "No injuries except to the head, as far as I could discern." Fleur's eyes opened wide when she saw Troy. "Breathing is regular, but labored. This was in his pocket." Bud held up Troy's phone. "I didn't want it digging into him. We can pass it on to the cops, when they arrive."

Fleur bent down to examine Troy's injury, and Bud used his own phone's flashlight to help her see better. She said, "It looks like it's stopped bleeding, which is good, and it's not actually that big. Head wounds can bleed a surprising amount, and I think that's the case here. It might not be very serious, after all. Was he alert when you found him? Able to speak?" She pulled open her little suitcase and poured distilled water onto a gauze pad.

Bud and I exchanged a glance, then he said, "Just about, but he was incoherent. Eyelids were fluttering, he was grunting, but that was about it. Closed his eyes when I shifted him to this position – big sigh. Maybe aware, and relieved he was being helped? Can't say. And you're right, the wound wasn't bleeding when I first saw him."

I wanted to ask Bud so much, but knew better; we needed to be alone for me to be able to do that.

Henri appeared at the door. "Ambulance is on its way – I stressed the urgency of the situation, and I think they took a bit more notice of me when I mentioned that this was the place where the Teriimana boy was found dead yesterday. I suspect the cops will show up, too. How is he?"

"Out cold, now, or at least asleep…but he's breathing okay." Bud stood and stretched out his back. "Fleur's doing a great job of cleaning him up – should make it easier for the paramedics to see what's what when they get here…though I reckon he's going to need some proper investigation; might have a cracked skull, for all I know."

Henri was shifting from one foot to another. "*Mon Dieu*. Yesterday? Now this? What's going on, Bud? I feel like…I feel like our whole world's caving in around us. If the Teriimana death wasn't enough to kill off this business, this should do it. All those stupid online rumors about a maniac on the loose out here? They'll have fun with this."

Fleur didn't look away from Troy's head as she said loudly, "Stop it, Henri. This isn't about us. Vaiarii is dead. This young man is…well, maybe halfway there. That's much more important."

I thought I caught a quiet "Not to me…" as Henri turned and left, but couldn't be sure.

Fleur stuffed the stained gauze into a small plastic bag, which she dumped into her kit. "That's all I can do. No point me covering up the wound, because that could interfere with what the pros will do when they get here. However, I…I can't remember if you're supposed to keep a person with a head injury awake or not. Oh no…look at me! The first real test of my training and I can't remember what's what."

Bud touched Fleur's arm. "Don't worry, that's natural. And we let him sleep…it's a good thing for someone in this state to rest. But I'll keep an eye on him, and I'll listen to his breathing; that's what matters most. You've done what you can for him. Thanks."

Fleur moved to stand, but toppled as she rose from the bed. Luckily, she managed to grab the bedside table to stop herself from falling, and Bud managed to catch her arm, too.

"Thanks, Bud." She pulled herself upright, and automatically repositioned the large, deep flower stone bowl that would, one day, camouflage an atomizer, which had shifted when she'd knocked into the table. Then we all spotted that she'd smeared blood all over both the bowl and the table. "Oh dear…"

Bud said, "It's okay, I'll clean it up."

Fleur wasn't looking quite herself. "No, I made the mess, I'll clean it up." She pulled some more gauze from her bag and wiped the table clean, then the bowl, then took off her sterile gloves and popped everything into the little plastic bag. "I'll dump this all when I get back to the main building." Once again she seemed to sway a little. "Oh dear, I'm feeling a bit overwhelmed. I hope the ambulance gets here soon."

She glanced down at Troy, then at her wristwatch, and noted, "The main road shouldn't be too bad at this time of day."

I knew what she meant: there was, essentially, just one road that circumnavigated the entire island, so the traffic into and out of Papeete could slow to a snail's pace at times; it all got snarled upon entering, and trying to leave, the main harbor and downtown areas. At least with the early rush being over by now, the ambulance should be able to get out onto the highway quite quickly, then they'd only be faced with taking it steady along the road that led to the resort – if what CeeCee had said about the state of it the previous night was accurate.

I suggested, "Let's leave Bud alone with Troy, so he can keep watch." I secretly hoped that, if we left, Bud might be able to elicit some information from Troy about how he'd ended up the way he was – if he hadn't already managed to do so.

Fleur hesitated. "It's our resort, Cait, so I really think he's our responsibility. I feel I should stay."

I replied, "Look at you – you need to clean up, and not here. Let's get you back to your apartment where there'll be soap and towels, and I think you might want to change your clothes."

Fleur looked down at her arms above where she'd removed the latex gloves she'd pulled on before attending to Troy, and her top; both were stained. She nodded. "Yes, you're right. I'll clean myself up, then – if the ambulance still hasn't arrived – I can come back." For all that she'd been trained in first aid, Fleur looked more than a little shaken.

She smiled warmly, then added, "Would you come with me, Cait? I could do with a bit of…company. Henri's so much more used to all this sort of thing than I am. He tries to be sympathetic, but I don't think he understands how terribly upsetting I find violence to be. Henri and Bud both dealt with the reality of it, and the threat of it, all the time. For we mere mortals, it's so…well, thankfully, out of the ordinary."

I didn't want to break the spell by telling Fleur that I, too, was more than passingly familiar with such unusual circumstances, so hugged her as we left, and made sure Bud saw me throw an exaggerated wink in his direction as I closed the door behind us.

Listening

There was nothing normal about the atmosphere at the bar when we walked in: CeeCee Ducasse was sobbing and screaming into her phone; Eloise and Nadine were huddled in a corner, whispering together in what appeared to be anger; Henri was pacing, while Edouard and Annette were flitting about the place moving things around on the tables and behind the bar itself, seemingly without purpose. At the sight of me and the rather bloodstained Fleur, everyone gave us their undivided attention.

CeeCee moved her phone away from her mouth and snapped, "How's Troy? Will he live? Did he say anything?"

Fleur replied with a concerned, "I believe he might make it. I hope so. And I hope the ambulance gets here fast. He needs to be in hospital, of that much I'm sure."

CeeCee relayed this information to whomever was on the other end of her call, then disconnected. "Papa will be here soon," she announced, as though that would put everything right. "I could help Bud with Troy," she added.

I said, "Fleur cleaned up his head wound, and I don't think there's anything else that can be done – at least, not without maybe getting in the way of what the professionals will want to see, and do. I think it's best if we leave Bud with him, alone, for now. Troy was responsive, but nonverbal."

"Will he be brain-damaged?" CeeCee's question surprised us.

"I have no idea," I replied. "We don't know if he's got a broken skull, or any associated internal injuries. So that's something we'll have to wait to find out."

"I hope he's not," said CeeCee. She added tearfully, "I don't know how I'd manage without him."

Fleur snapped, "I'm off to clean up," then she nudged my arm, and I followed her out of the bar, through the restaurant, across reception, and up a narrow staircase that led…well, I had to assume it was to the Legrands' own apartment.

When we reached the door at the top of the stairs, Fleur punched a number into the coded lock – the same type that all the bungalows had – and we entered what was, to my eyes, a tranquil haven among the treetops. Though the Legrands didn't have the view of the lagoon and the sea that Bud and I enjoyed from our bungalow, they had the delight of lush greenery and the mountainside beyond the windows of their main living room. Their furnishings were sparse, but adequate, and the kitchen was small enough to earn the *-ette* suffix I immediately gave it, though I could see that they had at least a peek-a-boo view toward the sea – and even the bungalows – from a small window above the kitchen sink which would make doing the washing up more than tolerable.

Fleur said, "I won't be long. Make yourself at home."

I wondered why Fleur had asked me to come with her; I felt I could have learned more about how people were reacting to Troy's condition if I'd stayed in the bar, rather than casting my eyes along the Legrands' bookshelves, and wondering how they managed to prepare anything more than a bowl of cereal in their apartment. As I looked closer, I could see that their furniture wasn't just sparse, but it had taken a lot of wear and tear. All the books were "well loved", and even the tiny kitchen cooker looked as though it were thirty years old – and yet it had been installed in this brand-new building. Shoved, almost out of sight, under the lumpy old sofa was an oversized pair of what I assumed must be Henri's flip-flops; he wore smart navy deck shoes around the resort, along with his inevitable navy shorts and white shirt, so I reckoned these must be what he wore when he and Fleur enjoyed what little time they had to relax.

Fleur appeared at the door of what had to be the bathroom, wiping her arms dry with a large navy towel which bore the yellowish scars of having been splashed with bleach, or something caustic.

She said, "I'll just change my clothes, then we'd better get back. I don't know why I wanted you to come with me, really – I'm quite alright, now. Why don't you go on down? I'll follow when I've decided the right sort of thing to wear for what's going to be another bad day – possibly even worse than yesterday, though I don't know how that could be the case. I do hope that poor young man will be okay."

Despite Fleur's assertion that she didn't need company, I could tell by her body language that she was on edge. I did my best to reassure her. "I hope so, too. You did a good job of getting him cleaned up, and I bet that means the paramedics will be able to get their work done faster." I didn't want to sound patronizing – Fleur certainly didn't need that.

Trying to distract her, I mentioned the view. "It's so lush out there. I know Bud and I have enjoyed being able to see the water for weeks, but I'm pleased to see this, now, and to know I'll be looking out at literally millions of evergreens in just a few weeks."

Fleur smiled; I was pleased she felt she could. "I think it's extraordinary that you and Bud own an entire mountain. This place is quite the responsibility, but that? It must take a lot of work."

"We've got a contract with a company that specializes in forest management; it's not something we could have done on our own. But our situation's not at all like you having this resort. You have people you're responsible for…their job security must weigh heavily on you. Not to mention the financial challenges you've told us you face. Our mountain? We love it, and the trees that have to be felled – to maintain the health of the forest – produce enough income to more than cover the management fees…but it's not something we ever would, or probably even could, sell, so it's not like the resort in that respect; it's not an investment. And I know that you and Henri see this place as that: something you've built, and will run to produce a profit, but also something that you can sell on, one day."

Fleur laughed harshly. "This – an investment? We thought so, yes, as we told you. But now? Now, I'm not so sure. Look, Cait – Henri mentioned something about you and Bud being caught up in that cold case that just made such a splash over in Australia. Do you think that Bud would…I mean, has he ever, well…you know…*looked into something?* Even though he's retired?"

I considered my response carefully, and decided that the best thing I could say was, "Why do you ask?"

Fleur stopped wiping her arms. "I think that Henri wants to ask Bud to help him to…investigate Vaiarii's death. And now, probably, this thing with Troy, too. But I don't want him to."

Fleur seemed to shrink into herself, and my heart went out to her.

Unusually for me, I gave myself a moment before I responded. "Fleur, Bud and I have…encountered…some tricky problems in the past, which we've faced together. Yes, as you say, we did get mixed up with a cold case in Australia, but it was just that – a cold case. The police weren't looking into it. I do think that the police are likely to want to investigate today's incident. And maybe they'll consider Vaiarii's death differently because of what's happened today, too. Bud would never want to meddle in a local investigation, and I bet Henri's the same in that regard. They both had careers where so many people were ready to criticize and think they knew better…so why would they do the same thing to what I know they'll think of as fellow officers?"

Fleur was still holding the towel in her hands, and now she began wringing it. "I only met Henri after his life as a cop. As we've told you, we got to know each other because we both ran bed and breakfasts and sat on some of the same local committees in Montreal. I have absolutely no background in law enforcement, or in criminal investigation. You all do. But I can't ask Henri to *not* try to work out what's going on here. He's terrified we're going to lose everything – and I mean that literally – and it's like it's burrowing into his brain. He's talking about it obsessively. That's not like Henri; he's bright, and usually thinks clearly. You know that, because you've seen him do it. And I certainly know it, because this place wouldn't exist if he didn't have that ability. I want to help him, to stop him being so overwhelmed by it…I want him to leave it to the locals, but I don't know how to do that. Bud would know what to say to him. And maybe you would, too. Would you both help us? Please?"

What could I say? "I'll talk to Bud. They were close, once. Maybe he can get Henri to…stand down."

Fleur burst into tears. "Oh, thank you, Cait. I can see how much you and Bud love each other – you're still like gushing newlyweds, even after three years. And maybe you don't see that…that same joy when you look at me and Henri. But it's there, deep down. It's just that we chose to do this with our new lives and it…well, it ground us down a bit, to tell the truth. Before Henri I had an existence, not a life, in the real sense. When we found each other, it was as though a light came on inside me – and I knew that my world would never be the same again. He really is my everything, Cait. My whole future. I'm not ashamed to admit that I love him with my entire being. But…but we don't gush, anymore. We haven't a giggle left in us, I don't think…but that will change. When this place gets going, we can pay down our debts, then we can realize our investment and go wherever we want, and do whatever we want…then we'll be like you two." She wiped her eyes and added sheepishly, "You two are adorable, really you are. So…so *sympatico*, you know?"

"Adorable?" I chuckled. "Well, I'm not so sure about that, Fleur, though we know how very fortunate we are to be together, and never take it for granted. I'm sorry for both of you that your choice to create this place has robbed you of some of your happiness. But I will say that you and Henri do seem to be on the same page – so, yes, I'm sure you'll both benefit when the weight of the resort lifts a little. You'll be fine. You complement one another very well."

Fleur smiled sadly. "We do, don't we? As do you and Bud. It's important, that. Henri's so…so dogged. Never lets up. Resolute. I'm sure he was a good RCMP officer. I know he was good at running his B & B, and I also know he's done everything possible for this place to be a huge success. He had a dream…*we* had a dream. You have to have a dream, don't you? To help you keep moving forward. And our dream will come true – if only Fate will allow it. Though not much seems to be going our way at the moment."

I agreed. "I think it's an observable truth that life can take us in directions we'd never imagined. But I believe that it's the unintended, and often unforeseen, consequences of our choices and actions that really make the difference…not Fate. To be honest with you, I don't really believe in Fate."

Fleur shrugged. "Call it what you will, Cait, but there's something that has the ability to get in the way of us being able to be the best we can – for ourselves, and for those we love – and it can come at you out of a clear blue sky, with no black clouds to warn you that a storm is on its way."

"Like me finding Vaiarii in your lagoon, you mean?"

"Yes. Then you have no control over how that storm might affect the person who means the most to you in the world."

"I'll talk to Bud about it." We hugged. I waited while she changed, and stared at Henri's sad, rather scruffy-looking flip-flops skulking beneath the battered sofa.

Tasting

When Fleur and I got back down to the bar, there was still no sign of an ambulance, and there was no sign of Eloise or Nadine either. I guessed they'd gone into the kitchen, so went there myself; despite my reassurances to Fleur, my plan was to try to get to the bottom of the situation that had arisen between the Trembley-Martins and Vaiarii Teriimana for my own peace of mind. The situation that the couple had described had bothered me…in more ways than one.

I walked into what appeared to be an empty kitchen, only to be surprised when Eloise popped up from below a counter with a giant stainless-steel bowl in her hands.

We both registered shock, then she said, "I know it seems heartless, but I have to get on. Me standing about in the bar wasn't helping anyone, and there are people coming who'll expect there to be food ready for them, so I'm attending to that. Nadine's gone back to our rooms to get herself changed so she can help with serving. It's going to be a lot for Annette to cope with on her own, and Nadine can turn her hand to most things."

I jumped right in. "Like defending your honor, for example?"

Eloise dumped ingredients into the bowl. "What?"

You know exactly what I mean, was what I thought; "When Vaiarii Teriimana threatened you," was what I said.

Eloise bashed whatever was in the bowl with the end of a rolling pin. "He didn't threaten me. He made a play for me…made filthy suggestions. Then he grabbed my bum, and I screamed."

"And Nadine came running? Laid into him?"

"She didn't even ask me what had happened. Didn't have to, I suppose. She could see that I was upset. She's my wife; wouldn't you expect her to defend me?"

"Of course I would. However, if my husband had heard me scream and came around a corner to see me huddled against a wall with a man standing beside me, I'm not sure that his immediate reaction would be to start hitting the man."

Eloise paused, her rolling pin at rest. "It's…different, for us. Bud's a man himself – he might feel he could reason with another man, get him to walk away just by using words and the threat of…something more. It's not that easy when you're two women. Men…stand their ground. Won't back down. And, in any case, Nadine's a bit…"

I chuckled, I knew what Eloise meant. "Yes, she does tend to leap before she looks, doesn't she?"

Eloise went back to her merciless domination of the contents of her bowl. "She does, but that's a part of why I love her. We'd only been together a few months when she gave up everything to move when I got a better job. And she's done that several times, since. She's not fearless, though – that would suggest she's foolish. No, she understands there are risks, but does things that need to be done anyway. She's brave."

"Do you think Vaiarii would have done more than grab your bum if Nadine hadn't arrived?"

Eloise didn't pause, but pounded the bowl harder. "Do you mean do I think he was taking the first step toward rape?"

"Did you then? Do you now? Two different questions."

Eloise nodded. "They are. I believe I did at the time: I didn't know him, and he was being aggressive in what I could only take as being a sexual manner – given what he was saying to me. Looking back, I have no idea how far he'd have gone."

"What was he saying?"

Eloise stopped, dropped the rolling pin. "The classic: 'All you need is a good man'. That sort of rubbish."

"So he knew that you and Nadine were married?"

"It's no secret."

I paused, knowing I didn't want to say the wrong thing. "Do you think that Vaiarii saw you, or possibly Nadine, as a specific target, because you're lesbians?"

Eloise shook her head with resignation. "He'd already been flirting with Annette, but that was…different. What she said earlier about that was true. We all heard him – he was annoying, but playful then. Which was why I didn't panic when he started on me. It was just silly stuff to start with, then…something changed in his eyes, and then he grabbed me and I knew I wasn't safe anymore."

I dared, "Can you remember what you might have said or done to make his attitude…change. Not that I'm blaming you at all – but I'm interested to discover if there was some sort of trigger for him."

Eloise glared at me. I knew I'd have to work harder to get her to understand why I was doing what I was. I added, "Sadly, I have personal experience of knowing how a completely innocent look, or remark, can set someone off…trigger them. I once had a boyfriend who'd start with a steely glance if I laughed a little too heartily at another man's joke in company, or if the toast was a bit too brown or…well, that was the problem, you see – I never had any idea what would set him off. There seemed to be no logic to it – though I'm sure he believed there was. But something flicked a switch so that the ugliness of what he was thinking suddenly showed in his eyes. And once I saw that, I felt unsafe. That's why I'm asking if you noticed exactly when you felt that the situation had changed – and if you can recall what you'd said or done just beforehand…because that might help me to better understand Vaiarii himself."

Eloise began to pound at the bowl again, "Whatever you might say, it sounds as though you *are* blaming me. Not him. And all I said was that the world might think he was gorgeous, but to me he was just another island boy."

"'Another island boy' were your exact words?"

Eloise paused, her rolling pin in the air. "Yes. And he was. But he was a pig, too. Though that might not be fair to pigs."

"And did he say anything to you or Nadine after she'd been pulled off him?"

"Other than wailing that she might have ruined him, ruined his career, by hitting his face? No. Nothing of substance…that I can recall. I was very shaken by the whole thing, you understand."

"And nothing of the same sort happened between you and Troy, did it?"

Eloise put down her rolling pin and wiped her hands. "Why are you asking all these questions? Do you think I'm some sort of tease? Why on earth would you think that two men would try to seduce me? Me! You're victim blaming."

I felt myself getting hot. "Eloise, I'm sorry that I've made you feel that way. It wasn't and isn't my intent. In my professional life – as I know you know – I'm a professor of criminal psychology. What you might not be aware of is that my specialism is in profiling victims of crime…usually murder victims. I try to work out how a person might have become a victim by delving into their lives to try to understand what it might have been about them – their habits, preferences, choices, and so forth – that might have brought them into contact with the person who did them harm. That's not about blaming them for becoming a victim, it's about trying to reveal clues that could otherwise go undiscovered about where their life might have intersected with their killer's. In this case I'm trying to understand why Vaiarii attacked you – why he made you a victim. You'd never met him before that day?" Eloise shook her head. "Okay, well, at least I know, in this case, why your paths crossed when they did: he was here to do a photo shoot, you work here. I also understand that he was flirting with other women, not just you. And I don't want to jump to the conclusion that he put his hands on only you because you're gay." Eloise looked up, her eyes telling me she at least appreciated that point. "I'm trying to work out if there was what he might have perceived as a cause – something specific that happened – to make him shift from flirtation to aggression."

Eloise shrugged. "We were alone. *That* was different."

"How do you mean?"

"When he was being a flirt, even though it was pathetic, it was sort of…oh, you know…the sort of thing a young man might think he needed to do because it was expected. Then? Then there was a crowd of us, all milling about, and he was getting lots of attention because he was being almost comically suggestive, you know? But I left the group and went around the side of the restaurant to get a bit of peace and quiet; the day had been madness, with people coming and going all the time, and everyone wanting snacks." Eloise sighed heavily. "Well, no, that's not true: I popped outside for a quick vape. But don't tell Nadine; she thinks I've stopped."

"Did Vaiarii see you vaping? Did he maybe think he'd discovered a secret about you?"

Eloise nodded. "He did, and he started off by teasing me that he'd tell Nadine. Then it was all about what would I do for him if he didn't. That's how it started. Then I told him he was just like all the other island boys…and that's when he got nasty."

"'Just like all the other island boys'? Or was it 'Just another island boy'? That's what you said earlier."

Eloise frowned. "They both mean the same thing. Why is that so important?"

I was honest. "I don't know. I'm just…trying to understand."

Eloise stuck her hands into the bowl and began to mix.

She didn't look up when she said, "Cait, I know you've spent a lot more time with Nadine than with me, and she's told me what you two have chatted about. So you know that we've run the gamut when it comes to how people react to us. Mostly we've been lucky – we've been able to be together, and get married. Both our families came to our wedding – which is not something all same-sex couples can say. We've been fortunate, for the main part. But there are still so many situations where we can't 'be us'. I know it's not the same for everyone, but we're not fighters, Cait, we like a quiet life…so we feel we have to consider every scenario and make complex decisions. For example, new workplaces have to be analyzed: what can, and can't, we do? Who's anti-gay? And there's always someone, trust me. Sometimes they have to fume at us silently, because the group we're with supports us and they don't want to be seen to be against us. Other times we simply make the decision to not put ourselves in certain circumstances, not go to certain places…or, if we do, to act like friends, not a couple at all, let alone a married one."

"I'm so sorry that you have to live that way." I was.

"It's been much worse for people like us in the past, and, of course, we always live in fear that it will become much worse again in the future. The hate is always there, bubbling away under the surface, for some people. And as soon as they feel they've been given permission to let that hate explode, out it comes. But – and I hope you've understood this from what you and Nadine have discussed – all we want is to be able to live a peaceful life…together. That's all. To be able to be us."

"That's all most people want."

"Cait, you need to understand that while we've had to stand up for ourselves, and for our relationship, like I said, Nadine and I aren't fighters. So even though she launched herself at Vaiarii that day, that was a spur of the moment reaction to her seeing me in what she could tell was distress. I know she can be a bit rambunctious, but she's arrived where she is by a different path than I did. I think she's told you about her time at school? What she went through back then?"

I nodded. "It sounds as though the all-girls set-up made life very difficult for her. That she learned back then that to attack was the best defense…though she also told me she mainly achieved that by aiming to be the best at everything she did."

Eloise smiled. "She did…and her mother has told me what that meant for her. Long nights studying, participating in almost every activity offered, pushing herself so hard that – as she probably told you – she ended up falling at the last hurdle, and was hospitalized before her final exams. She never did get over that breakdown… and she also never went back to that school." Eloise paused and her shoulders fell. "She can't even cope with the sight of a nun; they were so cruel to her at school. But now she's found her path – and she's an excellent practitioner in all her wellness disciplines. She experienced them on her own journey toward wellness, then she studied them and got all her qualifications, so that now she's able to pass on the benefits to others. It matters to her, and she's good at it: no longer because she wants to win, at any cost, but because she wants to help others. And she's helped me too. The vaping? It's a few puffs of the lightweight stuff nowadays, whereas I was a two-pack a day girl when she met me. Now? No cigarettes for four years."

"I've been pretty good for quite a while too," I admitted. "I yearn for a cigarette, but – for Bud's sake – I'm chewing the gum. It gives me something to do with my mouth."

"Addiction's a terrible thing," said Eloise, with a half-smile. "Non-smokers never get it, do they? Nadine used to smoke, but it was more about the rebellion for her. Gave up one day and says she's never felt like doing it again. Of course I'm pleased for her, but…well, she doesn't get it."

"Nor does Bud. Like Henri doesn't understand why Fleur is so rattled by Vaiarii's death, and now this attack on Troy. But even happy couples aren't expected to be in absolute synchronicity, are they? We'd all be less content if we were married to carbon copies of ourselves, right?"

Eloise let out a laugh. "Oh, you are so right." She leaned across the bowl, her hands still inside it. "Take Annette and Edouard. I like them both, but I can't imagine why they ever married each other, or how they've stayed together. They are the complete opposite of each other."

I was intrigued. "How so?"

Eloise dropped her voice. "This isn't gossip, it's what I've seen and been told by each of them – separately, of course. Annette used to be quite the party girl – nothing bad, just a great deal of dancing, lots of boyfriends, and generally always being out and about, whereas Edouard lived with his mother, and looked after her until she died. Cancer. It's…it's a terrible disease, Cait. It can't have been easy for him. It's never easy for the families. Then, apparently, he and Annette were set up on a blind date." Eloise grinned wickedly. "I can only imagine it was by someone with a cruel sense of humor, to be honest. But if it was some sort of joke, it backfired, because they were married in less than three months, and they've been together now for about four years. Personally, I think he's got a tiger by the tail, and I also think the reason they're here is because it's a nice quiet spot where he can keep an eye on her – not many chances for partying the night away here. But Annette? You must have noticed how she's like a wound spring all the time, and how Edouard always seems to be watching her. Though why he needs to bother at the resort I don't know."

I found Eloise's comments to be both interesting, and annoying – because I hadn't noticed anything of the sort when I'd interacted with Edouard and Annette. Had I really been that caught up in my own little world since I'd arrived? I supposed I must have been. Then I realized that I'd rarely seen them together, until this past day or so, so gave myself a bit of a pass on that one.

I heard a siren. "That must be the ambulance," I said, relieved that Troy would finally get the medical attention he needed.

"Will he be okay, really? He seemed like a pleasant man. Not the sort of person I'd have imagined as CeeCee's assistant, but steady, you know? Like all New Zealanders, in a way – they're generally polite, and just a little naïve, don't you think?"

"I don't know enough of them to comment," I replied carefully, "but this one needs to be tended to, so I'll just go and see what I can do to help."

"Yes, he really is a victim, Cait, so maybe you can find out how he managed to become one."

"I'll try," I said, "though why your first ever meeting with Vaiarii should have led him to victimize you, I really can't say. Look – just before I go, I do have one more question: *why* did you say he was like all the island boys? What was it about him, or about them, that made you say that? Have you been targeted before, by other locals?"

Eloise sighed. "Back to that again? No, I haven't been targeted by locals. Well, not recently. What I meant was that he was like all the boys here – the boys who used to tease me."

I was at sea. "Nope…I don't understand. Sorry, Eloise. What boys here used to tease you?"

Eloise puffed out her cheeks. "When I was little. The boys in school here teased me."

"You were here, on Tahiti, when you were a child? I thought…I assumed…you were born and raised in France."

Eloise shook her head. "I was born in France, yes, but I was the child of a military family, so we bounced around a great deal. My father was posted here from when I was about five until I was about seven. I was in the school system here at that time, in

Papeete, which is where my mother and I lived. My father seemed to always be on duty, so he preferred that we had a normal life, as he called it; didn't want us to get stuck in the military silo, he said. And I enjoyed my experience of Tahitian life back then, for the most part. But the island boys were merciless when it came to a tall, gangly, shy girl who didn't really think of anywhere as home. They picked on me – and I hated it. Hence my lack of love for the island boys."

"Did Vaiarii know anything about the fact that you'd been here as a child?"

Eloise shrugged. "No reason he should."

The siren was close, so I knew I had to go. "Thanks for that, Eloise. Much appreciated. I'd better get going now."

I left the kitchen wondering what Eloise's words about island boys had meant to Vaiarii, because I had a suspicion they'd meant something very different to the person who'd spoken them versus the one who'd heard them.

Stocktaking

The arrival of the ambulance led to a great deal of kerfuffle, and we all hung about in the bar waiting for news about Troy's condition. Bud came across from the bungalow where Troy was being attended to, to ask CeeCee if she had any information about Troy's next of kin, which didn't sound too promising. The request sent the young woman into another meltdown.

"I don't know that. Why would I know that?" CeeCee's wailing was annoying, and it got my goat that she didn't seem to know the first thing about the man she'd said was her "right hand". She didn't know where he'd lived in New Zealand, didn't even know if he had any family, and all she could do was offer his phone number and email address.

"I'm going to hunt through Troy's belongings to see if I can find any formal ID," said Bud – quite sensibly, I thought. "Cait, I could do with a hand."

I knew he didn't really need my help, but recognized a request from my husband that I should agree to. We both headed toward Troy's bungalow, but waited until we got there to talk. Arriving at Troy's door, we stopped.

"Of course, we don't have the code," said Bud. "I should have asked…Mahana, I guess…or did you see what she punched in when you came here the first time around?"

"The door wasn't locked, it was ajar. CeeCee just waltzed in…no code needed."

"Okay, you stay here, I'll go. Hang on – why was it open then?"

"No idea. Ours always shuts on its own when we leave, so maybe Troy meant to leave it unlocked when he left? Though that seems a bit odd."

"Never mind – I'll get that code."

When Bud had left, I examined the code pad. There was sand on several of the buttons. I took a photo, but didn't want to disturb the sand, so waited until Bud got back.

"One, one, one, one," he said with a roll of his eyes. "Master code which overrides everything, everywhere. A personal code can be set by each guest when they check in. Not a choice we were given, by the way – I was informed that ours was one, three, zero, six when we arrived."

Entering Troy's bungalow for the second time, I took Bud into the bathroom to show him the mess. He was also surprised, then snapped photos.

I noted, "The window being ajar has helped with the drying process, and nothing's different in here, other than the amount of water."

"He can't have pulled the curtain around the shower properly, before he used it," said Bud, which was exactly what I'd thought, "and it looks as though he used just two hand towels to dry himself off, which is a bit…odd."

"He's got a different bodywash to the one we've been using," I noted. "Ours is 'Ocean Life', but his says 'Calm Waters'. I know that Fleur told Edouard to bring the calming atomizer mist…maybe he also took it upon himself to bring the 'calming' toiletries too. Yes – see, the hand soap is the same, as are the shampoo and conditioner."

"All unused," noted Bud. "Looks like he brushed his teeth with his own supplies. Come on, let's check that backpack of his."

The contents of the backpack that I'd noted earlier were still strewn across the sofa at the foot of the bed. As Bud stepped toward the mound to pick something up, I shouted, "Stop!"

Bud turned. "Good grief, what is it?"

"Something's different…it's all different. Hang on a minute…you take lots of photos, let me have a think."

Bud nodded and I stepped aside, closed my eyes to the point where everything goes fuzzy and started to hum; I don't know why this technique helps with my detailed recollection, it just does, so I do it.

I took myself back to the time when I'd first seen Troy's room, and had noticed the pile of items on the sofa. I forced my memory to show me the collection, then to allow me to focus on each item, some of which were almost entirely covered by others, so I had to extrapolate what they were from the little I could see in my mind's eye.

I opened my eyes. "Okay, I'm sure."

"About…"

"This whole jumble of stuff has been rearranged since the first time I saw it. It's in essentially the same place, but it's been completely muddled about. I'd suggest someone's been hunting through it."

"Between the time that you, Mahana, and CeeCee first looked in here for Troy, and now?" I nodded. "That's an interesting period because, as far as I can tell, no one at all had an opportunity to be here."

"I agree…but we can think about that later. Is there a chestnut leather wallet there, Bud?"

Bud peered but didn't move anything. "There is — I can see the side of it, beneath a pair of socks, but that's all."

"Good. His wallet would be a logical place for us to look for his ID, so let's start with that. I'm doubly glad we both put on latex gloves before we came in here."

"Fleur's face when she handed them to me from the first aid kit was a picture," said Bud. "Have you and she been talking about this…situation?"

I filled Bud in on what Fleur and I had discussed, including her request for help with Henri, and he agreed it was something he'd do, to the best of his abilities. "For all that he and I have gone our different ways, I wouldn't want to do less than everything I can to help out him and Fleur. So trying to talk him out of investigating is something I'm willing to do."

"Thanks. Right, let's focus on what the medics need regarding Troy for now, eh?"

Bud pulled open Troy's wallet and found his driver's licence. Troy Archibald Wilson had an address in Auckland, and a date of birth that put him at a little short of forty-three years of age. He was an organ donor who was allowed to drive both cars and commercial vehicles, and his photograph made him look like a serial killer – as does mine. As does everyone's, I suspect; quite how the folks who take the photographs for drivers' licences and passports manage that trick, I don't know…but they do.

Bud said, "At least we have this. If they follow this lead, it might tell them who he listed as his next of kin when he filed his paperwork – if the New Zealand system works that way. Snap both sides, will you, Cait? Then we'll give it to the paramedics."

"Just before you replace the wallet, Bud – does it look as though anything might have been taken from it?"

Bud checked. "There's cash – though not much – and a few credit cards. I don't know how I'd know if anything had been taken, to be honest."

"Pass it over, and I'll take photos of everything in there, in case we get the chance to ask Troy himself if anything's missing." Bud handed me the wallet, which felt loved. The leather was soft and smooth, shinier in some parts, and it had the sort of indentations that develop over time. I pulled everything out, snapped, replaced everything. And handed it back to Bud.

I sat on the edge of the chair in the corner for a moment, thinking. Beneath the bed, I spotted something.

I said, "Look, Bud…under the bed. Is that one of those little plastic pots that camera films used to come in?"

Bud kneeled down. "It looks like it…though it's just out of reach. Back in the day I always used to think these things must have had so many potential uses. There, got it." He stood up, looking puffed.

I took the container Bud offered me, and opened it. Inside was a massive, truly black pearl – a dark, pearlized charcoal color, to be precise. I rolled it out onto my latex-covered palm. "Good grief, this must be worth a fortune. Look at the size of it, Bud."

We both stared. Bud said, "I've only seen the completely black ones, like this, in that really fancy store in Papeete…and they were all small, farmed ones. Do you think something this big could even be real?"

"Grab a coin or something, Bud…put them side by side in your palm, for a size comparison, then I'll take photos."

Bud stared at me as though I'd lost my mind. "A coin? Where would I get a coin?" He patted his boardshorts. "One – no coins. Two – no coins even in our bungalow because we spend no money here. The French Polynesian franc notes are beautiful, and the coins are so big they look like something you'd find in a pirate chest…but we both agreed we don't want to get stuck with any currency we can't exchange when we've left, so I've only used my card when we've had to buy anything. Have you got a secret stash of cash I know nothing about?"

I shook my head, handed Bud the pearl, and shoved my hand into my little cross-body purse where I found a stray Australian dollar; I'd kept a few, because I adore the engraving of the kangaroos on the back. "This'll do. Now hold out your hand."

I placed the dollar and the pearl beside each other in Bud's palm. The pearl was bigger than the coin, which meant it had to be more than twenty-five millimeters in diameter…huge, for a pearl. "Hold still," I instructed.

"This modelling thing's harder than it looks – my hand's starting to shake, and it never does that." Bud grinned cheekily as he spoke, and I poked out my tongue; it was the wittiest riposte I could manage.

I took several photos, then we returned the pearl to its container, and the container to the position it had been in when we'd arrived.

"Anything else…off?" Bud gazed around. "This is my first time in here. Same general set-up as ours, though a bit smaller. Fantastic view, much the same as ours. Is everything else the same here as it was when you first came in?"

I scanned the entire bungalow…now with fresh eyes. The way the curtains were hanging at the windows was a bit different; the mound of bedding had shifted a little; I sniffed the air as I went. "Those atomizers are spectacularly effective, Bud," I said, pointing toward the flower stone bowl on the bedside table. "When Fleur and I came in here last night to make the room up, the whole place smelled awful. Now it's really fresh. I wonder where she gets them."

Bud sighed. "Not the sort of thing we want to be trying to fit into our suitcases, Cait, okay? If you're that keen, get the details and we'll follow through when we get home."

I smiled. "Don't panic, I wasn't suggesting that. What I mean is…no, there's no way that an atomizer could be a clue to what happened to Troy. Besides, there's absolutely no reason to think that whatever happened to him happened here, in his own bungalow: it's much more likely that he was attacked while he was out on that boat. But…"

"But if that's where he was attacked, then why not just leave him in the boat? Set it adrift. Why bring him – or maybe what someone thought was his dead body – back to the resort? And how on earth did anyone get him from the boat to that other bungalow in any case? Oh – hang on – what about those housekeeping buggy things? That could work. But…why did he end up in bungalow number one? It's the closest to the main building…so, easy for anyone to notice even a buggy being pushed along."

I mused, "Right. Why *would* anyone bring him back to the resort at all if he were already incapacitated, or if they thought he was dead? And – possibly even more importantly – you're right…how did they get him into that specific bungalow? That was a high-risk move: if anyone at all was about, they'd have seen…well, whatever happened. Unless there's some sort of alternative route to the bungalows that we know nothing about."

Bud added, "Maybe it was a slightly lower risk to take him there than to bring him back here, to his own bungalow, when we, and CeeCee, were in close proximity to it. But no one saw anything. Or, if they did, they're keeping that knowledge under their hat. It was daylight, and we know that at least Henri and Fleur were about the place. And I'd have thought that Eloise would have been around, too…she'd have been getting breakfast ready, wouldn't she?"

I replied, "She's a bit more complicated than I'd thought, Bud. Which I understand could be said of anyone, the more you get to know them, but I was surprised to learn that she'd lived here, on Tahiti, as a child." I filled Bud in on my chat with Eloise.

Bud sighed, and looked a bit lost. "This is all feeling like a big, tangled mess, to be honest, Cait. You remember when we had to clear those brambles at home? Like that. A real problem to know where to start, when nothing's clear. We don't know what happened to Vaiarii. And we don't know what happened to Troy. What we do know, however, is that they have two things in common: CeeCee Ducasse, and a bash on the head. Not that I'm suggesting those two things are linked, in that CeeCee did it to them – but maybe they're linked in another way? Because both men were close to CeeCee?"

I could feel my frustration grow. "With Fleur asking us to prevent Henri from investigating, and with the police likely to want to immediately at least investigate what happened to Troy, we've really got no reason to…pry. I get that. But…oh, let's be honest Bud – we both want answers. Was Troy able to shed any light on what happened to him? Or did he really remain unresponsive all the time you were with him?"

"Grunts, in the main, though he mumbled some nonsense for a bit, and that was it. He was in and out of consciousness."

"What did he say?"

"He seemed to be talking about something to do with…I don't know…business reports? Something about reevaluating reports and scans. Like I said, it was gibberish, though he kept repeating it all the time, as though it was important to him. Re-evaluate reports and scans, I believe it was. And he said millions, too. Once. That I'm sure of."

I gave Bud's words some thought. "Reports? Scans? Scans of something he'd downloaded? Some report that needed to be reconsidered?"

"It could be something like that, but – come on – if they're waiting for some ID before they'll take Troy to hospital, we'd better get this to them. I know they said they wanted to check him over and stabilize him before they moved him, but they might have done that by now. We can come back here afterwards if we need to, and we can take ourselves off so we can have a fuller exchange of information and opinions later, too. Okay?"

We made sure the door locked behind us, and found the medics wheeling Troy on a stretcher from the bungalow where they'd attended to him; he was still out of it. Bud handed over the driver's licence, the paramedics and he exchanged a few words, then they left with their patient, and we rejoined the group at the bar. It had grown by one person: a solemn-looking woman wearing a startlingly bold lime green and cerise *pareo,* tied high around her neck, was sitting at a table, alone. I had to imagine it was Roimata Teriimana, though she looked about ten years older than Mahana, and I'd expected them to be contemporaries, given that Mahana had said they'd grown up together.

The woman looked at me, her face etched with grief and wet with tears. Her voice croaked when she said, "When you found my boy, was he wearing his crucifix?"

Now sure that this was Roimata, I shook my head sadly. "I'm certain he wasn't." *I was.*

"That is…very bad," she said. I watched her tears roll as Mahana joined her at the table, where the two women held each other, and wept on the other's shoulder.

No one spoke. No one moved, except for Fleur, who rubbed her breast and then crossed herself. I noticed that the birds had stopped singing; only the sound of sobbing filled the shimmering air, and I felt – for the first time – that Vaiarii Teriimana was being grieved for by someone who'd truly loved him.

Grieving

I wasn't surprised that it was CeeCee Ducasse who broke the grief-filled silence; however, the inappropriateness of her comment really floored me.

She cooed, "That's a stunning *pareo*, Roimata. Where on earth did you find that print?"

Everyone stared at CeeCee, who was clearly oblivious to the shock her words had caused.

Roimata answered evenly, "It was my mother's. Vaiarii's grandmother's. I wear it today to honor both their departed spirits. After what Mahana has told me about Troy Wilson, I pray it does not have to honor another precious soul today."

CeeCee replied cheerily, "I wonder if I could get someone to copy it. Retro is always…interesting."

I wanted to shake her.

Mahana said, "This might not be quite the right time for thoughts about fashion, CeeCee, dear."

CeeCee adopted a wounded expression.

I still wanted to shake her.

The young woman whined, "When Papa arrives, I think we should all go down to the beach. To the place where Cait and Mahana dragged my poor Vaiarii from the water. We should talk about a suitable place where we can set up a permanent memorial."

CeeCee's idea of how to handle a delicate situation wasn't shared by anyone else in the bar, it seemed. I could see Henri's shoulders hunch, but absolutely no one made a sound. Every eye turned toward the dead man's mother.

Once again, Roimata Teriimana impressed me with her dignified response. "I would like to see the place, but I would hate there to be a memorial. Vaiarii will always be with me." She touched her breast. "He is here, now, and there will be better ways to remember him, for others. I will have a shrine for him at my home. At what was our home. I have already spoken to a few people about setting up scholarships in his name, to support students from families who have very little, so that they can stay at school to graduate."

CeeCee snapped, "Vaiarii hated school. He left as soon as he could. Why would you want to have scholarships in his name?"

We were all watching the exchange between the dead man's mother and the dead man's fiancée with an increasing level of tension.

Roimata said quietly, "CeeCee, I know you loved my son, but I don't think you understood him well. He left school to work, to earn money to help us live. He enjoyed his schoolwork, and he was bright. Good at mathematics, especially. But he was also good at being a pearl diver, and he made money doing that. He would be happy to know that others would not have to make the same decision he did – to leave school because the family needed money. He would have made a wonderful teacher, if only he could have gained all the qualifications."

As a psychologist, I'm familiar with the concept that parents project their wants and desires onto their children – in many ways. I wondered if the life Roimata was describing as one Vaiarii would have been happy to live was, perhaps, the life she herself had desired for him; I hadn't seen anything of the young man online that suggested to me he was a frustrated educator. But I didn't say anything; I preferred to observe.

CeeCee piped up with: "I think it's you who didn't know your son, Roimata. I've always been polite to you, for Vaiarii's sake, but even he said you didn't understand what he wanted out of life. I did. He wanted to be able to make people happy, and he did that by sharing his smile with them. His smile was the most special smile in the world; you should see how many likes his smile gets online every day. Everything I post that shows his smile gets twice as many likes as anything else."

I wondered if CeeCee really judged the value of everything in terms of likes, and if she might even be addicted to the dopamine high that comes with seeing high numbers of views, likes, and comments. I'm familiar with the concepts from an academic point of view because I'm a psychologist first, and a criminal psychologist second, and I like to keep up with a broad range of psychological research. There's an increasing amount of it these days that focuses on the impact made on the human psyche by our online lives. It's all grounded in the most basic principles, of course: human beings naturally seek approval, and likes are a conveniently visible and measurable form of just that. But if that becomes a person's reason for doing something – anything – then they run the risk of losing sight of what truly motivates them, other than eliciting instantaneous and ephemeral positive feedback, which can stunt, and even skew, psychological development.

From what I'd seen of CeeCee so far – both in the flesh, and online – she certainly seemed to be teetering on the edge of perceiving herself solely through the eyes of others, but if she used her online presence to leverage business success – as Henri had suggested – then maybe the views and likes were a means to an end for her, which would put a different spin on her almost pathological desire to look perfect, and to post content on an alarmingly frequent basis. I wondered how she'd cope without Troy to point a camera at her all the time.

CeeCee stood up angrily, grabbing my attention. She pushed her chair aside and strode off toward the washrooms. She'd managed to avoid a lot of our search because she'd needed to use her bathroom, now she needed to go yet again?

Roimata said, "I hope she comes back with a more sympathetic face on her. These are terrible tragedies."

I suspected no one else dared comment.

Seeing my chance to grab a few moments alone with CeeCee, I waited a few seconds, then excused myself and followed her to the washroom; of course, I hoped people didn't think I was actually *following* her in there, just that I happened to need to use the facilities at approximately the same time.

To my surprise, when I entered the washroom, I was met by the sight of CeeCee speaking to her phone, obviously filming herself for her vlog. *Of course.* She was crying, and looking distraught. She was talking about Troy, and I suspected that might be something the police would prefer she didn't do, so I felt no guilt at all when I shouted, "Stop – don't post that, CeeCee. Don't post anything containing any information at all about what's happened to Troy." I even grabbed the phone from her hand, and looked at the screen. "Was that going out live?"

CeeCee looked horrified. Initially, I assumed it was because of the way I'd acted, but her reply changed my mind.

"Who on earth would post live? Unless they were in a situation where they had no choice, of course. I record everything, then at least check it before I post it, and usually edit it too. Well…Troy does that nowadays, but I started without him and I'm more than capable of doing it for myself."

I asked, "How long have you and Troy worked together?"

CeeCee stared at her phone in my hand but didn't make a move to get it back. "You mean how long's he been my assistant? About six months or so. He's good. I'm missing him already."

Oh good, was what I thought; "Do you have any idea what might have happened to him?" was what I said.

"How would I? I was the one who raised the alarm when I heard about the boat, if you recall. No one else even realized he was missing. Other than that, no, I can't even imagine. Papa's very upset."

I was surprised by CeeCee's final comment. "Your father understands how much Troy means to you?"

"Papa was the one who introduced me to Troy. He suggested I could do with some help to reach the next level with my online presence, and he was quite right."

I digested that fact for a moment. "Did your father meet Troy in New Zealand? Bring him here to work with you?"

CeeCee gave me a sly look. "You're clever at thinking things through, aren't you, Cait? You psychologists are very quick when it comes to making judgements, so I suppose it's helpful that you're good at other things too."

I bit. "It's sort of in our job description to assess people, and circumstances, and paint a picture that explains things."

CeeCee shook her head. "Not what I meant. You've taken a dislike to me, Cait, and I think it's because I pay so much attention to my appearance. Which I have to. It's a part of my job description, to use your terminology. You see, if they think I'm just some effervescent bimbo, they'll never expect me to get the better of them when it comes to negotiating a great deal."

I knew I was seeing – and hearing – the real CeeCee for the first time: her voice wasn't high-pitched and whiney like that of a petulant child; her mouth was no longer ridiculously pouty, nor did it come to rest in one of those bizarre "duck face" poses; even her alarmingly active, and aggressively "present", eyebrows seemed to have settled down a bit. It was a revelation.

"You're an excellent actress," I noted.

CeeCee laughed aloud. "Why thank you. Another skill in my armoury. Necessary, but underrated. Did I even fool you?"

I admitted, "You did." I felt my shame creep up my back.

"Good to know. Though I should tell you that I really am truly devastated by Vaiarii's death, because I did love him a great deal. And Troy's injuries are a bit of a…fright. You need to know that."

"Why?"

"Why what?"

"Why do you want me to understand that you wear a mask all the time, but that these particular emotions are true?"

CeeCee snapped, "Because they are. I've seen you staring at me with disdain – as so many people do. I don't care about that. I'm used to it. But I've also seen the way you look at everyone…and I know what you do, and what Bud used to do. Given that I'm the internet maven I am, I found out quite a lot about you two online. So I reckon you won't be able to help yourselves – you and your husband are going to want to get to the bottom of whatever is going on here at the resort, and I need you to know that it's got nothing to do with me. You see, even I can work out that Vaiarii and Troy had me in common, so you probably suspect me of…something. Well, you have to understand that I'm the only person who loses by what's happened – I have nothing to gain. No…I'm sorry, that's not fair – Roimata has lost a child, and that's dreadful, though what I said to her about her not truly knowing her son was correct; Vaiarii never had any interest in being a teacher, despite his mother having always gone on and on about that. Vaiarii adored being the center of attention – but he didn't want to stand at the front of a classroom. Oh dear me, no. He came alive in front of the lens. We were similar in that respect."

"So you were the one helping him to realize his true potential? You and he were achieving your own goals in slightly different ways, but as a team?"

CeeCee smiled. "There. Now you get it. And, yes, I was the one taking the lead; I know how the whole business works, but poor Vaiarii didn't have a clue. I was the one who got all his sponsorship deals, and I was the one spreading rumors about an international modelling career being in his future. I wouldn't have minded the two of us having the chance to travel the world together if I'd managed to land him a job with one of the big agencies. It would have played well with my followers. You see, Cait, I bet I'm as good a psychologist as you, but in a different way. I can get most people to do what I want, because I understand how best to get them to do it."

"Whereas I focus on victims of crime, and getting justice for them."

"In that case, maybe we should combine forces. I bet I could get everyone to tell me everything you want to know about them…whereas they'll be suspicious of you."

I didn't reply, because at that moment, Mahana bustled into the washroom. "Your father's just arrived, CeeCee and he's asking where you are."

CeeCee's demeanor changed in an instant. She ran out of the washroom squealing, "Papa! Where's my darling Papa?"

Mahana shook her head sadly, "That poor girl."

I said nothing.

Reassessing

When I joined the ever-growing group in the bar, I was still bemused by my heart-to-heart with CeeCee: I'd known she was a fake, but she'd managed to keep her true nature hidden from me for quite some time. I pulled out a chair at the table where Bud was sitting, and plopped myself down, chastising myself for being so dim.

Replaying all my interactions with CeeCee as I sat there, I realized I'd allowed my judgmental nature to get the better of me…again. I'd been so quick to be dismissive of the annoyingly false version of CeeCee, that I hadn't bothered to take the time to look beneath the surface. I was cross with myself: there was no one else to blame. And I knew I'd have to broach the subject with Bud at some point…though I didn't look forward to that, because he's always maintained that I can be too judgemental for my own good. Now there was more proof that he was right.

I was snapped out of my own little world by a hand coming toward me. I looked up and smiled politely at a face that was an excellent example of what most people would summon to mind if told to imagine a French man in his fifties with pots of money and the sort of appearance that might melt a woman's heart and make her feel quite fluttery – unless she happened to already be happily married to a ruggedly handsome man in his fifties. *Which I am.*

Charles Ducasse was a good-looking man, that was beyond question: graying dark hair, longish, and swept from his forehead in a style that looked natural, but was probably the result of a hairdresser's considerable skills; chocolate eyes that were doleful, yet still sparkled. He was dressed in a linen suit and shirt, and I saw – possibly for the first time in my life – how it's true that linen can crease elegantly. Charles was the full package, and

I could spot the resemblance between the man and his daughter; CeeCee had his eyes and nose, though her mouth was much fuller than his. I wondered what her mother, who I'd been told had died when she was a teen, must have looked like; I suspected she'd have been beautiful, too, because those beautiful people do tend to get drawn to each other, I've found.

"My daughter has told me all about you, Cait, Bud," said Charles Ducasse as he shook our hands in turn.

I bet she hasn't, was what I thought; "I hope she's been kind," was what I said.

Charles laughed. "But of course. My little girl is always kind, and polite. Besides, you are friends of Henri and Fleur, who are well known and respected by Mahana, and I have known Mahana since I was a young man and trust her opinions. So there is a direct path to trusting you too."

I wondered why on earth Charles needed to "trust" us at all.

"I need help," he announced, standing beside our table, but addressing the entire room. Everyone was there, and everyone gave him their attention. He continued, "One man has died, and one has met with violence at this resort. Two men whose lives are significantly connected to my daughter. I love my daughter more than anything else in the world, so I need help. Help to find out what's going on. To be sure that my child is not at risk here, or anywhere else. I need to be certain that this violence will not find its way to her. Who is with me?"

Roimata commanded the attention of the room when she said quietly, "But surely the police will be investigating what happened to Troy Wilson? They must. And with this…attack upon him, will they not now consider the death of my poor, dear son with fresh eyes?"

Charles replied, "It is true that we have an effective, though small, detective force on the island. The representatives of the *Officiers de la Police Judiciaire* – the OJP – are, of course, overseen by the *Procureur* in the initial stages of an investigation of a suspicious death, and I happen to know him personally; we dined together earlier this month. Later on, they work with the *Juge d'instruction* – also a close acquaintance of mine, and a true professional. I have faith in all of them, and in our systems, but, while it is true that they usually get their man – or woman – it is said that Canadian Mounties *always* get their man – or woman. Is that not correct, Henri? And both you and Bud here were once Mounties. This investigation should be something you can tackle."

Bud cleared his throat. "Monsieur Ducasse, both Henri and myself have retired, and there are professionals here whose job it is to investigate: we'd never want to tread on their toes."

Charles smiled. "It's Charles, Bud, and I am not suggesting treading on toes, I'm suggesting an entirely separate dance: an independent investigation. I have access to useful levels of government. I believe I could get you whatever information you might need, to be able to do as I ask."

I felt Bud's knee start to bounce next to mine, then he raked his hand through his hair – a sure sign that his stress levels are rising. "I don't think it's a good idea, Charles. Not something I feel I could get involved with. And certainly something against which I would counsel Henri." I was pleased that Bud had taken his chance to do what I'd promised Fleur we'd try to achieve.

"Ah, but Cait's already involved, Bud," said CeeCee confidently. "She was questioning me in the washroom earlier."

"She's been asking me all sorts of things, too," added Eloise. "Trying to blame me for Vaiarii being horrible toward me when he was here for that photo shoot."

"He wasn't horrible to you; you were horrible to him, and then Nadine attacked him," squealed CeeCee.

"He made me feel threatened. Nadine was defending me." Eloise sounded hurt.

CeeCee snorted. "Why would he want you when he had me? You don't even like men. And Vaiarii wasn't the sort to see that as a challenge."

Nadine countered with an angry: "Says you."

Charles held up his hands. "Stop. I don't know what you're all talking about, but this isn't the time for arguments. Troy Wilson has been attacked; we won't know how badly injured he is until they examine him properly at the hospital. We need to understand who did this to him, and why. We need to investigate."

Bud stood. "Charles – if I may?"

Charles Ducasse nodded, and took a seat beside me. The aroma of his aftershave, or cologne, was earthy, musky, and orangey. *Delightful.*

Bud made sure he had everyone's attention. "Look folks, I don't want to speak for Henri, nor even for my wife – they are both capable of speaking for themselves. But I must speak for *myself*. I understand your concerns, Charles, and I also understand that everyone here must feel the same way, generally speaking. It's not normal for there to be a tragic death one day, and an attack upon another person the next, in one small, out-of-the-way location like this wonderful resort that the Legrands have created. And, yes, Cait and I have a shared background in working on murder cases where we've pooled our resources and abilities to endeavor to get justice for the victim, or victims. But this is not a situation where I feel we should do that. We did it, once upon a time, professionally, and we've found ourselves having to do it when there was no possibility of the police being able, or maybe willing, to investigate. But this is not such a case. As Roimata said, the police are bound to look into what might have happened to Troy, and I agree with her – that, given what's happened now – they are most likely to take a different view of Vaiarii's death yesterday…or at least speed up the autopsy so they can understand how he died, and when. We have no role to play. It's not about interfering where we're not needed, it's about more than that – it's about all of us realizing we might be suspects. To try to 'investigate' might allow someone – anyone – who shouldn't, to skew the findings of a professional inquiry."

Charles Ducasse gave Bud a sideways glance. "You can't be serious? You think that someone here might have had something to do with what happened to Troy Wilson – or even what happened to Vaiarii?" He sounded truly astonished.

Bud nodded. "I do. And I don't think that can come as a surprise to anyone here. Look at where we are; it's incredibly unlikely that anyone could have come to the resort, then left again, without their presence being noted."

I wanted to say so much, but didn't dare.

Henri said, "That's not true, though, is it, Bud?"

Bud gave his ex-colleague a shrug. "How so?"

Henri continued, "Sonny Puletua said he saw Vaiarii in Papeete at three in the morning, then Cait found him in our lagoon around seven. Vaiarii got to here, from there, somehow, and no one knew about that, right? So…why couldn't someone else have done the same thing? Someone sneaked in here with Vaiarii's body, and someone sneaked in here and bashed poor Troy. It's possible – the facts prove it."

My heart sank. I knew this wasn't what Bud had wanted: a conversation like this, among such a large group, many of whom were – as he'd said – suspects.

"Well, it wasn't me," chipped in CeeCee. "I most certainly didn't kill my fiancé then incapacitate my assistant."

"And I did not kill my son," said Roimata quietly. She looked up with tears in her eyes and added, "And, in case you're interested, CeeCee, I wasn't here when poor Troy was attacked."

"Any one of us could have been here," said Charles, surprising me. "Even me. I have said that I have just arrived from Bora Bora, but I could be lying. I could have flown back at any time – there are enough flights each day, though, of course, there are records that will show I am telling the truth. However, as I said, anyone we *think* wasn't here could have been. Take you, Mahana: CeeCee told me you repositioned the boat that Troy had used early this morning when you yourself returned from Papeete. You could have been lying; you could have found Troy in his boat much earlier, bashed him, then taken his body to the bungalow where he was found."

I bit my lip. Obviously CeeCee had given her father a detailed account of everything that had happened, and it was clear that Charles was good at thinking through the possibilities of what that information might mean.

Mahana sounded mortally wounded when she replied, "Charles, what are you talking about? I did what I said I did. You know me…you have known me since I was not much more than a girl. I…I have been in your life for decades. Always there when you needed me. I…I have always believed that you know exactly what's inside me. You must know I am not a violent person, Charles. Why would I do all that to Troy Wilson? Besides, how on earth would I have managed to lift an unconscious man out of a boat, up onto the dock, and then get him from the dock to that bungalow? Look – it's right there. Anyone could have seen me do it. Anyone could have seen anyone else do it, for that matter. Which is what I've been thinking about: how did *anyone* manage to get Troy out of a boat and then into that bungalow? It's so close to the bar, the kitchen, the restaurant…so easily seen."

Nadine piped up and asked, "Could Troy could have been bashed over the head inside the bungalow, not in his boat? Was there enough blood on the mattress to allow for that?"

Roimata gasped and shook her head sadly. Mahana stroked her distraught friend's hand, then nodded in Nadine's direction.

Eloise added, "But, look…even if Troy was bashed inside that bungalow, why would he have gone there of his own accord? And how could he have got in? All the bungalows lock automatically, don't they?"

Charles asked, "Do you need a key to get into the bungalows?"

"A code," chorused Henri and Fleur.

Charles pressed with: "Who knows the code?"

Henri and Fleur looked at each other, then Henri replied, "All the locks are set with a master code of one, one, one, one. The plan is that when guests arrive, they reset the lock with a four-digit code of their choosing – one that everybody using the bungalow during their stay will share. Upon their departure, the lock will be reset again to the master code, which, at all times allows access for housekeeping staff and butlers, or for Edouard – if needs be."

"When you think about it, anyone could guess the master code. Troy could have worked it out. Let himself in there." We all turned. It was Annette speaking.

Bud sighed. "Look, folks, there's a real possibility that anyone who didn't know the master code could have guessed it, thereby being able to open the door of the bungalow in which we found Troy. We must also accept the possibility that someone could have arrived at the resort unseen – because we know that must have happened in the case of Vaiarii's arrival, as Henri pointed out. We also know that both Vaiarii and Troy have close associations with CeeCee. But we do not know of anyone who would wish to cause harm to either man. Is that a fair summation?"

Charles Ducasse said, "For a man who doesn't think we should investigate before the arrival of the police, you've made a good start, Bud. I shall tell you all that I had no reason to want Vaiarii out of my daughter's life: they loved each other very much, and all I have ever wanted is for my daughter to be happy. As for Troy? I introduced him to CeeCee because I'd seen his work in New Zealand, and I thought he'd be a great support for my daughter's online brand. He's certainly helped her in that regard. I am devastated that he's been hurt, and very much hope he makes a full and swift recovery. Anyone else want to speak up?"

CeeCee sighed. "Oh Papa, don't be silly. No one is going to stand here and say they hated either one of them, are they? All anyone's going to do is say good things about them. If they really did mean them harm, they'd lie, wouldn't they? And there's not a single one among us who can be sure they can spot one hundred percent of a person's lies."

CeeCee Ducasse tilted her head toward me, and I saw a quizzical look flit across my husband's face; he had no idea of what had passed between me and the heiress in the washroom.

I felt less than good about how I'd let one part of my nature defeat another, so I jumped in with: "CeeCee's right – there could be someone here who's such a good liar that we'd never spot their falsehoods. So there really isn't much point in asking you all, in public, to state your relationship with the two men." I didn't add that I'd welcome the chance to have a chat with everyone in private, because then everyone would have declined, and I knew that was exactly what I needed to engineer, if I was going to get to the bottom of things.

Unfortunately, the sound of an approaching vehicle made it less likely that I'd be able to corner people for a probing discussion; it had to be the police – they'd take over from here.

Explaining

I was surprised when Sonny Puletua entered the bar; I'd expected an officer from the Tahitian crime investigation department. Sonny smiled and waved his hands in a friendly manner, as though he were arriving for pre-luncheon drinks.

"Good morning, everyone, *ia ora na*." He beamed at the faces he knew, and seemed surprised to see that Charles and Roimata had joined our not-so-merry band. "I come first, more will follow – but I am here as reassurance that all will be well while we wait."

I thought this a rather melodramatic way of explaining his presence, but Sonny appeared to feel he needed to make an impactful entrance; he needn't have bothered – his physical presence alone demanded attention.

"I am Charles Ducasse, CeeCee's father," said Ducasse, approaching Puletua with an outstretched hand.

Sonny beamed and enveloped Charles's hand in his own. "Indeed, Monsieur Ducasse, I know of you, and have seen you in public several times. It is my great pleasure to meet you." He suddenly appeared to realize the situation and added more sombrely, "I am sorry for your loss, sir."

"Please, it's Charles," replied Ducasse retrieving his hand.

"And I am Sonny," replied the officer, beaming again.

"Thank you for coming, Sonny." Roimata's voice sounded weak. "Please tell your father that the flowers he sent to my home were beautiful, and I thank him for them."

Sonny moved to the bereaved mother's side and touched her gently on the shoulder. "Again, sincere condolences from our family to yours, Madame Roimata. You made good time getting here. I was held up at headquarters. There is…much happening there. The circumstances of your dear son's death, and now the injuries to Monsieur Troy Wilson, mean I was sent to formally request that everyone remains here at the resort until the detective assigned to this case arrives."

Annette laughed bitterly. "So you're here to make sure none of us run off, Sonny? That's rich. You think one of us has done this? We were all just about to share our alibis for the time when Troy was attacked – want to take notes? That would get you a few gold stars from the big detective, right?"

I wondered why Annette was being so scathing in her comments to Sonny, who, for his own part looked bemused.

The officer replied, "If you want to think of my presence as a politeness, rather than enforcement, then that would be preferable. And as for everyone's alibis – that will be something the detective will want to talk to you about. But he did ask me to warn you that he might not arrive for…" He checked his watch. "I hope he will be here in an hour. He was attending the…ahh…examination of your son's remains, Madame Roimata. Thanks to the urging of Monsieur Ducasse…Monsieur Charles…the results should be available very soon."

Roimata sobbed, and Mahana hugged her close. "My poor boy. He was so beautiful." Roimata hid her face in a large handkerchief, and shuddered in her friend's arms.

Sonny Puletua looked increasingly uncomfortable as he watched Vaiarii's mother dissolve. I felt sorry for her, of course, but I also realized that the officer was in a difficult position. As I looked toward Henri, our host – who must have been in such situations himself during his policing career – I could tell he wasn't likely to engage. Since the tragedy the previous morning he'd been in his own little world, and – according to his wife – spending most of his time trying to come up with scenarios that could explain away the presence of a corpse on his property.

When I turned to look at Bud, his expression told me he was battling with himself: normally he'd have stepped up, I knew that, but Henri's presence – and their shared past – meant he was probably waiting for the man who owned the resort to take the lead. I decided to jump in.

"Bud was just helping us all work through a few facts pertaining to the situation here, Sonny. Obviously, everyone's concerned about what happened to Troy today, and still reeling from yesterday's tragedy. But if you'd prefer us to not talk about what might have been going on here, then maybe it's best if we split up? That way we could each be alone with our thoughts, and less likely to discuss any topics that your investigative colleagues might prefer we don't."

"I'm not leaving Roimata," said Mahana.

"And I'm not leaving my daughter," added Charles.

"We could go back to my bungalow, together, Papa," said CeeCee. "I think that would be better for me. This is all too…upsetting." She glared at the woman who would have been her mother-in-law, had the marriage to her fiancé gone ahead.

Roimata lifted her eyes and looked helplessly toward CeeCee. "Upsetting? There will never again be any color in my life. No joy."

"Would you like to come to my rooms with me, my dear?" Mahana patted Roimata's hand. Roimata nodded dumbly.

Sonny finally said, "Maybe this is for the best – that everyone goes to their own place. But you must all understand, no one is to leave."

Eloise offered, "If you stay here, Sonny, you'd hear anyone leaving by car, and they'd have to pass you to walk out to the dock to be able to leave by boat. You can guard us all, and I could bring you some snacks while you wait."

Sonny's massive head bobbed up and down on his neck, and a ripple of relief passed around our tense group: the idea that everyone could get away seemed to go down well. It also meant that I could now choose who I wanted to have a private word with, which had been my intention. As chairs scraped, and folks rose to leave, I sensed a general urgency to escape.

I leaned across to Bud and whispered, "I'm going to try to get Annette alone; I'll ask if she can take me to grab some more of those atomizer pod things, okay? Can you do something similar with Edouard…peel off somewhere? Get what you can out of him concerning both Vaiarii and Troy, and whereabouts for critical times…you know the drill." I kissed him on the cheek, as cover. *And because I wanted to.*

Bud nodded his understanding. "Yeah, I think I might just about remember how to ask questions that lead to useful answers, Wife." He kissed me back.

I popped up before Annette could leave and nipped across to her. She seemed puzzled by my request for her help but agreed – which was a relief. I noticed Bud and Edouard heading toward the beach, which looked promising.

As Annette and I made our way toward the storeroom, I could see that Mahana was taking Roimata to the residential block, the grieving mother still visibly upset, and leaning on her friend for support – both physically, and emotionally. I'd seen Eloise and Nadine heading to the kitchen, presumably to prepare the promised snacks for Sonny, and sort out what was likely to be an extremely strange luncheon. I assumed that Henri and Fleur would go back to their apartment. With Bud off with Edouard, and CeeCee and her father back at her bungalow, we were all accounted for, which gave me a weirdly comforting feeling. I don't usually feel nervous when I believe myself to probably be in the company of a killer, so I challenged myself about why I now felt so…unsafe.

"It's terrible to think that someone attacked that young man," said Annette. "Knowing that – and not knowing who did it – has made me feel horribly unsettled, here, in my new home. I don't like it."

Maybe that's it? The violence against Troy feels more real to me because he's not dead, was what I thought; "I understand. What do you think could have happened to him?" was what I said.

Annette shrugged. "I don't know, of course, but I think he let himself into that bungalow for some reason, and someone attacked him there. No one's going to be able to get an unconscious man from one side of this place to another without being seen."

I sighed, recollecting Bud's observation about the housekeeping buggies, but realized that scenario was also unlikely. "You make a good point, Annette."

Just as we reached our objective, a couple of lorikeets flew out of the lush foliage growing behind the storage building. Though I'd become accustomed to their piercing calls, having them screech so close to my ear gave me quite a shock.

I ducked, and Annette swore. She noted, "Those things are very annoying, and so loud. They clawed at my head the other day when I came to get my supplies. Even drew blood."

"Might they be nesting nearby?" I had no idea of the mating habits of lorikeets, but it was late spring, technically speaking – though the lack of real seasons on Tahiti made it difficult to tell – so guessed they might be protecting their young.

Annette dismissed my idea with a wave of her hand. "There are so many of them in the gardens back there, and they are known to be territorial. Who knows what they get up to."

I was puzzled. "I thought the gardens only stretched from the restaurant and car park down to the dock and acted as camouflage for this place."

Annette rolled her eyes. "Back there is a huge part of the resort also surrounded by special planting – but it's the part that isn't for the guests. Our waste treatment tanks are there, as is our solar array, power storage, and our cisterns. Obviously, the waste treatment and cisterns are quite separate."

"Good to know." I giggled. Maybe a bit too much. "Oh, I say, Annette, I'd love to take a look behind the scenes. Would you mind showing me around?" Annette looked surprised, and rather unsure of how she should respond, so I pressed with a: "Pretty please? We're off soon, as you know, and I might never get another chance like this."

She shrugged. "I don't see why not, though I don't understand why you'd want to. Come on, if we go to the other end of this building, there's a path."

The path was much wider than I'd expected, and arced away from the corner of the square until we reached what was an impressively large, cleared area, that really took me aback. I knew the resort's water came from a well the Legrands had drilled, and that solar power was used, because Fleur had told us all about how she and Henri had wanted the resort to be as close to carbon-neutral as possible. Bud and I had listened patiently as both of the Legrands had bent our ears about the strict policies regarding sustainability that had to be followed for all new builds on Tahiti, but, seeing it for the first time, I was staggered by the scale of the undertaking, and I wondered just how far out on a financial limb Henri and Fleur had gone to be able to afford it all. The pressure upon them to make the resort successful, and quickly at that, was likely to be much greater than I'd ever imagined; I found the concept quite alarming.

Three dozen solar panels, all mounted on angled metal frames, sat beside two gigantic tanks, and a substantial building constructed from serviceable blocks. Whatever could be painted had been, in a dark green, though it didn't really blend in at all.

Annette pointed to the tanks. "Those are the water tanks. The treatment plant to purify the water is in that building, as are all the batteries needed to store the power. There's also a system in there that takes in all the wastewater, then churns it around, so it can be separated into liquid that's purified and used for gray water uses here – like watering the gardens and so forth, and then solids, which are composted, again for use in the gardens. Edouard's got training in managing it all."

"That's a lot of responsibility," I noted. It made more sense to me now that I saw so little of Edouard – he was probably back here monitoring all the systems every day.

"My husband is a very responsible person," noted Annette. She didn't make it sound like it was a good thing.

"Is it difficult, being out here at the resort all the time? I mean, you don't get into Papeete very often, do you? Don't you miss family? Friends?"

Annette pushed a bit of dirt with her toe. "My parents are both dead. Cancer. And I never had many…real friends."

"I'm so sorry to hear that about your parents. That must have been terribly difficult for you."

Annette half-smiled. "It's something we're used to here. My mother was a child living on Mangareva, in the Gambier Islands in the 1960s. In 1966 the French began nuclear testing, from the Mururoa Atol. They didn't even build a shelter on Mangareva until after the first test. By then the damage was done. All the people who lived on the Gambier Islands were impacted, though they were told they'd be safe. They kept on testing for almost ten more years, sending poison into our air. All our islands were affected. Our land, our water…all contaminated. There is so much cancer here. Everyone who is from these islands has had someone they love die because of it…or, sometimes, many members of their extended family. Even Tahiti was hit by a cloud from a big test in 1974. 'Centaure' is a word we hate. It was the final test, above ground, in this area. July seventeenth, 1974. We will never forget. My mother had moved to Papeete by then, but not even Tahiti was safe. They said the cloud would go toward a few small islands as though the people who lived there did not matter. But the wind brought the cloud to Tahiti.

Everyone here was exposed. The dust covered the fruit, the vegetables, and was forced into the soil by the rains. They stopped testing above ground after that, but carried on testing below ground until 1996. We all live with that. And many die because of it. It is not something that tourists think of."

Annette's tone had become scathing as she spoke, the rawness of her emotions clear. I grappled with what to say: I recalled the facts of French nuclear testing that I'd gleaned through general knowledge over the decades, but I'd never thought about the specific impacts, though the growth in the popularity of French Polynesia as a holiday destination only since the turn of the century made much more sense in the light of me putting all those facts together; no one would want to travel to a place where there was a chance of lingering nuclear contamination.

I said, "When Bud and I came here, on our way back to Canada, we arrived as know-nothing visitors. We hadn't expected to be coming here, you see, so neither of us had really done the sort of research that someone planning to visit might do. It was kind of Henri and Fleur to offer us a place to stay for the period we had to wait between ships that could get us from Australia to Canada, but we could have spent some of our time here bothering to find out more about the history of the islands. And not just the bits that most travelers know about – the Gaugin years, for example."

Annette laughed cruelly. "Gaugin? Don't mention that man to me. He left his wife and children in Europe to follow his dissolute ways here. He took what he wanted from our culture – inventing his own ideas of what it should look like and passing them onto the world as real – and he took our women, and made many of them sick. Right here on Tahiti he fathered children by two girls who were not even fifteen years old, then had another fourteen-year-old 'wife' when he lived on Hiva Oa. They were so young. Just children themselves. He even named his home in Atuona *Maison du Jouir* – the House of Pleasure. He deserved to die of syphilis. He was a bad man, who could paint a bit, though his flat daubs, and even his carvings, have none of the real vibrancy of our home. There is no light in any of his work; he paints women, and roads, and trees. Our life comes from our light, and from the sea. It is as if Gaugin never saw that light, never understood the importance of the sea. For him it was all about the pleasures of the flesh, not the beauty of nature. I wish Henri hadn't chosen to put those paintings on display inside all the bungalows."

I'd been completely unprepared for the way the conversation between me and Annette had gone, and I cursed my own shortcomings. Annette and I had been in each others' company so often during the past few weeks – why was this the first time I was discovering that she had such strong feelings about so many complex topics?

"I appreciate you being so open with me," I said.

Annette shrugged. "You'll be leaving soon. And the past couple of days have reminded me that life is short, and being inauthentic is hard work. Edouard and I don't talk much, because there's so much we don't need to say to each other. We had a similar upbringing and share a great deal of common history, so that we do not need to commiserate about lost loved ones, or how and why they died. We don't even need to talk about how tourism is changing our islands, nor of how the resources used by those who come and go means that those of us who live here will have to change every part of our lives to accommodate the tourists' needs. Edouard and I will have no children – we don't want to create lives that our own genes might then destroy. No, we will only ever be us. And the chances that one or both of us will become sick later in life is high, because all four of our parents were poisoned. Our lives are in paradise, but we have a bleak future. The trouble is that Edouard thinks this means we should be serious about our lives all the time, but I think we should celebrate the happiness we have, now, while we can. On this, we differ a great deal."

I acknowledged that what Eloise had pointed out as Annette's "party girl" background might have been nothing more than a young woman with an obviously fatalistic view of life making the most of her opportunities to escape from…well, a life more than tinged by tragedy, by the sounds of it.

As I thought this, I realized that I was talking to yet another person who had pulled the wool over my eyes. I'd believed that I'd come to know Annette, that she was a warm, jolly woman, going about her duties with few cares, a genuine smile, and always ready to chat about whatever subject I raised. This visit to a part of the resort I'd never seen had also revealed to me a woman I'd never truly met, and I felt panic in the pit of my stomach.

Just how blind had I been since I'd arrived in Tahiti?

My pride at having graduated from sploshing in the safety of the pool to risking the lagoon seemed petty; my delight at seeing my husband's health improve, and relishing that, less so; my determination to take up my teaching duties again, despite being thousands of miles from my place of work had been necessary; my granular attention to detail when it came to the workings and service delivery at the Legrands' resort had been fair payment for the hospitality of our hosts. But that having become the totality of my world for the past few weeks had robbed me of my usual attention to the *reality* of the people around me. For all that Bud's always encouraging me to be less judgemental, I'm keenly aware that observing, questioning, analyzing – and judging – people is what I do all the time. It's what I've done since I was a child – the child no one understood, who always seemed to end up watching, rather than participating.

I felt as though I'd just found a part of myself that I'd temporarily misplaced…and it hit me with quite a jolt.

I gave myself a rapid talking to, then decided to do what I'd intended – focus on the knotty problems surrounding Vaiarii's death and the attack upon Troy. That was why I'd asked Annette to bring me to this part of the complex – to see if there might be some way that a person, or persons, unknown could have found a route by which they could somehow bring an incapacitated – or, in the case of Vaiarii, dead – human being into the resort without being seen. I scanned the area with eyes that were now looking for something that could be useful to my investigation – which I was determined would now progress without delay. Yes, there was a possible path that could be taken from the dock to the top of the walkway to the bungalows that would be mainly out of sight, as long as the person pushing a housekeeping buggy knew about this area – and I assumed that everyone who worked there did.

"Can we take a look inside that building?" I asked Annette the question abruptly, clearly taking her aback. I reckoned she'd expected a response from me regarding the opinions she'd just shared, but that wasn't where I needed to focus for the moment.

"No reason why not," she replied, and we approached the bleak looking structure.

The door wasn't locked. I asked, "Is that normal?"

"I think so. This is Edouard's domain. He's good with these systems. It's why we're here: he came to help the Legrands set the whole thing up, then they asked if he'd stay when they opened. He liked the idea, and sold it to me. I went to college to study hospitality and tourism – just a diploma, not a full degree, like Mahana. But there's not much I can't turn my hand to, and it's expensive to live in a nice place in Papeete. Our accommodations here are good, and they're free. It won't hurt us to be away from the hustle and bustle for a while."

I took Annette's comments on board – now wondering if the loss of four parents to cancer might well make a couple want to withdraw from society for a while, to tend to their emotional wellbeing.

I replied, "There's no code pad here, though the handle has a keyed lock within it. Let's be wary, Annette – anyone could have got into here."

Annette leaped backwards. "You mean the killer might be in there?"

"Troy's not dead – he might have nothing more than a nasty bump on the head."

"I don't mean Troy, I mean Vaiarii."

I paused. "You think Vaiarii Teriimana was murdered?"

Annette's expression suggested she was addressing a small child. "Of course I do. We all do. None of us have talked about anything else since you found him."

"Cait? Cait!" Bud was calling.

Thankful for the interruption – thereby removing the need for me to respond to Annette – I shouted back, "Coming."

Before I left, I pushed open the door to the building: all its walls were covered with large, flat, white boxes, the markings upon which told me they were the storage batteries for the solar power system; there was a dizzying amount of pipework – the pipes painted in various colors, to allow a person to know which pipe was carrying what, I assumed. I recognized the water purification system, because the filters and UV lamps were larger versions of exactly what Bud and I had at our home, to clean up the water from our well. There wasn't a single place for a person to hide in there, and the entire area was gleaming – without even a cobweb in sight. I closed the door, accepting I couldn't lock it, then headed off to find Bud, with Annette trailing behind me, and possibly wondering what on earth had got into me.

I was on a mission, and nothing could stop me, now.

Waiting

Annette and I found Edouard and Bud hovering outside the storeroom. They both looked a bit sweaty – which wasn't exactly unusual – but they were both out of breath too. I noticed the concern in Bud's eyes.

"What's happened?" I knew something was up.

"Big smash on the main road. Two dead they think." Bud's tone matched his bleak news.

"That's awful. It wasn't…it wasn't the ambulance with Troy in it, was it?" I had to ask.

Bud smiled, looking tired. "No. But two people won't be getting home today. And it means that the detective coming to head up the investigation will have to drive all the way around the island to get here. Sonny informs us that traffic chaos has already ensued, so there'll be even more of a delay."

Annette asked, "Why doesn't the detective come by boat?"

It seemed a sensible question, so I backed it up. "Yes, wouldn't that be easier?"

Edouard grinned wickedly. "Sonny told me that the one they are sending gets seasick just looking at a boat. Has to come by car."

"How can they send someone to work on Tahiti who can't use a boat?" Annette sounded disgusted rather than surprised.

Edouard shrugged. "Let's go with 'he was the best man for the job', like they always say, eh?"

Bud had clearly picked up on Annette's unusual mood, but didn't comment, instead he said, "Why don't you and Edouard head back to your place, Annette, while Cait and I do as we all agreed and go back to ours? I've taken enough of your time, Edouard. I appreciate you explaining to me how the security cameras work."

As Bud mentioned cameras, I kicked myself for not having thought of them before, so – as soon as we were making our way back through the garden to our bungalow alone – I hissed, "There are cameras? Where? Why didn't we know?"

"There are only a couple: one points toward the dock, you know – the jetty beyond the beach. That's in case any of the guests have problems there, and to allow the reception desk to spot any comings and goings. And there's another that faces the parking lot, for the same reasons."

"Have they recorded anything useful?" I hoped they had.

"They aren't being used at all, at the moment. Not turned on. Edouard told me that right away, but I used the set up to keep him chatting – and to give you more time alone with Annette. Then Sonny came and found us, told us about the smash…so Edouard insisted we came to find you two. I hope you had long enough alone with Annette to…well, find out something useful."

We'd reached our bungalow, and I plopped onto the sofa. "Keep the doors shut, Bud – we'll enjoy the air conditioning more that way, and I don't want us to be overheard by anyone, especially CeeCee and her father."

"Want anything from the fridge?" Bud had already pulled out a bottle of water for himself.

"I'll have a water too, please." I sipped, feeling my innards cool as I did, even as the sweat on my body enjoyed the effects of the almost chilly air being pumped into our room, then circulated by the overhead fan. It was bliss.

"Sonny reckons we're in for another storm," observed Bud. "At least, that's what his father says. In about –" he checked his watch – "forty-five minutes, to be precise. And Sonny's father – via Sonny – was exceedingly precise."

"I didn't see any clouds above Mont Orohena when Annette and I were out looking at the cisterns."

Bud chuckled, "You were looking at what? Cisterns? Why on earth were you doing that?"

I explained to Bud about the area set aside for all the systems that allowed the resort to function, then filled him in on what Annette had told me – all about her tragedy, and anger.

"The whole thing's a bit of a problem," I admitted.

"How so?" Bud settled beside me on the sofa, though we were both happy to not touch each other, so we could cool down properly.

"You know I was talking to you about the development of self?" Bud nodded. "Well, as you know I can't help but observe and analyze all the time, so when I make judgements about the words or deeds of a person – or even their body language and micro-expressions – my analysis is based upon my knowledge to date of that person's psyche: is their reaction to be expected, for *that person*, or is it out of character, for *that person*, understand?"

Bud tutted. "Might have learned a thing or two about it during my…how many years was it of interrogating suspects, Wife? Feel free to continue – I'll do my best to bumble along behind you." He winked and threw me a kiss, and I gave my best cute smile as a response.

I said, "Look, this is me eating humble pie, Husband…I've messed up. And rather badly, at that."

Bud sat a little more upright. "Again, how so?"

"I've been distracted…for all the right reasons, yes, but I'm starting to believe that the people who live and work here – who I'd come to think of almost as part of an extended family over the past few weeks – aren't the people I thought they were at all. I've accepted the public persona they've chosen to project as being not only a true representation of their personality, but also a full one. I've been doing my usual assessment thing since I found Vaiarii's body, but I've been weighing them up against completely erroneous, so dangerously useless, base criteria."

Bud nodded. "You're saying that you can't be sure that what you've been judging as being normal or unusual responses from everyone are accurate, because you don't know the people you're judging as well as you thought you did?"

I nodded. I felt guilty about having done a poor job.

"I see," said Bud, thoughtfully. "Come on, Cait – don't look so down. First of all, none of that is your fault – we're here, being us, taking a break, so you're allowed to get to know people you'll see for a few weeks, then never again, on a relatively superficial level. That's what the rest of the world calls 'normal'. As for what that means, going forward? Well, I have two suggestions."

I smiled, my love and respect for my husband welling up inside me. "Pray tell, oh wise one," I mugged.

Bud grinned. "Get everyone on their own – drill down until you believe you've discovered a big enough part of the real person to satisfy yourself that you can move on with assessments on a firmer basis."

"I agree that's a good idea, but it might be easier said than done, what with Sonny here, and all of us in our own 'lairs', contemplating tragedy. But I can give it a go, and I know you'll help." Bud nodded. I asked, "And your second suggestion?"

"You know I talked the other night about that old RCMP trainer Henri and I 'experienced'? George."

I pointed at my head, smiling. "Eidetic memory, Husband."

"Good. Well, think about what I said that old George told us, and interpret it your own way: our gut instincts are worth something, Cait. We can't always have all the information or insight we'd like in a certain situation, but we can sense when things are right…or off-kilter somehow. By all means use your academic vocabulary, and that planet-sized brain of yours, but also allow yourself to listen to, and learn from, those cues you've already been picking up here, even if they were subconsciously collected. And not just since Vaiarii died, but before that, too."

I nodded, but had to reply, "I understand what you mean, but that's exactly the ability that's let me down, Bud. Annette? Not a happy, chatty, ex-party-girl, but a young woman who's acted out in potentially dangerous ways because of the desperate tragedy that's befallen all her nearest and dearest, with a bleak view of her future, and a slightly contentious relationship with her husband. See? She'd hidden all that from me."

Bud leaned toward me. "Think, Cait – did she really 'hide' it from you, or did she choose to 'not show it' to you? There's a big difference. Don't forget, she's a service provider and you're a guest…okay then, a 'test guest'…but Annette's employed by Henri and Fleur to deliver good service, and she'll be judged by them on that basis, in terms of keeping her job. I'm pretty sure they wouldn't want everyone who works here to burden guests with insights into their lives that are so…well, deeply personal, and with the potential to impact a guest's ability to enjoy their vacation, because they're thinking about nuclear testing, cancer…oh, and Paul Gaugin's questionable morals and the impact they might have had on the Polynesian population. But, either way, you've got nothing to blame yourself for."

I mulled over what Bud had said, then chuckled. "This situation makes me think of the way a pearl is created, with a small foreign object – an irritant – entering a mollusk and causing trauma. The mollusk creates layer upon layer of *nacre* to surround the irritant, to try to protect itself from the nastiness that's got inside its shell, thereby making something that's smooth, shiny, and beautiful. It's not totally dissimilar to what we humans do, when we're psychologically traumatized: we build layers around that irritant to protect ourselves – maybe we wrap it in a layer of denial, another of diminishment, another of rejection – just so it doesn't hurt as much anymore, doesn't continue to cause more damage. And we humans are very good at also wrapping ourselves in shiny layers of protective *nacre*, too.

The problem is that I've made the mistake of accepting the perfectly smooth and shiny pearlized versions of people that have been presented to me without question. Good grief, Bud, I know the way it works well enough from my own life; I built up layers of protection to allow myself to keep going despite all the psychological damage Angus did to me, while we appeared to the world to be a 'happy couple'."

Bud reached out and hugged me. "The Cait I first met was tough and shiny, alright…though I wouldn't say you were smooth; you came with spikes." He winked. "But I knew that wasn't the real you – the whole you – though you didn't dare show me even a glimmer of the true person you are, the warm and loving one, until we finally got together. But, like I said, my instincts – my *gut* – told me she was always there."

I patted my husband's tummy. "Back to trusting this fellow again?"

"I could do worse. Trouble is, it's telling me it's empty right now. Aren't you hungry? You're usually hungry before I am."

"Oi, you…I've been incredibly good since we got here. Have you seen how much fruit I've eaten?"

Bud laughed. "Seen it? I haven't had to see it, because you comment every time you eat some. The juice in fruit isn't some sort of poison that you have to avoid at all costs, you know…as I hope you've learned these past few weeks. It can be delicious, and very good for you. You know you're glowing these days, right?"

"That's sweat, Husband dear."

Bud hugged me again. "Oh, come on now. See? That's a bit of a hangover from your self-protection armory right there. You just cannot take a compliment, can you?"

I shook my head. "I am working on it, honestly. I know it bugs you that I can't accept what you say and be happy about it. But being told for years that you're fat and stupid, as well as both headstrong and annoyingly pedantic, simultaneously – which is almost impossible, by the way – grinds you down, as I've said when we've talked about me, and Angus, in the past. You and I haven't been married for three years yet, Bud; I think there might be new things I'm still finding out about myself in terms of being half of a loving couple…so don't panic if you see a few more parts of me emerge over the – hopefully decades – ahead. But we've been through enough that I believe you've met the real me – that I've done all I can to show you the traumatizing irritant at my core that led me to transform myself into the hard, and essentially fake, person I chose to show to the rest of the world for all those years. And, having known Jan before she died, I think I can understand the hole she left in your life when she was gone: the irritant at your core isn't the hate you felt for the man who killed your first wife, but the fact you felt you were to blame for her death. And we've both done a great deal to tackle that one head on. So now it's time for me to search out the imperfection – the damage – at the core of everyone else here, so that I can better evaluate them as a suspect in our case."

Bud stood. "Cait, it's not 'our case'. You know that, right? Sonny's here now, and a detective is on his way, so – while I agree we should gather whatever insights we can – let's also agree that the solving of all of this mess likely won't be down to us."

I popped up off the sofa and clung to my husband. "We'll see. How about we stroll over to the restaurant to find out if there's any food available? On the way, you can tell me whatever else you managed to learn from Edouard."

"Sure, but that won't take long: Edouard's clearly happier here, now, than he's ever been in his life. He's lord of his own domain; Henri trusts him; he's comfortable in his accommodations, able to live within his limited means, and delighted to see as much as he does of his wife."

I smiled. "Don't you think that might be the 'pearlized' version of his life that he's shown you there, Bud?"

"Touché. However, in my defense, I didn't say anything that set him off on a major rant. What was it you said to Annette that made her decide to share her real thoughts with you in such a seemingly aggressive manner, by the way?"

"I asked her if she missed family and friends, which led to her telling me that all her family had died of cancer, and that she had no friends."

Bud closed the door behind us. "Hmm…that's where she was still not being as open as she might have been, it seems. One of the very few things I learned from Edouard – other than how blissfully happy he is here – was that Annette and Vaiarii knew each other when they were young: Annette's brother and Vaiarii were close friends. Now, I know that Annette mentioned this in passing yesterday, but Edouard said the three of them were really close. In fact, Vaiarii and her brother did a great deal of diving together until Annette's brother got into a difficult situation – eventually died. I wondered if that might have been the 'incident' that meant Vaiarii stopped working for that pearl diving concern."

"Did you put that to Edouard?"

"I did, but he said he wasn't sure if Vaiarii had been there on the fateful day. Said that Annette hardly ever mentions her late brother, because his death still makes her so angry. What he did tell me, however, was that he was horrified when Vaiarii turned up for that photo shoot because he'd believed that by coming here to live, Annette would be able to 'escape the clutches of' – and he used that very phrase – the people who made her miserable in Papeete. Which included, apparently, Vaiarii Teriimana."

I paused, and whispered, "How did Vaiarii make Annette miserable?"

"Big picture? Unintentionally, I believe. Edouard told me about a support group that Annette joined before her parents both died of cancer – while they were both undergoing treatment. It seems there are quite a few such groups on the island; they act as a resource for those facing the blight of cancer within their family, helping them face their impending loss, and are led by those who've already navigated that journey. Edouard told me that Annette bonded closely with quite a few of the people in her group, but that she left abruptly when Vaiarii joined it about six months ago when his mother was diagnosed with thyroid cancer. She said she needed a break from the intense situations that could arise in the group for a while – before planning to go back to help others, one day. However, unfortunately, every time Annette ran into Vaiarii in Papeete after that he'd end up asking her to spend some time with him, talking about how the disease can affect family members, forcing her to drag up emotions she was still struggling with. It wasn't helping her healing process. In fact, it was making her miserable. This according to Edouard."

We walked on. I mused, quietly, "Talking with others who are facing a tragedy that you've been through yourself, can help some people with their own progress toward better mental wellbeing, but it sounds as though that wasn't true for Annette. The rawness of her anger about her parents' deaths was clearly fresh when she spoke to me about it. Maybe Edouard was right to convince her that coming here was a good idea. But…if Roimata is sick, and her diagnosis was about six months ago, that might explain what I observed online: the shift in the way Vaiarii acted in public became apparent about six months ago, too. That could have been a response to his mother's diagnosis. I thought when she arrived that Roimata looked a great deal older than her contemporary, Mahana; cancer treatment could explain that."

"But none of this can be connected to Vaiarii turning up here, dead, surely? That seems so…unlikely."

As we approached the restaurant, I could see that CeeCee and her father were already seated at a table. "Fancy joining those two for lunch, and a bit of digging?"

Bud kissed my cheek, then made a face. "Oh, you're quite…moist. They're sitting toward the back, near the air conditioner…so, yes, let's invite ourselves to their table. Not our fault they've picked the coolest one, right?"

Peeling

I decided to be the bubbly version of myself as Bud and I approached the Ducasse family, and my husband followed my lead, beaming with bonhomie.

"How wonderful that we get the chance to have lunch with the famous Monsieur Charles Ducasse himself, and his even more famous daughter," I said.

I knew my gambit had worked when Charles gallantly rose and motioned to the chair beside him – he and CeeCee were facing each other. I took the seat offered, and Bud sat beside CeeCee, who was the only one at the table not grinning like a Cheshire Cat.

It was Fleur herself who scuttled into the restaurant with luncheon menus. "Due to the rather unusual circumstances, we hope you all understand that a very simple menu has been prepared for today. I trust you'll all enjoy our chicken *fafa*; our chef insists upon using traditional taro leaves, not spinach, and we grow the taro in our gardens, here at the resort. We also grow our own ginger, and garlic."

"And what was the name of the chicken we shall eat?" CeeCee sounded deadly serious.

Poor Fleur panicked. "We don't raise our own chickens. The chicken is of the highest quality, but I don't think we ever asked the names of the birds."

"My daughter is being wicked, Fleur, pay her no heed," said Charles, flashing a warning look across the table, which CeeCee studiously ignored. "Of course we understand the strangeness of the situation here, and are grateful that you're able to provide us with any luncheon at all. But we are not guests, we are merely visitors, to your family. Will you and your husband join us to eat?"

Fleur looked even more alarmed. "That's most kind of you, but…maybe we could join you for dessert? Eloise, our chef, has prepared a gelato that's quite exceptional, even if I say so myself. As you can see from the menu, we've agreed it should be called 'Gelato Legrand'. I won't tell you any more about it, but my husband and I would be happy to be with you when you taste it for the first time. Coconut bread and fresh baguettes will arrive in a moment, then Annette will see to drinks all round."

Fleur all but ran off, and the four of us passed around the jug of iced water and sipped, doing our best to cool down.

"It is sweltering," announced Charles…as though we didn't already know. "This is a technical term, you understand, and it means high humidity and high heat. It is not as bad as the technical term 'unbearable', which I hope is not something we discover for ourselves today."

The poor man seemed desperate to fill the silence, and we were all relieved when Annette arrived with the promised sweet and plain breads, took drinks orders, then got to work on a round of chilled, fruity refreshment at the small service bar at the back of the restaurant. We all took bread: great globs of butter with the baguette for me, but without for Bud and CeeCee; I smiled when I saw the glee on Charles's face as he helped himself to a large wedge of coconut bread and slathered it with the coconut cream Annette had also delivered to our table.

Sighing with satisfaction after the first bite, the man leaned back and said, "So much better than *brioche*, and the chef has made an excellent coconut cream. These flavors take me back to my youth."

CeeCee tutted. "All that is bad for you, Papa, you know that."

"Not when it's just once in a while, child."

With our drinks in front of us, breads to nibble, and Annette back in the kitchen, I dared to say, "It's been our pleasure to meet both you and your daughter, Charles – not that the circumstances are ideal, of course – but what meant even more to me was that CeeCee dropped her mask and allowed me to meet the real person under there. You must be incredibly proud to have such a savvy, successful daughter."

I wondered if Ducasse would bite.

He did.

He roared with laughter. "CeeCee allowed you to see that she's got more brains than looks? You're honored, Cait. That's not something a lot of people get to experience – though many feel the truth of it, while not understanding why such success flows toward her. I am, indeed, proud of her. She is very much like her mother, having both an excellent brain, and a stunning physical presence. Francine, too, was always proud of her daughter, and would not have been at all surprised to see what a wonderful young woman she has become."

Bud asked, "You're a widower, Charles?" Charles nodded. "It's a difficult path to tread, as I know myself. I hope that one day you find someone who will make you as happy as Cait has allowed me to be."

"Papa's far too fond of playing the field to ever get trapped into marriage again, aren't you, Papa?" CeeCee placed a sliver of bread into her mouth.

I wondered why a young woman whose fiancé had just died was referring to marriage in such a way. I said, "But you were planning to marry Vaiarii, CeeCee. Surely you didn't see that as a 'trap'?"

CeeCee took a sip of her daquiri. "Of course not – it wouldn't have been a trap for us. But Papa always calls it that, don't you? Maman was the only one for him, isn't that right, Papa?"

Charles looked at Bud. "My wife Francine, CeeCee's mother, died six years ago, but the wounds have not healed. They might never heal. I have come to terms with this. But having a daughter to raise, when you are a man alone, is difficult. Francine had time to help me, and our child, to prepare for us having to continue without her. That was a blessing." He raised his glass toward his daughter. "But CeeCee had to become mature beyond her years. At sixteen she took on the responsibilities of overseeing our three homes, and staff. We had all agreed this would be a good thing for her to do. When she chose to leave school at eighteen and not go to university, I accepted she would be better equipped for the future by continuing with her own business ideas rather than having her creativity stifled by a system of education that is organized to produce people who all think the same way as each other. And her success means that her mother and I were correct; CeeCee just needed the tools, and the confidence, to be able to be her true self. When she turned twenty-one last year, she was already a wealthy woman in her own right."

So CeeCee Ducasse was only twenty-two? No wonder she looked so youthful without all that make-up...and no wonder she wore it; people might not take such a young-looking "influencer" as seriously as one who appeared to be a little more experienced.

I decided to try to dig deeper. "Your daughter might be wealthy, but we all know that the persona she adopts on camera isn't real. CeeCee – how did that work with Vaiarii? Did he get engaged to the real you, or the fake one?"

CeeCee sipped her drink. "Both. But we're all more than one person, aren't we? You're a psychologist, you know that. And Bud's been a cop, so he knows that too. Vaiarii was...complicated. Everyone is."

"He'd been acting a bit differently, in public, over the past few months," I added. "Do you know why that was? Any reasons for his altered behavior?"

CeeCee's sharp glance told me she knew what I was talking about. "He'd become a bit wrapped up in…things. His mother isn't well, you see. I talked to him about it, of course, and offered to help. Papa and I have been through it all. But Vaiarii didn't want our help. Said he was just fine. But…well, yes, he was drinking more. And he lost his car deal, which was a shame. It was a nice car."

"CeeCee," chastised her father. "He drove his car when he was drunk. Much worse could have happened than that little bump into a tree. He could have hurt someone, or himself, or worse."

"He's dead anyway, Papa."

CeeCee's tone and affect was so completely different now that she wasn't being the "public CeeCee" that I felt I was starting to get the measure of her somewhat. Like Annette, she'd built layers of protection around herself; her life was cushioned by money, and celebrity, so that differed, but the end result was the same – she was cocooned, and safe from the damage that was at her core.

"You say that so harshly, *mon ange*, as though it's…well, as though it was Vaiarii's fault that he is dead, somehow," said Charles. "I know you loved him, and you will miss him. It is acceptable to admit that, without it having to be a drama. As I do, with your mother's loss."

"Oh please, Papa, you surround yourself with young women – not quite as young as me, thank heavens – but that's how you insulate yourself from the real world. We all do it. Why wouldn't we? The real world is horrible. Full of people who are unpleasant to you…tell you that you can't do this, or that. When CeeCee Ducasse turns up somewhere she can do whatever she wants – everyone knows she can make or break their business."

I jumped in with: "Your father said that your online presence had strengthened because of what Troy brought to the table.

Was he a gifted videographer? Was it something he'd done a great deal of? You met him in New Zealand, is that right, Charles?"

Charles nodded, still slathering coconut cream onto bread. "I could see that CeeCee's online life was about to take off, and I'd been keeping my eyes and ears open for someone who could help her up her game when it came to editing her video content – adding in layers that are generally missing in the content of her competitors…an artistic edge, if you like – that sort of thing. I initially heard about Troy through a friend of a friend; they'd used his video-editing skills for some sort of corporate job and had been both surprised and impressed…they thought he was a gifted filmmaker. I liked the idea that he was a bit more mature, too; when you've been in a business for a while, you know a few tricks of the trade, and I reckoned that was what CeeCee needed – someone who'd got a good bit of experience under his belt, not another young person, like her. It's not bad for CeeCee to have a wise head to turn to when I'm not around – which is quite a lot of the time. Then I discovered that Troy was also a photographer – you know, real cameras, real film; he had his own studio at the same place he had his editing suite, and made large-scale prints. Troy sees the process of the development of film, and printmaking, as an art in its own right. I eventually met him at an exhibition in Auckland where a few of his pieces were on display. Even bought a couple, for the apartment we have in Nagasaki."

"That sounds exotic," said Bud.

"There's a large center for the pearl business there, and we export a lot of our stock to Japan. It's practical to have a little place of my own when I need to be there. Hotels get so…stale."

Just as Charles made this comment, Annette appeared with our food. She was being helped by Nadine. Both of them were wearing matching *pareos* that I'd not seen on them before, though they were similar to the one Mahana usually wore. I imagined instructions from Fleur about presenting a professional service front were at work.

"This looks and smells wonderful," said Charles as the food was presented to him. "Just the way I like my *fafa*. Hearty, and fragrant. Doesn't it remind you of the way Maman used to make it, CeeCee?"

CeeCee looked at her plate of what was an artful presentation of a relatively simple dish, with vivid green leaves draped across the golden chunks of shallow-fried chicken breast, all sitting on a bed of fluffy white rice, with the fragrance of the ginger and coconut sauce wafting up. My mouth was already watering at the sight and aroma of mine.

"It's a large portion," noted CeeCee, making that sound like a bad thing.

Though the heat of the day meant I'd have preferred something chilled rather than steaming, I dug in, but I didn't want to get distracted from my plan to also dig into the relationship between Vaiarii and CeeCee, so I managed to ask between mouthfuls, "Will Roimata find it difficult to manage, with her son gone? Are you and she close, CeeCee?" Given the abrasive nature of the interactions between the two women earlier in the day, I wondered how CeeCee would respond.

"Mahana is a strong woman. She'll be strong for Roimata as she has been strong for others before," said Charles, who was clearly enjoying his meal.

CeeCee was poking at her plate with her fork. "Mahana was wonderful when Maman died. She came to visit every day for weeks. It was a difficult time for us."

Now that CeeCee wasn't play-acting, I could spot the hurt in her eyes – and behind her words – and I was interested that neither she nor her father had answered my question about the relationship between her and her dead fiancé's mother.

I pressed with: "If it was Vaiarii who was the glue between you and Roimata, will you not see much of her from now on, then, CeeCee?"

The young woman finally put a tiny piece of chicken that she'd surgically removed from a chunk on her plate into her mouth – quite determined to not answer me, it seemed.

Her father responded, "Sometimes it is difficult for a mother to accept that her son has another woman in his life who is important to him. It was like this with Roimata. But she always was a woman who believed that her way was the only way."

Bud said, "Cait was telling me that you, Roimata, and Mahana were close, back in the day, but that Roimata's choice of a husband was not very popular."

Charles's steely smile spoke volumes. "Pai and Roimata never married. Vaiarii was born out of wedlock. I did not hold this against him, as many did. Pai never renounced his Muslim beliefs, and Roimata accepted this. However, despite the fact she raised Vaiarii as a good Catholic boy, he didn't attend a Catholic school. This…hurt Roimata, I believe."

Hoping this might prove a useful vein of inquiry, I asked, "In some of the online candid posts of Vaiarii, he seemed to be expressing his discomfort with the way he was being treated. He felt discriminated against. Was that because of his mixed race, his father's beliefs…or because he was illegitimate, maybe?"

"Troy didn't even know who his own father was, so I don't know why he even had to mention this to Vaiarii."

CeeCee's remark threw me a little, but I decided to take the path she'd offered. "Troy and Vaiarii didn't get on? Wasn't that awkward for you?"

CeeCee tilted her head. "Not really. Vaiarii was my fiancé; Troy is my employee."

"And now they've both suffered blows to the head, though one of them has survived," observed Bud.

CeeCee gave up any pretense of being interested in her food. "A blow to the head? Vaiarii? I didn't know that. I thought he'd drowned. Why didn't anyone tell me about that?" She stared at Bud, then me, then her father. "Did you know this, Papa?"

Before Charles had a chance to reply to his irate daughter, we were all startled by a massive clap of thunder. I had my back to the open end of the restaurant, so turned; the dazzling blue sky had been darkened by black, roiling clouds. There was a wall of rain approaching the lagoon from the direction of Moorea – which had disappeared.

"This is not an island storm, it's a sea storm," noted Charles. "This could last some time."

"Sonny's father said this would happen," noted Bud. He checked his watch. "That's…a bit spooky. It's arrived exactly when he said it would."

"Julius Puletua is a legend," replied Charles. "One of those people it's wise to never disagree with, because he is invariably right…about everything that is connected to nature."

A flash illuminated the restaurant, then there was a cracking sound, followed by a groaning noise, and an almighty crash. The smell of burning filled the air. All four of us pushed back from the table, immediately wary.

Bud rose. "Stay here – I'm going to check what's happened."

He moved quickly to the front of the restaurant, then disappeared outside, around the corner. We heard raised voices – Bud and Henri – then Bud reappeared. "We should be okay here. That lightning hit a palm tree, which splintered at the top, then came down onto the corner of the reception area. No one's been hurt, but a section of the roof structure's been hit. Henri's using a fire extinguisher to make sure there are no sparks left and, of course, the rain's on its way."

As Bud retook his seat, I observed, "Poor Henri and Fleur. Haven't they had enough misfortune already?" It was out of my mouth before I could stop it. I mentally kicked myself, and rapidly added, "Not that Vaiarii's death is a mere misfortune – it's a tragedy for all those of you who loved him."

"Vaiarii's death is both a tragedy and a mystery, Cait," said Charles heavily, pushing away his half-eaten meal. "I hope this detective they're sending can sort it all out, because there's no way that Vaiarii should have drowned. Not him. And not here. Doesn't anyone know what he was doing here?"

Bud answered, "Everyone who was here when Cait found the body said they hadn't invited him. No car. No boat. No idea how he got here, or why."

"He could have swum here," said CeeCee.

"From Papeete?" I was surprised. "That would be an incredibly long way to swim."

CeeCee smiled sadly. "If you'd ever seen him swim, you'd know what I mean. Vaiarii Teriimana made swimming look as easy as walking is, to you or me. He moved through the water as though it were there to help propel him forward. It was an enthralling sight. Then he'd disappear beneath the surface, only to reappear so much further away than you could imagine. And he could do that for hours. Never even seemed to be out of breath when he walked up onto the beach afterwards."

Charles reached for his daughter's hand. "He was an incredible young man, you're right…and blessed with a unique skill set. If only he'd continued diving for natural pearls, he might have made some more significant finds in his career, not just that one pearl that lit up the industry some years ago."

A kaleidoscope shifted in my head, and I could see possible links between several of the elements that had come to my attention since I'd found Vaiarii's body. But…I needed more information before any of it would make sense.

I was just about to ask more about the relationship between Vaiarii and Troy, when Fleur entered the restaurant.

She looked frazzled. "I'm sorry to interrupt your lunch, but the weather's looking bad. Would you mind if Henri and Edouard closed the shutters? We don't want the place getting inundated by the rain."

Charles and Bud both rose and immediately offered to help.

"No, please, continue with your meal. They're attending to the little shutters over at the bar at the moment, and Eloise and Nadine are out on the beach grabbing anything that might fly away – Sonny volunteered to place all the beach umbrellas on their sides, too, because we don't want them to snap. Mahana and Annette have gone to the dock to make sure that everything's properly tied up."

"In that case, I insist we help here," said Bud firmly. "Tell us what we need to do, and we'll do it."

With Bud, Fleur, and Charles all working to close the shutters, I knew we'd be enclosed in a dark space within moments, so I wandered behind the restaurant's little service bar, where I'd seen Mahana turning on lights in the restaurant on previous occasions. I stared at the row of switches, but none were labelled. I flicked one, with no apparent result, then spotted that the ceiling fans were slowing, so flicked it back on again. I finally found the one that made the lights come on in the restaurant, just as the shutters were closed.

Although the restaurant was large, I felt…trapped. The noise as the rain slammed into the shutters was astonishing, and I knew that, from then on, any truly insightful table conversation would be difficult, because everyone would have to talk loudly to be heard over the tattoo of the storm's anger, and that wouldn't be conducive to speaking frankly.

Charles and Bud returned to the table, and Fleur quickly assessed that it was time to clear away our food. I thought it best to allow her to do what she wanted without offering to help. It was an awkward situation: were we now supposed to act like guests, or friends? If Charles and CeeCee hadn't been there the answer would have been simple – act like friends and pitch in. But with them in the mix? Hmm…

"Henri and I won't join you, after all, if you don't mind," announced Fleur upon her return, this time with a tray of desserts. She placed the bowls in front of us, and stood back, her eyes gleaming with pride. "Gelato Legrand. I hope you all enjoy it. If you do – please consider this: we would be happy to rename it Gelato Ducasse Pearls…because of how it looks."

The dessert was a work of art: Eloise had excelled herself. An almost completely spherical hard shell of dark chocolate – within which there were swirls of iridescent colours – made the dessert look as much like a giant Tahitian peacock pearl as it was possible for a dessert to be. A piece of gold foil topped the sphere, upon which the letters DP had been piped in dark chocolate.

Both CeeCee and her father seemed impressed – CeeCee less so, possibly, because she immediately hit the shell with her spoon and dug inside. I followed suit, and then lost myself for a moment in the sweet delight of creamy banana and coconut flavors, perfectly balanced by the bitter chocolate coating, and there was a hint of something that was familiar, but I couldn't put my finger on it for a moment. *Then I had it.* "Is there maple syrup in this?"

Fleur nodded excitedly. "Eloise used it as a nod to Henri and me being from Canada, but I don't think that should stop you from saying yes to it being named after you, if you like the dessert well enough, Charles, CeeCee."

Charles said, "It's quite delicious, isn't it, CeeCee? CeeCee has great experience when it comes to desserts; she has had a sweet tooth since she was a small child."

CeeCee's eyes were closed, and I could tell she was showing a genuine emotion as she smiled with complete contentment.

"It's a perfect dessert." CeeCee opened her eyes. "But call it Gelato C. Ducasse, with a CD on top of the gold foil. That would be better. It would sound too commercial, otherwise, and we wouldn't want that, would we? This way it would be personal."

Fleur beamed.

"Are you certain you won't join us?" Charles was almost pleading.

Fleur shook her head. "Henri wants to do what he can over at the reception area – clear up the worst of the mess before anything can fly about and do more damage – and I shall help him. But thank you."

Mahana's entrance drew our attention. "Roimata's gone. She's not in my rooms anymore. Has she come this way? I can't find her."

Hoping

Fleur immediately phoned everyone, and it seemed as though they all arrived at the restaurant at once. As soon as Sonny appeared we gave him our attention. Mahana explained that Roimata's car was still parked outside the reception building, and had escaped being damaged by any of the debris created by the collapse of the tree that had been hit by lightning; Mahana had checked that, and had let her friend know, then she'd headed to the dock to work with Annette to ensure that all the boats were safely tied up at the dock. When she'd returned to her rooms, where she'd left Roimata, her friend wasn't there.

Sonny asked everyone to sit down, so – for about the first time ever – the restaurant looked quite well attended. With the shutters closed, and the lights on, it even looked quite festive. It was a strange atmosphere.

"Roimata said nothing about an intention to go somewhere, or do…something?" Sonny sounded as though he were begging Mahana to come up with a useful insight.

Mahana replied desperately, "She was in pieces. She didn't say much about anything – she just cried. But, no, she didn't tell me she had a plan to go…anywhere."

Sonny asked the room in general, "Did anyone see Roimata? After the tree had fallen is the critical time. Anyone?" Everyone shrugged or shook their head.

Eloise said, "Nadine and I were on the beach – with you, Sonny, and none of us saw her."

Edouard said, "I was at the reception area with Henri, we were clearing as much debris as we could. We didn't see her, right, Henri?"

Henri shook his head. "Didn't see anything, except a great big mess."

"The four of us were here, and we didn't see her," offered Charles. "None of us saw her come in here, or even pass by – correct?" Bud and CeeCee shook their heads. He added, "I wouldn't have seen her even if she had passed, because I had my back to the open end of the restaurant, the same as Cait."

I was nodding my acceptance of the facts, when it dawned on me that Charles was wrong. I added, "No – after the tree had come down, Bud went outside to see what was happening – we all turned at that point. After that, Fleur came in, then you and Bud helped with the shutters…so you, Bud, and Fleur would have seen Roimata if she'd passed by then…until the shutters were closed."

Charles looked puzzled. "Well, it's much the same thing – I didn't see her. Did you, Bud?" Bud shook his head. "There you are."

"Madame Cait is correct, Monsieur Charles," said Sonny. "It is important to be accurate in our recollection of events."

Charles shrugged. "Very well. But we still didn't see her."

Charles Ducasse clearly liked to have the last word on a matter.

Sonny clarified, "So, no one saw Madame Roimata after Madame Mahana left her to go to the dock?" More head-shaking. "This is difficult. Madame Roimata is grieving her dead son. Tell me, is there somewhere here at the resort that meant something to Vaiarii Teriimana? Somewhere his mother might go because it had meant something to him?"

CeeCee answered, now in "public CeeCee mode". "Vaiarii visited here only once, Sonny. The place was unknown to him. Nowhere here meant anything to him. Roimata knew that, so there's no reason for her to go to any particular spot. Unless she's floating in the lagoon, of course, like my poor Vaiarii was."

As CeeCee's words hit home, the sense of dread among our group became palpable.

Sonny said, "I shall go."

Bud and Henri were on their feet.

"We'll come with you," said Henri, glancing toward Bud, who nodded. "You might need…help."

The rest of the group remained frozen in their seats. Beyond the shutters the rain was beating against the walls, and the palms cracked like whips as the wind toyed with them. I looked at Bud's feet, and was grateful he was wearing deck shoes, not his more casual flip-flops, which might have been dangerous in what were likely to be treacherously slippery conditions.

Henri announced, "It should be easy to see if Roimata is in the open lagoon, but we should check around, and underneath, the bungalows in case…" He didn't finish his sentence.

Fleur and I exchanged a worried glance as our husbands accompanied Sonny toward the bar, where Henri said the small shutters would offer a better way to get out than opening the large ones at the front of the restaurant.

I was desperate to know what was happening. I asked Fleur, "Is there no way we can keep an eye on them?"

"No windows in the restaurant – just one wide open end, and the view to the lagoon."

"There are windows in the kitchen," said Eloise, "though you won't see much from there – it's stuck between this place and the bar, so it doesn't have any sort of view at all, in any direction…just walls."

I hate not knowing what's happening and could feel my frustration building.

Seemingly out of the blue, CeeCee said loudly, "Did one of you kill my fiancé?"

Given the tension in the room at the time, CeeCee might just as well have dropped a stick of dynamite into a fireworks store: everyone went off at once.

I was fascinated.

CeeCee's father immediately reached out and patted his daughter's arm, quietly remonstrating with her, while she looked away haughtily, a wicked glint in her eye.

Edouard grabbed Annette, and told her to not get upset.

Fleur stood and patted at the air, trying to get everyone to calm down.

Nadine jumped up and started pacing, then shouted that CeeCee had no right to accuse Eloise of such a thing, while Eloise tried to get her to sit, and calm down.

"Don't shush me," snapped Nadine. "That horrible man attacked you. Why is everyone acting as though he was some sort of saint? He wasn't. Who knows how far he'd have gone if I hadn't arrived on the scene."

CeeCee shouted, "Don't be ridiculous. Vaiarii wasn't even slightly interested in her. He told me all about it."

Nadine snarled, "Bet he didn't. He grabbed Eloise's bum. Didn't tell you that, did he?"

CeeCee growled. "He told me that he blamed Eloise's father for signing his mother's death warrant. Did you know that your father-in-law oversaw the nuclear tests carried out here that poisoned so many families, Nadine? I can tell by your face that's news to you – so maybe ask your wife about it."

Everyone turned to stare at Eloise, including Nadine, who said, "That's not true, is it, Eloise?"

Eloise bounced a knee beneath the table. "He wasn't in charge. He was following orders. It was before I was born. He was posted here twice in his career, you see – once when the tests were above ground, once when they were underground. I'd been born by the time of his second deployment, and spent a couple of years in Papeete with my mother. You know about that, Nadine."

Nadine looked as though she'd been kicked in the gut. "But…but your dad, your mum…you…you never told me what he did here. Just that he was 'military'. We've never talked about it, I know, though your dad doesn't really talk about anything much. He…he didn't really do that nuclear testing, did he?"

Eloise rose. "No, 'he' didn't do it, the French government did. Like so many other governments did, the world over, in their own ways. He was just one of the people told to do his job, his duty. The army, the navy…they were the ones who had to enact what the government said. It wasn't his fault. I told Vaiarii that, but he wouldn't listen. He was shouting that my father was killing his mother and had also killed him. He was attacking me because of something my father had done, when my father had no choice."

Nadine looked confused. "Vaiarii didn't…he didn't really try to force himself on you? That wasn't why you screamed?"

Eloise shook her head, tears running down her face. "I was so shocked by what had happened…by what Vaiarii was saying – his anger was astonishing – and you made an assumption, and…and it just spiralled. Then it was too late for me to change what I'd said, so I just kept repeating it. I feel…awful about it, especially now that Vaiarii's dead."

Nadine was incandescent. "You lied? To me? To everyone. About a man attacking you, when he didn't? That's…" Nadine shook her head with disgust. The apples of her cheeks were puce.

Eloise took a deep breath. "Oh God, I've been a terrible person, I know, Nadine. Please forgive me." She looked around the room. "Please, all of you…I'm so sorry. I…I made a terrible mistake."

Nadine snapped, "A mistake?"

Eloise sagged. "No…worse than that. Oh my darling, I shouldn't have allowed you to believe that Vaiarii was being sexually aggressive…nor should I have elaborated, because then the whole thing took on a life of its own. And, yes, I do know how awful it is when women – straight, or gay – do this sort of thing, because it affects the way people react to truthful allegations. I know all of that…and yet…I did it. I've let so many people down. Poor Vaiarii himself, of course, but all of you too. You most of all, my darling. I'm so terribly sorry." She stared bleakly at her wife; Nadine's chin was quivering with a mixture of rage and sadness.

I knew I had no choice…I pounced. "Eloise – what exactly did Vaiarii say about your father killing his mother…and him?"

Eloise's glance was venomous as she wiped her tears. "There you go again, asking for exact wordings. What's so important about exactly what was said? It's the meaning that matters."

I smiled sweetly. "The words matter, Eloise, believe me."

Eloise tutted loudly. "He said…" She closed her eyes. "He told me he'd found out who my father was, and what he'd done, from a group of men at some club. I *think* he said, 'Your father's killing my mother and he's already killed me', which made no sense, because he was standing there in front of me saying it. And – before you ask, Cait – did I ever really tell him he was like all the island boys? Yes, I did, because I was just a little girl when they found out what my father did, out at Mururoa, and they were horrible to me back then and – judging by what Vaiarii told me they'd said – they were still blaming me, and picking on me now. Vaiarii was attacking me verbally when I said that he was just like them, then he flailed toward me. He didn't actually touch me. But he might have done at any moment. It was my terror that he would strike me that made me shout out, which brought you running, Nadine. And you…assumed what you assumed. And I…went along with that. Then – well, I couldn't say anything different, could I? So I stuck with the lie."

Nadine covered her face with her hands. "Oh Eloise."

Eloise whispered a guttural, "I'm so sorry."

My attention was drawn by the sound of labored breathing.

Annette was seething, that much was clear, and her husband was trying to keep her in her seat.

When she spoke, her voice trembled, but she didn't shout. "They've been busy reevaluating recently declassified reports into the testing, you know. Many lies were told, many truths hidden. I understand that your father had to follow the orders he was given, Eloise, but you need to understand how finding out all this about him must make us feel…those of us who've lost loved ones because of those tests. Those of us who truly fear for our own future health."

Charles said, "My poor Francine." He grabbed CeeCee's hand.

Eloise sobbed, "They lied to everyone, Annette. My own father is sick. He is…he is also dying. It wasn't just the people who lived here who were impacted, it was the people they sent here…the people they ordered to stay at their posts…they were poisoned, too."

Nadine sounded horrified. "Your father's got cancer? I didn't even know your father was sick. Why haven't you said anything?"

Eloise replied quietly, "He's begged me not to. He hates being pitied. Says he wouldn't be able to bear what he'd see in people's eyes when they look at him. He wanted to keep the information private, and Maman agreed."

"But I'm your *wife*," wailed Nadine. "I thought we told each other everything. We've always said we'll be open and honest with each other about *everything*. We've…we've only got each other…and the truth." She sounded completely desolate.

The shift in the atmosphere inside the restaurant was significant: the anguish of loss, and betrayal, sucking what little air there was out of the place.

I grappled with the enormity of the situation. Was French Polynesia really paradise? Yes, nowadays…but just beneath the gleaming surface, was a deeply embedded wound, that was still significantly impacting the people who'd seen it inflicted – and those who came after them, too.

I dared, "CeeCee, was Vaiarii sick?"

The young woman scoffed, "Even if you've only seen him online, you could tell by looking at him that he was as healthy as an ox."

Her father held her hand tightly. "My darling, cancer is invisible…even in those close to death. It's usually the treatment that makes a person look sick. Your mother? She never looked sick for one day, did she? She was always beautiful. Then she was tired for a few weeks, then she died. You remember that, right? Beautiful to the end. No treatment, you see. She didn't want any. That was her choice. She had so much cancer, in so many parts of her body, that the treatment would have been devastating. She didn't want that. She wanted to spend the time she had with us, being herself – a loving mother, and wife. I begged her to reconsider, for…too long. I hope you remember nothing of the fights we had, my dear child, nor the tears and the pleading. Eventually, I backed down. I came to realize that I was being selfish by asking her to fight it. We both knew that she would be extremely debilitated by the treatment, and that her extra time with us would be…very different from living a normal life. So, instead of maybe a year or two, much of which would have been spent in hospital, she had only a few months, with us, at home. I…I wish, even now, that she'd loved me enough to fight, and stay with me…with us."

CeeCee whispered, "Don't say that, Papa. She loved us so much that she chose to spend all of her time with us, and you loved her enough to let her go, on her terms…as much as was possible."

"It's a choice everyone must make for themselves," said Edouard quietly. "My mother chose the other way. She valued the extra time she had with her family, and we valued the extra time we had with her. Even so, it was hard for everyone…very hard. But in a different way."

"There is no right answer," said Eloise, "but Charles is correct; my father looks as he always did, just a little older, and more…tired isn't the right word, but he looks more wizened, and maybe even wise, when I talk to him on screen. He has made his choice."

CeeCee looked confused. "Why are you all saying this, as though my Vaiarii might have been sick? He wasn't. He'd have told me. We were *engaged*."

From my point of view, that belief on CeeCee's part didn't hold much water; I'm only too familiar with how many secrets people keep from their nearest and dearest, sometimes for what they believe are very good reasons.

CeeCee added sullenly, "Anyway, he wouldn't have been able to go back to his diving if he'd been sick." She glanced guiltily at her father.

Charles snapped, "What do you mean? He was diving again? Is he the one who's been selling those large, natural pearls? He's been hunting? You know how hard I've had to work to make sure that all the people we buy from are using sustainable methods of production and harvesting – divers shouldn't be ripping as many oysters out of the sea as they fancy…it's not good for anyone. Not for the markets, and not for the ecosystem. And you knew about this?"

"I couldn't stop him, Papa. He said it was something he had to do – to prove himself. Said he needed to do it while he could…oh! Do you think he meant…?"

"We'll talk about this later," snapped Charles. "No business talk in public."

I said, "I think it's a bit late for that, Charles. Are you saying that the man I found dead, yesterday morning, was involved in some sort of illicit pearl trading? That might be a motive for murder, don't you think?"

Fleur wailed, "Vaiarii wasn't murdered – he died, that's all. No one's been murdered here."

I replied evenly, "Troy was bashed over the head here, Fleur. I believed him to be dead when I first saw him, so I don't think it's too big a leap to believe that the person who hit him also thought they'd killed him. So…intended murder, here, in the case of Troy, at least. And, on that note, CeeCee – did Troy know about Vaiarii's pearl-diving excursions, by any chance?"

The young woman thrust forward her chin and held her head high, when she said, "He might have done."

Every micro-expression I could detect through her heavy make-up was telling me that Troy had known all about it, and that CeeCee knew that to be the case. But I didn't press the matter; I needed to do some research before I asked any more questions.

Sonny Puletua filled the door from the kitchen and announced, "We have located Roimata Teriimana. She is being helped to come here by Monsieur Bud and Monsieur Henri. We are all very wet." He looked down at his large body, as he dripped on the floor. "Are there towels?"

Mahana leaped up. "I can go to the stores, but…well, the towels would be wet before I got them back."

"Stuff them into one of the carts – they have lids that close," said Annette. "Don't bother, I'll do it." She stood, passed the dripping gendarme and disappeared.

Mahana hovered. "If only I could get to the beach towels – but the same thing applies…by the time I got them back here they'd be soaked."

Eloise stood. "I have a stock of cotton towels in the kitchen – you can start by using them, come with me, Sonny."

Mahana called, "Where was Roimata? Is she alright?"

Sonny nodded. "She was in the garden, praying."

"In this weather?" Mahana sounded as surprised as I felt.

Sonny replied, "She said the rain did not matter to her, that she wanted the anger of the storm to hear, and to swallow her own anger. So maybe she wasn't praying as much as berating."

He followed Eloise into the kitchen, and an uneasy silence befell our strange, but now diminished group, as we waited for Roimata's arrival.

Collaborating

When Bud and Henri accompanied Roimata into the restaurant, we all rose to greet them. Mahana fussed about with the tea towels and napkins Eloise had brought from the kitchen, then Annette arrived with a buggy full of bath sheets, so they could all dry themselves off, which was just as well, because there was a puddle at Henri's feet. He kicked off his deck shoes and Bud did the same – it was going to be more pleasant for them to be barefoot with dry feet, I reckoned. Both pairs of shoes were now black with the rain, rather than the navy they'd started out as, but I could see that Bud's were a fair bit bigger then Henri's so I grabbed his and dumped them beside the wall, out of the way, where they could drain off a bit.

Mahana was in tears, chiding Roimata in a loud whisper that she'd been worried about her, that we'd all feared for Roimata's safety. Roimata herself looked largely unconcerned, indeed, she seemed to be a great deal calmer than I'd seen her at any time since her arrival. She clearly didn't feel the need to apologize for having been the cause of such alarm.

Bud ambled across to me, giving his hair a final towelling off. I asked, "Was Roimata really praying in the garden when you found her?"

Bud shook his head, then ruffled his hands through his hair; it was a fair bit longer than he usually wore it, and I liked it: it made him look as though he truly lived the island life – which we had been doing. *Well, for a few weeks, anyway.*

"She said that was what she was doing. She appeared to be howling into the storm to be honest…raving, more than praying. Then she kinda crumpled when we found her – maybe she'd worn herself out? I don't know. Obviously she's soaked through, but then we all are. It's easing off a bit out there now, by the way. According to Sonny's father's predictions, the storm will have passed in another fifteen minutes, and I'm not going to bet against him…so it shouldn't be too long before we can open up those shutters and get some air into this place. This heat and humidity is wretched."

"As Charles said earlier, it's 'unbearable'. Though bear it we must – and at least we have the air conditioner in here. But keep clear of it – you don't want to get too cold, being as wet as you are."

"I dream of being cold, Cait. I swear I've forgotten how it feels."

I asked, "Did Roimata say anything that might be…useful? Or did Sonny?"

Bud glanced around, to make sure we couldn't be overheard. "He's a great guy, Cait – big heart, lovely personality. Obviously a family guy, and eager to be seen to do well at his job. There's a messaging system that's keeping him apprised of developments in the case – not all the ins and outs, but enough – and he let slip that a car's been found that belonged to Vaiarii. It was in a parking area beside a public beach about half a mile farther along the coast – away from Papeete. Located this morning, found all locked up. Phone in the glove box. Been there since first thing yesterday."

I mused, "So that might be what happened: Vaiarii drove there, then swam here. Given what CeeCee was saying, half a mile would be well within his ability in terms of swimming. But I keep coming back to why. I need a word with Roimata, but it doesn't look as though I'm going to get close to her any time soon; Mahana's all over her. Sonny didn't mention anything more about the fight he had to break up at that club, did he? The one Vaiarii was involved with?"

Bud shook his head. "Nothing. To be honest, we all had to shout to have any sort of conversation at all. He only mentioned the car thing because he got the message while we were out there. I was surprised he had a signal at all, given the weather."

"Bud, how approachable do you think Sonny is?"

"He's approachable alright, but I dare say a lot would depend upon what you approach him about. You want to winkle information out of him he might not want to share, right?"

I grinned and hugged my husband. "You know me too well. Could you tag team with me a bit? Try to help me out as a 'fellow officer', albeit retired?"

"You know I will. Want to try now, before the seasick detective arrives and blows any chance we might have of extricating confidential information?"

I grabbed Bud's hand, and headed toward Sonny. "Could we have a private word, please?" I used my sweetest smile, and even batted my eyelids – in a comedic way, of course – which at least made Sonny smile.

He pushed open the door to the kitchen, and said, "Welcome to my office." We all trooped in, and stood as far away from the door as possible, to allow for some privacy.

Before I had a chance to say anything, Sonny held up a massive hand. "Please, Madame Cait, Monsieur Bud – let me tell you that, since I met you yesterday, I have done my due diligence and I realize I find myself in the company of two impressive investigators. I have read about the case you became involved with in Australia, and I have also found your names mentioned in…situations where the police have eventually been involved in several other parts of the world too, including in the south of France."

Bud and I exchanged what I knew was a panicked glance.

Sonny added, "Do not be alarmed. This information is not widely available, but I have a background in computing – something I brought with me into this new career I have taken up – and I am sometimes able to find out things that others would not happen upon. I am good at making connections, though, of course, my responsibility is to keep the peace, and maintain safety and security for the people here on our island. But tell me, are you about to invite me to help you…make some connections?"

I wanted to kiss the man, but decided that an excited "Yes, please," would suffice.

Sonny beamed. "Excellent. But I can break no laws, you understand."

Bud patted Sonny on the arm – he couldn't reach his shoulder. "We'd never ask you to do that."

Sonny nodded graciously. "What do you want to know?"

Bud nodded at me, and I began. "The fight at the club that you had to break up – who was fighting with Vaiarii?"

Sonny shook his head. "I did not break up a fight. The fight had finished. I was asked to take Monsieur Vaiarii from the club and escort him home. He was drunk. He had a bloody nose. His knuckles were scraped, his clothes torn. I did not see a head wound, but Vaiarii had very thick, long hair, so it is possible it was there, but I could not spot it. The man who provides security for the club told me that Monsieur Vaiarii had been fighting with a tourist – which is why we were called. It's important for tourists to know they are safe. Of course. I know no more than this."

I was disappointed. "No description?"

"He said 'a tourist'. It was a man."

"So…white?"

Sonny shrugged. "Probably. Most tourists here are white."

"Would the security guard be likely to think of any white person at the club as a tourist? Even if they lived here? You know – if they were a resident on Tahiti?"

Sonny gave the matter some thought. "It's a small island, and many of us have been here for generations. We tend to know island people, or at least know of them – whatever ethnic mix they might be; we have a wide variety on this one small island, including, of course, many white residents. So, no, I think there must have been something about the man, other than him being white, that made the person I spoke to believe he was a tourist."

I asked, "Is there any way you could find out more details?"

Sonny looked surprised, then checked his watch. "I think maybe Hiroiti will be awake at this time of day. He is married to a cousin of mine. I have his number. This will be one family member chatting to another, of course."

Bud grinned. "The security guard is married to a cousin of yours? What a stroke of luck. Thank you."

Sonny bowed. "Not as much luck as you might think; I have almost one hundred cousins…people I know as cousins. Let me do this now. We do not know when our detective friend will arrive. I can at least help with this – since you think it is important." He stepped aside, dialled, then spoke fast and low in a mixture of Tahitian and French which I found dizzying.

Bud whispered, "You haven't cracked understanding Tahitian yet, have you…with that memory of yours?"

I replied, "I'm doing well with reading it, but I just can't catch the words when they're spoken. Mind you, maybe it's no surprise that I can read it, because it was a Welshman who first encoded the Tahitian language."

Bud's shoulders shook. "You're making that up."

"Am not. Bloke named John Davies – of course – from *Llanfihangel-yng-Ngwynfa* in Montgomeryshire, came to Tahiti as a Protestant missionary in 1797. Spent a lot of his time translating various religious texts into Tahitian. In fact, you could say he invented the Tahitian language as it's written today, because he had to come up with a set of vowels and consonants that he used to phonetically transcribe a language that, essentially, hadn't been written down before then. Even came up with a spelling book, a dictionary, and a grammar primer – which were what Tahitians used to learn to read and write from then on. Weird, isn't it?"

Bud shook his head. "Good grief, you Welsh get about a bit, don't you?"

I laughed. "The original influencers, us Welsh. We've managed to stick our fingers into all sorts of pies over the centuries. However – talking of pies – it wasn't a Welshman who invented the symbol for Pi, though a Welshman by the name of Robert Recorde did invent the equals sign, back in 1557."

"Really?"

"Really."

"I bet you've got a ton of bits of information like that tucked away in those memory banks of yours, right?" I nodded. Bud chuckled. "Well, if it's alright by you, you can keep them there."

I play-thumped him.

Sonny returned. "The man was short, weedy-looking, and sandy-haired. Not a young man, not an old one. Hiroiti marked him down as a tourist because he'd never seen him before. The man was gushing over Vaiarii and buying him drinks before they clashed. This also made Hiroiti think he was a tourist; many tourists gushed over Vaiarii, because of his photograph being everywhere on the island."

I asked, "How old is your cousin's husband?"

Sonny smiled. "Around forty."

"Thanks. And at what time would your cousin's husband usually start work at the club, Sonny?"

"I know this: he starts at midnight. Before that, there isn't much trouble. After that, people are coming from bars, so are screened at the doors. It is a new club. Not much trouble. Yet. Though that might change."

I said, "Thanks that helps. And one more thing: I don't know if you have any way to find out if Vaiarii Teriimana spent any money on medical bills, in Los Angeles, about five months ago, but that would be very helpful."

Sonny's considerable brow furrowed. "This is very specific information you are asking for, and highly confidential."

"So you wouldn't know?"

"I might have seen some paperwork on a desk before I left the office this morning. But…I couldn't say."

"So…you do know, but you can't tell me?"

Sonny said nothing.

I continued, "Okay – just tell me if I'm wrong: about five months ago, Vaiarii spent one very large sum of money, then several smaller ones, in Los Angeles, on his credit card or cards, and the payments were made to several different medical establishments – maybe clinics, or maybe hospitals."

Sonny said, "I think your wife is…unusually clever, Monsieur Bud, or else she has some secret powers."

Suspecting that was all I was going to get out of him, I thanked Sonny just as he gave his attention to his phone.

"Ah, the detective we have been expecting is close now. The weather is clearing – as my father said it would – and he will arrive in no more than thirty minutes. Have we made useful connections, Madame Cait…Monsieur Bud? I am not clear about how my talking to a family member, and not answering your questions, has…helped." He grinned.

Bud asked, "Do you have any suspicions about who might have harmed Troy Wilson, Sonny?"

Sonny pursed his lips. "Me? I am a lowly gendarme. I am no detective, Monsieur Bud. How could I possibly work out who might choose to do harm to this man? I have never even met him, though I have seen photographs of how he was found. I know nothing of him, except that he is Mademoiselle CeeCee's assistant and that he is from New Zealand. I have been told that he is not yet dead – which is good news. Now…maybe we should join the others, before people start to wonder why we have been in here, together, for so long."

I said, "You go on ahead. I just need a quick chat with my husband, Sonny."

The officer replied, "*Bon chance,*" and departed with a wave.

Bud said, "Okay – tell me what you're thinking."

I grinned. "In a nutshell, and referring to Vaiarii's death – who might have hated him enough to…somehow create the situation whereby I found him dead in our lagoon?"

"Do you want to do one of your list things? I know you must have one already in your head."

I grinned. "How well you know me, Husband. Shall I begin?" Bud nodded, so I did. "Right, first of all, we don't know how he died, so we'll have to work without method and means for now. So let's focus on potential motives…though, while it's a starting point, it really isn't the best way to begin, because we don't know what actions we're looking for a motive *for*. Pre-meditated murder? A violent altercation? A crime of opportunity?"

Bud nodded. "I know, you always used to say that when we were working an official case together, but – as then – I'll say this: it's all we have, so let's at least make a start."

We shared a smile, and I began. "Right…Annette: possibly Vaiarii was mixed up in her brother's death – that diving 'incident' Vaiarii was involved with years back could have been the 'accident' that involved her brother. He's also a sad reminder of the loss of her parents. Edouard: might he act to protect his beloved Annette from more hurt? Other than that, we're not aware he had any direct connection to the dead man. Did you get the impression that Edouard's love for his wife was such that he might act out of love for her, rather than for his own, unknown, reasons?"

Bud raked his hand through his hair. "I'm going to give you the only answer I can to that one, Cait: none of us know how far we'd go if we thought someone we loved was in danger of being hurt – be that physically or psychologically. Yes, I'd say that Edouard is devoted to Annette. The way he looks at her when we're in company with them speaks to that, I'd say. But, as for how far he'd go? I couldn't say."

"I know what you mean, and totally agree. Okay then, Eloise: Vaiarii angrily blamed her for his mother's illness, and clearly touched a very raw nerve for Eloise when it came to her father's involvement with the nuclear testing in the area. Might she feel strongly enough to want to shut him up…just one too many 'island boys' picking on her because of her family, and now she's big enough to do something about it? Then there's Nadine: first, we have to consider whether she knew the truth about Eloise's father, and might have acted to save her wife from hurt? Or – and I think this is more likely, because I don't think Nadine is good at camouflaging her true self – she knew nothing about the role Eloise's father had played, but really believed that Vaiarii had sexually threatened her wife, and wanted to attack back."

"I'd agree with you about Nadine," said Bud thoughtfully. "Her demeanor when Eloise told us about the work her father had done in this region was one that I'd judge as being truly astonished. An honest response – I don't think she knew."

I nodded, and continued. "Next, what about Mahana? She's obviously devoted to Roimata – so is there maybe something we haven't yet discovered that Vaiarii might have been doing that could have hurt his mother, and Mahana acted because of that? But…we have to balance that with how Mahana feels about CeeCee; would she hurt the girl that much? Or did she think that Vaiarii was a poor match for her? Then there's Roimata herself: the relationship between a mother and her child is one of the most complex…but I certainly haven't spotted any specific reason why Roimata might want to rid herself, or the world, of her son. Have you?"

Bud shook his head. "No, though the woman's…look, I know her son is dead, so she's grieving, but there's something else there, under the surface, that I can't figure out. Do you know what I mean?"

"I do, and I can't fathom it, either. She's lost her son – her only son – yes, but she's…she's utterly desolate about it. I have to fall back on my psychological insights here, Bud, because I don't have my own children, but her state of mind seems…beyond that which I've seen grieving parents present on other occasions. Though, of course, every individual is different." I sighed with frustration. "Anyhow, onto CeeCee. She says they were a happy couple, but maybe Vaiarii wasn't faithful, and – even if it's not what happened between him and Eloise – he might really have been more than a flirt, and CeeCee simply had enough of it. And then there's his return to pearl diving…might it be something to do with that? I know she's got pots of money, but when did that ever stop someone wanting more? Or Charles might have acted to save his daughter from a marriage he was against, or which he believed would make her unhappy."

Bud said, "And then, though I hate to say it, there's Henri and Fleur to consider."

"Indeed. Henri seems unimpressed by Vaiarii, though had nothing specific against him…though Vaiarii did flirt with Fleur. Might that have set Henri off? And as for Fleur herself? Do we think there might be…what, a potential fling there? Older woman dumped by young stud? Henri said she got fluttery when Vaiarii was flirting with her at the photo shoot. Might he have turned up here to offer himself to her, and she reacted badly? Or Henri did?"

Bud snorted. "I think you're clutching at straws when you're talking about Henri and Fleur that way. But don't forget Troy, if we're talking about Vaiarii's death: he's mousy, and white…it could have been him fighting with Vaiarii in Papeete, and we found that black pearl in the film cannister in his bungalow. Might he have been involved with Vaiarii's death…and then someone found out about that and bashed his head in this morning? That…could make sense."

"Fair enough. But…I feel we're missing something. Or a lot of somethings. Because we don't even know how Vaiarii died, which is really annoying. See…both Troy and Vaiarii were hit on the head, and we know what that did to Troy, but we have no idea what it did to Vaiarii – or do we need to use the dreaded 'C' word, and I don't mean 'cancer'."

"Coincidence?" Bud sounded suspicious. "Or an actual *modus operandi* for a killer? I can't see it, Cait."

"Me neither. But I also don't see a connection. Or else I see too many. It's all a tangle."

Bud hugged me. "Hey, let's get in there – we don't want to miss anything that might…help."

Rethinking

When we re-entered the restaurant, Sonny was doing his best to gain everyone's attention. He cleared his throat extremely loudly. "The detective assigned to the case will be arriving in approximately twenty minutes."

Fleur jumped up. "I'll just…um…tidy myself up before he gets here. He's bound to want to see us all."

Various people rose to also use the facilities, which wasn't something that had occurred to me; personally, I needed coffee, or something to pick me up. I'd hardly slept, the humidity was draining, and it had been a grinding day already. I asked Mahana if coffee might be available, and she took my suggestion as a good one and headed into the kitchen, followed by Eloise.

I whispered to Bud, "Let's see if we can get into the bar to be on our own for a bit. I don't want to miss the arrival of the man who's going to solve all this, but I do need to think. Even twenty minutes would help."

We passed through the kitchen, ignored Eloise and Mahana 'discussing' the coffee-making responsibilities, and headed into the bar from there. A good deal of rain had managed to wash underneath the shutters, and the front of the bar was quite wet. Bud suggested he open things up to allow the place to dry out, while I settled myself in a chair at a table, and began to organize my thoughts.

When the daylight finally streamed in, the air freshened a great deal, and I allowed myself to focus on what I knew…or didn't know. I'd decided it was time to use the technique I've found useful in the past – wakeful dreaming. By allowing my thoughts to flow freely, without me trying to interpret them, I find I'm able to see connections and understand relationships in ways that logical thinking doesn't allow. I knew I was safe because Bud was there — I have no idea what's going on around me when I do this — so allowed myself to become unfettered by reality…

I'm on a beach, but it's not the beach at the resort — this beach is made of millions of pearls, of all colors, and they're incredibly difficult to walk on, especially since they are being washed over all the time by a sea that's made of grapefruit juice, making the going sticky underfoot.

The first figure I see is Mahana, though she's got a tiny body and a giant head, and she's carrying a tray of *pain au chocolat* in each hand, which she throws toward me. They fly into my mouth, and I eat them until I can't breathe…but I still want more because they are so fresh and delicious and warm. Eventually, I can take no more, so I bat them away with my hands which are trailing bandages and pastry flakes fly everywhere. They're caught by CeeCee who is floating toward me plucking individual flakes from the air with her long, long fingernails, and she places them on her forked tongue, which she snaps back inside her mouth. When she lands on the pearly beach, she transforms into a snake, then slithers away from me, crying tears that turn into more pearls as she sheds them, until she is completely buried in pearls, and cannot move.

Then Vaiarii Teriimana emerges from the mounds of pearls beneath her — he is alive, and vibrant, except for one leg which isn't a leg at all, but a massive golden crucifix. However, he manages to move easily, and is trying to pull CeeCee the snake out of the pearls, but there's nothing for him to grip onto so he calls for help, and his mother arrives. I know it's Roimata, though it looks nothing like her — this person is no more than Vaiarii's age, and she is stunningly beautiful. Her strength helps her son to get the slithery CeeCee out of the mounding pearls, then they throw CeeCee toward me and she wraps herself around my throat and tries to strangle me. I call for help, but Vaiarii and Roimata have vanished, and it's Troy who comes to my aid. But he's a miniature version of himself, barely reaching my knees, so he can't help…however, he snips at CeeCee the snake with a massive pair of shears he's holding, and screams in a squeaky voice that people must come to see the reports that have been re-evaluated, which I know means I will be saved. I join in crying out with him, and it's Edouard and Annette who arrive. They are literally joined at the hip so have to move as one to be of any use, but they don't…they pull against each other, and I shout instructions about how they need to work as a team but they can't hear me, then Eloise arrives carrying a massive chef's knife and slices them apart…when they are carried away by a wind I didn't know was blowing, but appears from nowhere as billowing smoke and fire…then they are gone. Eloise waves the knife in the air, though it has become a glittering sword, and screams, "I've killed them all", and I see blood drip from the sword, before it dissolves and becomes a cloud of dust that consumes Eloise…who is now a weeping Nadine, fighting with the dust and making it swirl. I grab the dust and throw it at CeeCee, who is still wrapped around me, but she uncurls and envelops tiny Troy, who disappears completely, to be replaced by Charles who grows within his daughter's coils until he's so big she splits open and becomes more pearls…but these are massive and black and they split open too, and are full of…gelato which rains down upon me, drowning me in what is now a raging sea…where I find Vaiarii who is grinning – though his teeth are not white and pearly, but black, and his mouth is full of French pastries and now I am inside his mouth and eating…pearls that taste of grapefruit…and I know that I'm going to drown until I hear Fleur's voice telling me to be calm, that her brave husband will save me, and he does…appearing from within Vaiarii's innards sprinting toward me on tiny feet which are moving so fast that they become a blur, then we both shoot out of the mouth of what has become a giant fish arcing above the lagoon, that's shaped like a pair of flip-flops that are snapping and gnashing at us as we fly into the air...

"Cait, he's here – I heard a car arrive."

I opened my eyes. I felt a bit wobbly, as I often do after I've been "doing my thing".

Once I felt a bit better, I asked, "Bud – *exactly* what did Troy say to you when he was babbling?"

Bud stared at me. "You okay?" I nodded. "Right. Good. It's weird, seeing you there, but not there...you know what I mean. Okay, what did Troy say? 'Re-evaluate', 'reports', and 'scans'. I think that was it. Kept repeating those words. And he said 'millions'. Oh...do you think that's connected with the nuclear testing? Annette said there's been a recent re-evaluation of reports no longer classified as secret by the French government...could what he said be something to do with that? Scans could be scans for cancer? But why would that bother Troy so much that he used those critical moments to keep repeating those words? Do you think he had some reason to be worried about that, on his own behalf? Maybe he, like Eloise, was here on Tahiti many years ago, and he might have been affected himself? Or maybe his parents were here, like Eloise's father was? But...how's that linked to him getting bashed? Or to Vaiarii being dead? Even if we don't know how he died. I wonder if this guy's going to know that. If he stayed on for the autopsy, he must, I guess."

"Let's go and ask him, Bud, because that's absolutely critical information. And here, take a look at this, will you?"

I pulled out my phone, scrolled to one of the photos I'd taken of the tattoo that the Vaiarii had had removed from his leg, and used the pencil app. "See?"

Bud smiled warmly and hugged me. "Yes, it's the overall shape that means something, right? They weren't letters, after all. You've put it together, haven't you?"

"That totally depends on Vaiarii's cause of death, Bud. So, come on, let's go and play nice with Mister Detective."

Still hugging me, Bud said, "I have just three words for you, Wife."

I pulled back, to be able to see his face. "And what are those?"

"What three words do you think? I. Love. You."

I kissed my husband's cheek. "You've done it again, Bud – just the thing I needed to hear to push me over the edge. Thanks. I needed that. Right…I just have to check something on my phone, and – while I'm doing that – could you do me a favor, please? Then…let's go and grill a detective."

Accusing

When Bud and I entered the restaurant, neither of us was prepared for the sight that met our eyes. Well, I certainly wasn't…and the expression on my husband's face suggested that neither was he.

I'd expected to see everyone there, and everyone was. Some were sitting at tables, a couple were standing, there were drinks, coffee, and snacks dotted about the place, and Sonny Puletua was there – as imposing a figure as ever. What took me completely aback was the fact that Sonny was holding onto Henri Legrand, who was struggling.

The room was completely silent, every face agog with shock…then Fleur let out a wail that could have cracked glass. After that, everyone was shouting at once, and their venom was all being directed at a figure whose back was toward me. I assumed this was the almost-mythical detective who'd been originally sent to Tahiti from France, and had now arrived from Papeete, having had to drive around almost the entire island. The small man was wearing long cargo pants and a short-sleeved shirt, both either navy or black, and both completely soaked through. There was a puddle at his feet upon which were, rather surprisingly, a pair of sturdy hiking boots. The rain had stopped some time ago, so I judged he must have got wet through at some earlier point in the day. His hair was collar length and hung in dripping rats' tails. Even from behind he looked…morose.

"Is Sonny arresting Henri?" That was what it looked like to me, but I wanted to check before I said, or did, anything.

Bud shrugged. "I guess so…or maybe not? No cuffs. I thought the French used cuffs. I can't see you'd get very far trying to arrest people without them. Though, given Sonny's size, they might be superfluous."

The small man raised a hand, and everyone shut up, even Fleur, who stopped squealing. "Monsieur Legrand, you will come to headquarters with me. You have been informed of your rights. You have many questions to answer. Now you must all be quiet and allow us to depart, peacefully."

I said loudly, "I'm sorry we missed your arrival. We also missed hearing what Henri is suspected of doing."

The man spun around, and I was looking at a face that made me so vividly recall a day when I was looking for a book to read in Brynhyfryd library when I was ten years old that I could hear the librarian stamping a book at the counter. On that day, I managed to reach up to a volume titled *Goldilocks*, by Ed McBain. I'd been surprised to find it had nothing to do with three bears and a girl with an inability to realize that items in someone else's home were not hers to try out, then discard as not being up to snuff. Then it was ripped from my hands by a shocked librarian exclaiming that the book contained scenes and words I shouldn't be subjected to at my tender age. Later in life, I went on to read all the books featuring the character of Matthew Hope, whose law-firm partner Frank Summerville always said you could classify people's faces into two types: pigs or foxes. While I've learned to disagree with this view and now see it for what it was – a writerly device – the man staring at me across the restaurant looked more like an ageing fox than any human being I had ever seen: sharp features, graying, reddish, close-clipped hair and beard, and tiny teeth glittering in his mouth. The effect on me was electrifying.

"And you are?" Even his voice sounded like the sort of thing you'd expect to come from a sly old fox. It was…unnerving.

I beamed and bounced forward. "Professor Cait Morgan, University of Vancouver. Here on a break with my husband, Bud Anderson." I didn't use Bud's background to try to impress the detective – I felt it best to keep that quiet. "And you are?"

Beady eyes gleamed. "Allard." It appeared that he didn't think that his rank, or role, needed to be shared.

"Ah, Detective Allard, a pleasure," I said, my hand still stuck out in front of me, waiting for him to shake it. *He didn't.*

I continued with: "You've decided that Henri might be implicated in a crime?"

With a wary expression, and in nasal tones, Allard replied, "As I have just informed him. He is suspected of murder."

Fleur wailed, "Henri couldn't have killed Vaiarii Teriimana. He…he wasn't even here that morning. He was at the fish market. Ask any of the traders there – they'll tell you that they saw him. If he didn't get the fish yesterday morning at the market, where did it come from? You ate the fish for dinner last night, Cait…Bud. Tell him it was fresh. Henri couldn't have killed Vaiarii."

"Whether the fish you served these people last night was fresh or not, Madame Legrand, is of no importance, because where your husband was yesterday morning is of no importance. Your husband is not suspected of killing Monsieur Vaiarii Teriimana. He is suspected of killing Monsieur Troy Wilson."

CeeCee leaped from her chair. "Oh my God, no. Troy's dead? Why on earth didn't you tell us that? Did he say anything before he died? Did he send a message for me? Or…or for Vaiarii's mother?"

Allard looked puzzled. "You are CeeCee Ducasse – the fiancée of Monsieur Teriimana, yes?" CeeCee nodded. "Why are you so upset by the death of Monsieur Wilson?"

CeeCee sat down, hard. "Troy and I were very close. He worked for me. He was my right-hand man. I thought he might have…sent some sort of message for me, or maybe he wrote me a note. He'd have known how worried I was about him."

In flat tones, Allard said simply, "Monsieur Wilson did not regain consciousness. He said nothing. He wrote no notes."

CeeCee hit the table with her fist and buried her face in her hands. Charles put his arm around his daughter's shoulders. She didn't push him away.

As a ripple of shock ran around the restaurant, I saw Eloise and Nadine grab for each other, as did Annette and Edouard. Mahana and Roimata held hands until Roimata broke free and began crossing herself and mouthing words silently, while Fleur looked absolutely desolate, and Henri's pulsing temple told me he was doing all he could to not explode.

I knew I had to do…something…anything. I shouted, "CeeCee – did Vaiarii recently have a tattoo removed from his leg?"

Everyone looked at me, seeming to momentarily forget their shock at the news of Troy's death and Henri's arrest due to the strangeness of my question.

CeeCee looked bewildered. She nodded.

I barked, "Was it a tattoo of a cross…a crucifix?"

CeeCee nodded again. "He said that once his mother was diagnosed, he didn't want it any longer. He was angry. Very angry that his mother was sick."

"I shall not die of this cancer, CeeCee," said Roimata quietly. "My surgery was a success. They say I am doing well…that the cancer was found early, and is gone, Vaiarii knew this. Yes, I must take hormones for the rest of my life, but I will be well. I believe them when they tell me this."

CeeCee snarled, "Your illness upset Vaiarii a great deal. It…it changed him."

I asked, "Were you diagnosed with medullary thyroid cancer, Roimata?"

The woman looked puzzled. "How do you know this?"

"A colleague who teaches at my university has a wife who had the same disease. I read up about it at the time she was diagnosed, so know it's often the form of cancer found in those who've been overexposed to radioactivity. She had a thyroidectomy and is now enjoying her ninth year free of cancer."

Roimata nodded gracefully. "It was stage one for me. My prognosis is good. As I said, Vaiarii knew this. I knew about the tattoo removal, though, which is why I gave him my gold crucifix to wear. It was originally his father's; I had it made for him, and he always wore it, though he never was able to give up his own beliefs. It was the one single thing that he left behind when he went away. He placed it on the table in our small home, and left us, to go back to his sea life. Being here, on the land, with us was…too much for him. Vaiarii knew how very precious that crucifix was to me, because I never took it off my own neck until the day I gave it to him. He wore it for me, because he knew how much it meant to me, and I was grateful."

I said, "I'm glad they caught your disease early, and that you have such a good prognosis. I wish you luck with the hormone therapy – it took my friend's wife's body a while to become accustomed to it, and she hated the strong opioids she was prescribed after her surgery."

Roimata held her head high. "I look old now, my hair is thin, my skin is like rice paper, and I must take medication for the rest of my life. But I am alive, and I can cope with my pain. I put those horrible pills into my bedside drawer and took none of them. I am a strong woman."

Allard sneered, "Stop. These questions…these matters…are personal. They are not appropriate for this moment. Come, Puletua, we are leaving. Bring Monsieur Legrand to my car."

Henri looked up at Puletua and barked, "I didn't kill Troy Wilson, Sonny. You must know that. Why would I? How could I?"

Allard smiled. "This is for the investigation to discover. Which is why we must go."

I said, "Detective, do you really think that a retired Royal Canadian Mounted Police officer would commit murder at his own resort? That he would kill a man he'd met only twice? Why do you believe this to be the case? Are there no other suspects? Why Monsieur Legrand?"

Allard almost smiled. "We have evidence that Monsieur Legrand and Monsieur Wilson were previously acquainted, and that there was bad blood between them."

Henri fumed, "I met the man for the first time when he arrived here with CeeCee for that photo shoot a few weeks back, then he showed up again last night. The first time he was here, we hardly exchanged a word. Last night, much the same. He was a quiet man. I have no relationship with him at all, let alone one that would allow for bad blood."

I noticed a flick of Allard's tongue before he spoke: he couldn't wait to show us how clever he was. "You had a business relationship with him, Monsieur Legrand. Indeed, you denied him a significant amount of money when you turned down his offer to become one of your suppliers."

I was puzzled — as was Fleur who asked, "What did Troy Wilson want to supply us with?"

Even CeeCee piped up. "Troy worked for me — why would he be trying to do business with the Legrands?"

Allard spoke with confidence. "Photographs. He put in a bid to supply this resort with all its artwork, for the guest rooms, and so forth. You turned him down. The contract would have been for a great deal of money. Anyone would be angry about this. And then he comes here — twice — to take the opportunity to tell you how angry he is that you have not allowed his business to thrive. You are a large man, Monsieur Legrand, he was not. You took advantage of this when you two fought, and you hit him, maybe with the intent to kill him…this is what our investigation will ascertain."

I didn't take my eyes off Henri as Allard spoke, and I saw the horror creep across his face.

"What's he talking about, Henri?" Fleur's anguished voice rang out across the room.

Henri sagged. "He must be talking about the company I had a few conversations with – exchanged a few emails with – about supplying photographic prints for all the bungalows rather than those Gaugin prints. Remember? We looked into it together."

Fleur nodded, but still looked truly puzzled. "I remember. They were good photographs of places all over Tahiti, but we went with the Gaugins. But that was a studio in Papeete with the name of a person – the photographer, I assumed – but it was nothing like 'Troy Wilson'. It was…umm…"

Charles Ducasse asked, "Was it Grey Lynn?"

Henri and Fleur both exploded with: "Yes!"

Charles added, "That was, indeed, Troy Wilson's studio. Grey Lynn was the area of Auckland where he was raised. Hence the name. Troy was a photographer of some note. He had a small studio in Papeete, didn't he, CeeCee?" His daughter nodded. "Though I didn't know that he was using his downtime from working with CeeCee to have this sideline, I'm not surprised. His photographic art was his passion; his video editing paid the bills."

"As I said," hissed Allard, "Monsieur Legrand had a business relationship with the deceased, that went sour. Leading to friction, and, ultimately, to Monsieur Wilson's death."

A rumbling of dissent rolled around the restaurant, until it reached Fleur. "It was a few emails. There was no friction, just a polite: 'Thanks, but no thanks'. That was it. You can't think that my husband would kill someone because of that. You must be mad."

I wondered how the detective would react to such a disparaging remark.

I saw Allard's chin lift, then he replied with a cruel: "I have evidence of a relationship. Monsieur Wilson was a hot-headed man. A fight broke out. A death resulted."

"What do you mean, Troy was hot-headed?" This time it was Charles who sounded incredulous. "He was a quiet, somewhat timid man. My daughter ran rings around him, and he took it. I love her dearly, but when CeeCee wants something, she goes about getting it in a very forthright manner – she'll bark her instructions. Troy always did what was required of him. He was placid, patient, and highly talented. He didn't have a bit of temper in him. What evidence do you have to support your theory in that respect, Allard?"

Allard's lip curled. "Monsieur Wilson has been apprehended, twice, in Auckland, for having participated in brawls, usually in bars…or else just outside them."

CeeCee tutted loudly. "Troy got bashed by people dealing drugs. Quite often. He didn't like drugs – and if he saw that people were dealing, he'd point out that what they were doing was illegal…and dangerous. He got beaten up for his efforts more than once, and, on a couple of occasions, your lot hauled him in as though he'd been the troublemaker. Typical."

"This is not helpful," snapped Allard.

Fleur stood and shouted vehemently at the detective. "It's helpful if it proves that my husband had no reason to have a fight with Troy, and that Troy was unlikely to fight with him."

I said, "I think I might be able to help."

Allard swung his mocking gaze in my direction. "And how might you help, Madame Morgan?"

I replied coolly, "It's Professor Morgan, actually."

Allard's smile was steely. "And of what, exactly, are you a professor, Madame Morgan?"

"Criminal psychology."

His smile froze. "An interesting academic field."

I added, "I've often applied my learning in the real world."

Allard's eyes narrowed as he said unctuously, "And how exactly did you do that?"

Bud replied, "Professor Morgan was hired as a consultant by the integrated homicide squad in British Columbia."

"Ah, how nice. And this was because…?"

Bud spoke gravely, "Because as the person who had oversight of more than eighty officers focused solely on solving homicides, I knew that her expertise was second to none when it came to helping our investigations by profiling the victims of violent crime. Her insights allowed us to focus on *real* suspects more rapidly than we might otherwise have done, and allowed us to thereby use our resources more efficiently, and wisely. Though I retired four years ago, my experience is significant. I suggest you listen to what she has to say."

The expressions on the faces around the room made it clear that only Henri and Fleur had any idea about Bud's specific background. I was so proud of him in that moment.

Allard smarmed, "This is very interesting, but we are in a part of France, here, not Canada. And even if *Professor* Morgan has worked for you – her retired husband – in the past, it does not mean she has any insights into this case that might be useful."

I asked, "Did the autopsy on Vaiarii Teriimana show that he died of drowning? That he had sustained scraped knuckles and a slight head trauma several hours before his death? That he was suffering from cancer in several parts of his body, and that he had taken a large quantity of opioids not long prior to his death?"

Allard shot a venomous glance toward Puletua. "This is a confidential matter."

I said, "Don't blame Sonny, he didn't tell me anything. I surmised it, from what I have learned about Vaiarii Teriimana." I turned toward Roimata and added, "I'm so sorry, Roimata. It was bound to come out."

Roimata was dry-eyed but looking completely blank…empty. "I know. Though I had hoped it would not. My poor, poor boy. His death is my fault. It is a stain upon my soul that will never be erased."

Mahana drew back from her friend as though she'd been scalded. "What do you mean, Roimata? Are you saying that you killed your own son?"

Roimata gazed at us all in turn. "I did not. But I…I very much fear I created the hand that did."

Allard looked annoyed. "Stop it. This is none of anyone's business."

CeeCee leaped up. "It damn well is. Vaiarii was my fiancé. How dare you say that the way he died is none of my business. We were going to spend our lives together, have children together. Build a life…together. How dare you say this has nothing to do with me. It has everything to do with me. Vaiarii was my future…and you know how he died, and you weren't even going to tell me? But…Cait…what do you mean – cancer? Vaiarii wasn't sick; we talked about this before."

Charles put his hand on his daughter's arm, encouraging her to retake her seat. "We did, child, and remember what I said about your mother? Tell us everything, Allard – and remember that I am the one who had enough influence on this island to get that autopsy rushed through. Tell us how the young man who will now never become the father of my grandchildren died." CeeCee sat, and he hugged her close.

Allard appeared to weigh his options. "It is true that Monsieur Teriimana drowned, that he was under the influence of the many painkillers he had taken a little time before his death, as well as there being high levels of alcohol in his body, and the belief is that he took his own life. It is also true that signs of cancer were found in many parts of his body. The young man would not have had a long time to live even if he had not made this choice." Allard finally showed some compassion and nodded toward Roimata, then CeeCee. "I am sorry that this must be very difficult news for you to hear."

"It's even worse than knowing he's dead," said CeeCee flatly. "That he was dead was difficult to process. That he was riddled with cancer, and took his own life is…unbelievable. Well – not that he took his own life, but that he was that sick. He looked so…vibrant. Always."

Charles looked shocked. "Why are you not surprised that Vaiarii would take his own life? He was raised in the church."

CeeCee looked sheepishly toward Roimata. "When you and he went to the clinic, and they told you what was wrong with you, Vaiarii was devastated. After that, he really…well, I can't say he lost his faith, because we never really talked about it beforehand. But it was while he was on a trip to LA, around that time, that he got that tattoo of a crucifix removed. He was so angry after that…so sad, and angry. I know that when you had your surgery he was a little happier for a while, but then he got very stressed again and…oh…*that's* why he…oh, no…" I saw the light of realization in CeeCee's eyes, then she shut down again. "He never told me he was sick. I…I can't believe he felt he couldn't. Why didn't he want to tell me, Papa?" CeeCee dissolved – a sobbing child in her father's arms.

Nadine asked quietly, "Was that why he was so angry with you, Eloise, and your father?"

Allard's eyes slid toward the couple who were holding hands at a table. "Who are you, and why does this matter?"

Eloise sat upright. "I am the Legrands' chef, Eloise Tremblay-Martin."

"And I am their wellness treatment specialist, Nadine Tremblay-Martin."

Allard sneered, "And what do a cook, and a masseuse, have to offer that could be of any value in this matter?"

Eloise spoke with sad gravitas. "When Vaiarii was here for that photo shoot several weeks ago, he lashed out at me. He'd discovered that my father was one of the military personnel stationed here who took part in the nuclear trials. He blamed me for his mother's illness and – with the information you have just given us – I can now understand that he must have blamed me for what he must have known was his own impending death. Oh God…that poor young man. I…I had no idea."

Nadine stroked her wife's arm. "You couldn't have known. Please…please don't blame yourself, my darling."

Bud said, "None of us can be blamed for what our parents have done, Eloise – it's not our choice. Sometimes, it's not even theirs. But Vaiarii's anger toward you might explain why he chose to die here."

Henri shouted, "He drowned himself in our lagoon because he blamed Eloise's father for his own illness? That's…that's…"

"He was lashing out at the only target he could find," said Fleur quietly. "I…I see that, now."

"Well…it was the wrong target, and it's hurt a lot of the wrong people, that's all I can say," snapped Henri. He looked guiltily toward Roimata when he spoke, then added, "I'm sorry."

"Let me tell you a story," I said.

"There will be no 'stories'," shouted Allard.

"I have the *Procureur* on speed dial," said Charles in a threatening tone.

"Then make your little story fast," replied Allard acidly. "I want to be away before the sun goes down."

I didn't respond to him directly, instead I addressed the room. "I know that when a person is diagnosed with medullary thyroid cancer, it's recommended that the rest of their family is tested too, because it can be a hereditary cancer. I'm guessing that Vaiarii told you he wouldn't get tested – is that correct, Roimata?"

Roimata nodded. "I begged him, but he said he'd…he'd know in his heart if he was sick."

I continued, "This was about six months ago." I didn't want to get Sonny into trouble, so chose my next words carefully. "I can't be sure about this, Detective Allard, but if you check Vaiarii's financial records, you'll probably find a payment from him to a place in Los Angeles where he bought himself some pretty expensive, and comprehensive, medical imaging. This would be when he was there about five months ago, which is when I believe he discovered his own condition. It's when he got his crucifix tattoo removed, and it's the point in time when he decided that he needed to make a plan for his mother's future security…because it was also about then that he knew she'd have a future – right, Roimata?"

She nodded. "My surgery was almost immediate."

I continued, "So he knew his mother was safe, for now, but also knew he wouldn't be around to look after her in years to come – be those years healthy for her, or not. She was the woman to whom he owed everything, and with whom he had a close and enduring bond. And that's when he came up with the plan to go back to free diving for pearls, in areas where he'd dived as a boy, and where his father had dived before him. He told you about the fact that he was doing it, CeeCee, but I don't believe he told you why. However, he needed a helper – someone who could cover for him, if needs be, or who could lend a hand with the whole undertaking…and that's where Troy came in."

"Troy and Vaiarii weren't that close," said Charles, sounding puzzled. "That's right, isn't it, CeeCee? You told me there was some friction between them."

I could tell that CeeCee wasn't going to reply to her father's question, so jumped in with: "I'm sure it was a coincidence that Troy entered Vaiarii's life, through you and CeeCee, at just about the time that Vaiarii really needed someone he could trust. It's odd, but, sometimes, we human beings find it less difficult to share our darkest fears with a person we don't know well…we don't want to burden those we love with the weight of our worries. Obviously I can't say for sure, but maybe that's how it began. A few beers, a heart-to-heart…maybe discovering the common ground of Vaiarii's father having left him at a young age, and Troy never having known his own…then the genie is out of the bottle, and Troy knows about Vaiarii's health challenges, and his determination to set up his mother as best he can before he's out of the picture, and no longer there to earn an income to help keep her safe, and comfortable."

Annette asked, "Do you *know* that Vaiarii was diving for pearls again? He hadn't done that since my brother died."

I asked gently, "Was that about five years ago, Annette? And was Vaiarii involved with your brother's diving accident?"

Edouard grabbed his wife's hand. "This isn't something we need to talk about now."

Annette smiled sadly. "It's alright, my dear. First of all, I am sorry to hear that Vaiarii was sick. I…I didn't know. I feel guilty, now, that I didn't let him talk to me when he'd wanted to. Maybe I could have…well, maybe I couldn't have solved the problem, but talking about his illness might have gone some way to allowing him see a different…path. I didn't dislike the man, indeed, yes, Vaiarii was involved with my brother's accident; he saved him. You see, my brother Jean was older than Vaiarii, a much more experienced diver; he had been diving for many years. It is a sad truth that some free divers suffer because of their time beneath the surface. Vaiarii and Jean were underwater together, and Vaiarii brought my brother up, unconscious. The doctors told us, later, that Jean had suffered a stroke. Vaiarii saved his life in that moment, but…but poor Jean died when he had another stroke, some months later. It was a tragedy, and

Vaiarii said that pearls were not worth a life, so he never dived for them after that. If he had started again, it must have been for what he believed was a good reason."

CeeCee nodded. "I didn't know about your brother, Annette. Vaiarii told me he'd stopped diving because of an incident, but never explained more. But when he started again, he told me he found it…freeing. And, yes, he told me that Troy would go with him, sometimes. He said…oh dear…Vaiarii said he wasn't as young as he once was, that he liked to have someone reliable on the boat. Troy grew up around the water – he was just the right person for Vaiarii to depend upon. I travel such a lot, and I didn't always need Troy with me. Quite often my sponsors will only spring for a flight for one, or one room, so I would do my own recordings and send them back to Troy for him to edit and upload. And…yes, Troy and Vaiarii got on much better than I led you to believe, Papa. In fact, I know that Troy had been spending more and more of his free time over at Vaiarii's home, and even at yours, Roimata, isn't that right?"

Roimata nodded silently. She was crying again. Mahana's mouth formed a little "O" as she grabbed at her friend's hand. Roimata looked a little sheepish. *Which made perfect sense.*

Edouard asked, "Did Vaiarii actually find any pearls?"

Charles answered, "I know of half a dozen rare-sized natural examples that have popped up in the market recently. They've gone for large sums. Roimata – if Vaiarii left that money to you, you shouldn't have anything to worry about. They fetched about a million dollars."

A gasp ran around the room.

"What have these pearls to do with anything?" Allard sounded angry, but I didn't let him throw me off my stride.

I hit the ground running again. "CeeCee, you asked if Troy had said anything before he died, or sent a message for you. I think now's the time when you tell us all why you did that."

CeeCee had hardly any make-up left on her face; she'd cried off the false lashes, her lipstick had been erased when she'd been blowing her nose, and she looked younger by many years for it. Now she also looked unsure of herself – a unique peep into her psyche.

She stared at the table as she said, "I thought…Troy and Vaiarii said…oh alright then, why shouldn't I tell you all? Vaiarii said there were lots more pearls, that he'd put them somewhere safe until he could sell them, one at a time, so he wouldn't flood the market. I don't know how many there were, though I believe there were a good number – maybe dozens. Enough that he'd given one to Troy, who'd said he wanted to give it to someone very special, if she'd have him…though I haven't the faintest idea who she was because he wouldn't say. He was very secretive about it all. Maybe he was making it all up, I don't know. And I have one, too." CeeCee looked at her father. "Don't be cross, Papa – I know I can use any of our merchandise whenever I want, but it is rather wonderful to have my very own pearl. And it's quite beautiful. Not as stunning as my engagement ring, but almost. As for all the others? Troy knew where they were, but when I asked him about them – after Vaiarii had…died – he said that I didn't need to know, that the pearls were for Roimata, now, because Vaiarii was gone. He said he'd tell her. But he…obviously didn't. And now? Now we'll never know where they are. I'm so glad Vaiarii sold the ones he did, because now at least you'll have something, Roimata. Look, I know we haven't always got along really…warmly. But Vaiarii was a good man, and I truly loved him, and I know he did everything he could to be a good son, and he would have been a wonderful father for our children. Oh, God…why did he have to get sick? And then why did he choose to…?"

I turned to my husband and nodded. He passed me the film cannister I'd asked him to retrieve from beneath Troy's bed. I handed it to Charles. "We found this in Troy's bungalow. You're an expert – could you tell me the value of what's in that container, please?"

As Charles Ducasse rolled the massive black pearl onto his hand, everyone peered to try to see what he was holding. Having stared at it for a few seconds he held the pearl between his thumb and forefinger and lifted it up.

Nadine gasped, "Is that real?"

Eloise said, "That's the biggest pearl I've ever seen."

Edouard stared at Annette and grabbed her hand. He whispered, "I thought he was lying."

Annette nodded, her eyes wide. "Me too."

Fleur seemed…*bemused?*…while Henri and Sonny both stepped forward to get a better look. Only Mahana and Roimata completely ignored the jewel, while Allard feigned disinterest, but glanced at it out of the corner of his eye.

Charles said, "One, it is real. Two, it is an exceptionally large specimen. Three, it looks perfect, but I would need to examine it more closely to be sure that is how it would truly be assessed. Finally, I would say it would fetch approximately…well, it would depend on how many people wanted it, at auction, but it might go for as much as two or three hundred thousand. And, to be clear, I am speaking of US dollars, not French Polynesian francs. And you say that Troy had this?"

Bud nodded. "We found it in his room."

"It must be the one that Vaiarii gave him," said CeeCee.

I asked, "Edouard, Annette – did Troy tell you he had something like this?"

The couple shared an anguished glance. Annette spoke quietly, avoiding the gaze of the irritated Allard. "He did. After the incident when CeeCee burned her hands, when everyone went to bed, Troy came from his bungalow to the reception area and he was…well, skulking about there. I saw him. It was very late – or maybe I should say very early. It had been a strange day, and I was having trouble sleeping. He asked if I'd seen…"

I prompted, "Did he ask you if you had found a gold crucifix? Vaiarii's gold crucifix."

Annette nodded. "Exactly. He was desperate. He seemed certain that Vaiarii would have had it here with him when he…died…and said that he knew how very much Roimata would want it, because – after her son – it was the most precious thing in the world to her. I didn't really understand why that meant so much to him, but he was a nice man. He asked me if I could let him into the empty bungalows so he could search for it, but I didn't want to say yes. He said that he would give me a pearl big enough to set Edouard and me up for life if I helped him. I…I didn't believe him, but he was desperate so…"

I said, "So you took him into each of the bungalows so he could look for Vaiarii's missing crucifix, didn't you?"

Annette nodded. She looked at Fleur, her eyes full of tears. "I did. But I didn't believe what he said about the pearl, so I asked him for cash instead. Not much, just a little. Please don't fire us for this. Troy seemed very upset about the crucifix, and I stayed with him the entire time. He was very tidy when he searched, and we were very quiet."

Fleur nibbled her lip. "What you did was wrong, Annette, but I can understand why you did it. Let's say no more about it."

I pounced, "But we must, Fleur. You see, while I concede that Bud and I managed to sleep through all of the stealthy searching that Troy and Annette undertook – we had the doors closed and the air conditioning cranked up, it was such a humid night – I believe at least one person was woken by their sortie. That person probably saw a flashlight in the darkness, or heard doors opening and closing…and once they were alerted to the fact that Troy was hunting for something, they'd have known what it was…because they already had it."

Finally, Roimata's head came up. "Someone has my boy's crucifix? My Pai's crucifix. Vaiarii *was* wearing it when he died? Someone took it off him? Why would a person do such a thing? It is valuable only to me."

I noticed that even Allard's expression had shifted; he looked truly intrigued.

I said, "The night before he died, Vaiarii Teriimana went to a club in Papeete where he had a few drinks with a close friend. Troy. He was the small, weedy 'tourist' the security guard there saw with Vaiarii. Yes, CeeCee, I know that you and Troy were at the club that evening, but you both left early, and you stayed at home, whereas Troy returned. Vaiarii and Troy were having fun, drinking together, then they had a falling out…and Sonny here was the person who had to take Vaiarii home after a bit of a brawl, during which he sustained some superficial cuts and bruises, and a nasty bump on the head. Of course, I can't be sure, but I have to wonder if maybe Vaiarii was getting a little maudlin, and mentioned to Troy that he'd been thinking about ending his life. Anyway, after the fight, Sonny drove Vaiarii to his home at the apartment block where he and his mother lived. If Vaiarii made a will, I'm sure he'll have left it to you, Roimata. If he didn't, everything he owned will become yours anyway. But I'm pretty sure that Vaiarii didn't believe that would be enough of a cushion for his beloved mother…who he now knew would live a possibly long, and hopefully healthy, life – hence, the plan to gather the pearls."

CeeCee spoke quietly, and – this time – in her normal voice. "I can't believe that Vaiarii would have made the decision to end his life without…telling someone."

I said, "I believe he wanted his death to mean something, which is why he came here, CeeCee. I agree he was wrong to focus on you, Eloise, but that's what he did. He swam here from the beach where he'd parked his car – it wouldn't have been the first time he'd driven when he was drunk, and I suspect he was past caring, in any case. He brought the strong opioids that will no longer be found in his mother's apartment, then took them, and waited for them to have their effect. Psychologically speaking, I believe he came here to die for two reasons, though I'll admit that the first one is a bit of a leap on my part. Sonny, you told us how you and your father used to come to this lagoon when you were a child. You told us it was a secret place, for fathers and sons alone."

Sonny nodded. "We did. It was. Not that women were not welcome, but – sometimes – it is difficult for fathers and sons to be completely alone. This was our place."

"Do you think it might have been possible that Vaiarii and his father came here, too?"

Sonny smiled. "They would have been unusual if they did not. Especially given that Pai was Pai, and Vaiarii was Vaiarii – they both loved the water, and this place would have called to them, I believe."

"Do you know if they ever came here together, Roimata?" I had to ask.

The poor woman managed a shrug. "I do not know. They certainly spent a great deal of time with Pai passing on all his knowledge of the sea to Vaiarii. I know they had a special place to do that, but I do not know if it was…here…where he died. But, yes, that would make sense."

I allowed a moment for the room to take in the idea, then said, "So, that would be my first point – that Vaiarii came here because of happy memories of times with his father in the lagoon. However, I also believe that – however unfairly – he would have made an effort to let you know, Eloise, that his death should be laid at your door…literally…because of your father's role with the nuclear testing which Vaiarii saw as having signed his death warrant. However, he didn't know where you lived, but he did know where you worked, so I believe that he would have placed his crucifix somewhere in your kitchen. Now, the only way into the kitchen, when the bar and restaurant are closed up, is to open at least one shutter to gain entrance…and the easiest shutters to open are the small ones at the bar, not the massive ones at the restaurant. He'd have needed light, so turned on the lights at the bar. They were still on the next morning. Then he left his crucifix and his flip-flops in the kitchen."

Allard couldn't contain himself. "This is ridiculous. Flip-flops?"

Charles tapped his phone, which was on the table in front of him, and glared at the detective. Allard did his best to contain his obvious displeasure.

I continued, "Vaiarii's father was a *Bajau Darat*. When they dive, they use wooden hand paddles to help them swim. When Bud and I were in Australia recently, I saw quite a few people use their flip-flops – or thongs as they call them there – as hand paddles, when they swim. They give the swimmer a bit of extra propulsion, and there's the added advantage that – whenever the swimmer choses to leave the water – they have their shoes with them. And, yes – Vaiarii's flip-flops are still here, as is his crucifix. Aren't they, Fleur?"

Everyone turned to stare at Fleur, who, in turn, was staring at her husband, who was still being held by Sonny.

Fleur spoke in a flat monotone. "Sonny, please let go of Henri's arms. He's not going anywhere."

Sonny did – without even checking with Allard if he should.

Fleur gazed at her husband with a tired smile, then said, "I went to the kitchen yesterday morning – dear God, was it only yesterday morning? – to bake the *chocolatines*, and I found the crucifix and the flip-flops in the kitchen. Of course, I had no idea what they meant, so I ignored them and got the baking done, then went through the bar to open up the shutters for the day. I noticed that the lights were on, and meant to turn them off…but as soon as I opened the shutters, that's when I saw the body. You all need to know that the first thing I did was to run to the lagoon to try to save whoever it was. I waded in and saw that it was Vaiarii but…but he was dead. I hate myself for having done it, and hate myself even more for saying it now but, honestly, I panicked. It was as though my brain just switched off. I literally couldn't think of anything other than all the ways in which a drowning could be bad for you, Henri. Bad for the resort. I still couldn't work out exactly what the flip-flops and crucifix meant, but I could only imagine that they belonged to Vaiarii, and that he'd *meant* to leave them in our kitchen…but I couldn't make sense of any of it. I couldn't help Vaiarii, but I could help you, Henri. I could help us. I had to do at least that much. I knew people would be arriving at any moment, so I just scooped everything up and ran back to our apartment. I had to get myself changed – I was soaked through, and covered in sand, of course – and when I'd done that, I had a bit of a think about things. I was terribly shaken, Henri, my darling. All I could imagine was that Vaiarii had gone into the kitchen and had left those things there on purpose…and I thought he'd done it because they would tell everyone that he meant to be where he was. That he'd meant to die where he had died. And I knew that would look dreadful for the resort. This place is everything you've ever dreamed of, Henri – I couldn't let all that be undermined. Then Mahana texted me to tell me what had happened and I knew I had to make decisions, so I…I did what I thought was best, Henri. I put the crucifix around my neck, where it would be safe, but hidden under my top, and I stuffed the flip-flops under the sofa in our place, meaning to slice them up and dispose of them in the recycling bin later on, when I had time. You have to understand…I thought that if people believed it was an accidental death – that he was in our lagoon by chance

– it wouldn't look as bad for us as if he'd *meant* to die here for some reason. That would seem…personal, and the blame would fall on us. An accident isn't personal."

Fleur looked at me. "You saw the flip-flops when you were in our apartment, didn't you, Cait?" I nodded. "I meant to get rid of them, like I said, but…well, I just couldn't think fast enough in the morning. I only had moments to calm myself down and respond to Mahana's text. I knew Henri had left a couple of hours earlier – before it was light; he wouldn't have seen the body in the lagoon, because he'd have simply left our apartment and got straight into the truck to drive to Papeete. I was the only person who knew anything about it. But…but how did you know about the crucifix, Cait?"

"When it was mentioned earlier today, you made a reflexive movement toward your chest, then crossed yourself. I didn't think too much of it at the time, but – later – that reaction took on a new significance, especially when I recalled that you were the person who was always first to enter the kitchen, to bake the pastries for your staff. Anyone seeing the lagoon that morning would have seen Vaiarii's body, and you'd have been there before even me."

Henri shouted, "But Fleur did nothing wrong. Except that maybe she shouldn't have kept the crucifix. I'm sorry, Roimata – I understand how much it must mean to you, but now you can have it. Give it to her, Fleur."

I said, "Just a moment, Henri. That crucifix has even more significance than you think: Troy wanted it, and went looking for it, because he knew how very much it meant to Roimata. And I believe that Roimata herself meant a great deal to him. He's been spending a lot of time at the Teriimana apartments, and I believe that Roimata has recently been receiving the attention of a new man in her life…giving her more hope for her future happiness – something her friend Mahana has noticed. Thinking about how Troy acted when he was with CeeCee – and, by the sounds of it, with Vaiarii, too – he was adopting what I might call a 'paternalistic stance'. Maybe he had some hope of, one day, offering his heart, and a rather large pearl, to you, Roimata…so Vaiarii and his wife would be, truly, his family too."

Everyone looked toward Roimata, and Mahana gave her a bit of space as she turned to her friend. "Is this true, Roimata?"

The grieving woman nodded, teary-eyed. "It is. I…I liked Troy very much. He was, indeed, a gentle man. And I think that, maybe, I even loved him. So, yes, maybe one day we'd have been together."

Mahana shook her head in disbelief. "I don't understand, Roimata. What were you thinking? With your illness…a man? Really?"

Roimata managed a smile. "Oh, my dear, dear Mahana…it is my illness that has shown me how precious life, and love, can really be. I loved a man once with such a passion that I was prepared to lose my family for him, my career too – but I never regretted it. Not even when he left me and my darling boy. I understood why he had to go…he was missing an entire part of himself. He had to get back to the sea. He gave us more than ten years. They were hard work, but wonderful. It's never been easy for me, but I knew true joy, because I followed my heart. But not all passion is the same…some smolders, and waits. Sometimes for too long. Listen to me, Mahana – seize joy, grab it when you can. Look at you – in love with a man for years who never knew, then he married someone else, so you buried yourself in work, in your career. Now here you are, with a new resort to open up – and I know you're excited that you'll be able to set up this place just the way you want it, which is wonderful for you, and I really do admire the way you've worked so hard to be the best you can be. But you're alone. And the man you've loved since you first met him is also alone, and has been for years…and he still has no clue how you feel about him. Seize joy, Mahana. Speak up for yourself. You deserve happiness, my dear. Like I once had. I had hoped I might have a version of it again; not a youthful passion, but something more wonderful in its own way…an understanding between two people who had grown to know themselves fully. But now…no, that will not be. My life was saved by the surgeons and the doctors, but my son, and the man I was starting to love, have both gone now, so there will be no light, or flavor, or color in my life for some time. Maybe forever. Never underestimate the importance of joy, Mahana. Never."

I said, "I'm so terribly sorry, Roimata. Your losses are truly devastating, I know. And I'm not sure that what I'm about to say will help you at all."

Roimata said, "It will. The truth is as important as joy, and also must never be taken for granted. It, too, must be hunted out, and seized."

I acknowledged her comment, then said, "Once Fleur knew that Troy was hunting for something, she must have guessed it was Vaiarii's crucifix, so she had to come up with some sort of plan that was better than just hiding it on her person." I turned to Fleur and said, "Why on earth didn't you just drop the crucifix somewhere where you could have 'found it' later on? I wish you had. But you didn't."

Henri growled, "Where are you going with this, Cait?"

Bud looked across the restaurant at his old comrade and said quietly, "Where she must, Henri. Where she must."

I continued, "This morning, when you saw Troy and he asked about the boat, Henri, you said he took some fruit with him, but declined pastries. Is that correct?"

Henri looked puzzled. "I did, because he did. What of it?"

"Did he and Fleur chat together, alone, for long?"

Henri shrugged. "No more than a couple of moments; I went to fetch fruit from the kitchen, while Fleur offered the *chocolatines,* then he left. He was very cheerful."

"Did you ask him to meet you in bungalow number one after he'd taken his photographs, using that boat, Fleur? And when you met there, did you ask him to stop looking for the crucifix? Did you even tell him what had really happened, and ask him to keep quiet about it? And did things…get out of hand?"

Fleur stared at Henri. Henri stared at Fleur.

I watched as Henri's eyes filled with hope, then anguish. He shouted, "What? No! What happened, Fleur?"

Fleur pulled down the mock-turtleneck of her top to reveal a red welt. "This happened. Troy and I were standing beside the bed, and I was offering him the crucifix, and I was explaining what had happened, and I was apologizing for having held onto it, and I was fiddling with the clasp…and Troy grabbed for it…or maybe he even meant to help me – I don't know now – but I couldn't help myself, I just lurched backward, trying to get away from him…but he was holding onto the chain by then – it's really heavy and thick – see? And when I pulled back, he didn't let go to start with…and he fell forward. He let go as he fell, but my neck was already like this. I didn't really pull him over…he just lost his balance as I stepped back, and he toppled forward and sideways and hit his head on the flower stone bowl that was on the bedside table…and I heard a dreadful cracking sound. He just…he crumpled onto the floor. It was as though he were a puppet, and someone had cut all his strings. He went right down. Just like that. I thought…I *believed* he was dead. He had no pulse. Wasn't breathing. I was convinced of it. Honestly – I truly believed he was gone. So…so I managed to roll him up onto the mattress and I…I left him there. Thinking about it now, I have no idea why I put him onto the bed. It just didn't seem right to leave him on the floor, I suppose. But, truly, I didn't think for one moment that he was still alive. I'd never have left him alone if I'd thought there was a chance for him. When you came in and told us all he wasn't dead, Cait, I couldn't believe it. When I tended to his wound, I hoped that he would survive – it didn't look as bad as it had…sounded. I hoped he'd be able to tell everyone that it was an accident. But…but he didn't. I…I'm so sorry, Henri. All I wanted was for everything to go well for us. I know how much this place means to you – we've sunk everything into it. We're in so much debt."

I said, "You weren't so unaware of your actions that you didn't take the time to try to cover them up, Fleur. That little stumble when you had bloody hands after tending to Troy's wound? How fortunate that you 'accidentally' smeared blood on the flower stone bowl and table."

Fleur whispered, "I know, that…that was bad of me. You're right, I did do that on purpose. But by then…well, I'd lied about the crucifix…and I had to keep lying. I said all that to Troy. Tried to explain to him. But Troy couldn't see that…all he wanted was this." She fiddled about at her neck and eventually unclipped the heavy gold chain, then flung the crucifix onto the table. "There. Is everyone happy now?"

Henri was weeping. "Happy? Oh Fleur…I'll never be happy again. That poor man, Troy…he might have lived…if only you'd dropped that crucifix in the garden, like Cait said…or at least if you'd called an ambulance when he got hit…oh my Fleur…"

Nadine whispered, "You…you really did this?"

Fleur rallied. "You defended your wife when you thought Vaiarii had attacked her. I was defending my husband, because Vaiarii had attacked him…in a different way. You lashed out at Vaiarii; I didn't even lash out at Troy…I was trying to get him to see my point of view. We each defended the person we love most in the world but…but for me, the outcome was different. But you have to believe me, Henri…it was an accident."

Allard stepped forward and cautioned Fleur; I noted that he'd waited to do it. Then he spoke forcefully, "Puletua, you will take Monsieur Legrand in your car, I shall bring Madame Legrand in mine. They will be questioned separately at headquarters. We will get to the truth of this matter." He glanced toward me and snapped, "The parlor games are over, *Professor* Morgan. Now the professionals will step in."

I wanted to say so much, but Bud placed his hand gently on my arm, so I literally bit my tongue.

As Sonny steered Henri toward the door – his massive arm enveloping the man's entire back – Henri wailed, "No!"

Allard himself took Fleur by the arm – too roughly, I felt.

Not one word was uttered by anyone as Allard and Fleur walked behind Sonny and Henri, heading to the car park. There wasn't a breath of wind. All I could hear was myself breathing.

Then Charles shouted, "I know some good lawyers. I'll send them to you in Papeete. Neither of you say anything…more. To anyone."

Henri looked over his shoulder and shouted back, "Thank you, Charles. Mahana – you're in charge."

Consoling

The mood of complete shock reigned for at least five minutes, which is a long time when you're in a room full of people who are doing a great deal of soul-searching.

I'd noticed Charles texting – presumably to the lawyers he'd mentioned – and I could sense that CeeCee had something on her mind. I could guess what it was.

Eventually, Charles put down his phone and said, "So Troy took the secret location of the rest of the pearls Vaiarii had found to his grave. If only he'd been able to tell someone…something."

"Or if he'd left a note…or a map with a great big 'X' on it, or something on his phone…just…anything," said CeeCee, looking frustrated.

I asked, "Is that what you were hoping to find when you rummaged through Troy's belongings in his bungalow? You slipped away from me and Mahana to 'use your bathroom' when we were searching the bungalows so you could try to find his phone, or a note, or a map…a clue?"

The fresh-faced young woman's neck flushed. "You knew I did that? How could you tell? His stuff was all in one big messy pile to start with, and that's how I left it."

I nodded. "Same size of pile, but different arrangement of 'stuff'. But let's not worry about that. You didn't find anything, did you?" CeeCee shook her head. I added, "Well, in that case, it's just as well that Troy managed to whisper three words to Bud, over and over again. What did he say to you, Bud?"

Everyone stared at Bud. "He kept repeating 're-evaluate', 'reports', and 'scans', and he mentioned 'millions', once, too. At least, that's what it sounded like to me."

CeeCee snapped, "What on earth does that mean?"

I replied, "At one point Bud suggested it might be a reference to the work that's been done recently to re-evaluate the reports about the nuclear testing that went on here – that Annette had referred to – and therefore, possibly, something to do with scans for cancer…and maybe millions that were, or weren't spent, in the right way. But something else that my husband said sent me to a website where I spent a little time earlier on that was very helpful. Did you know that there's a system in place whereby every three-square meters of the globe has a unique three word designation? The system is called 'What3Words'. I tried a lot of combinations of slight variations of the words that Bud told me Troy had managed to whisper to him. I found, for example, that 're-evaluate' didn't work, but that 'revalue' followed by 'reports' followed by 'scans' was a spot not far from Nagasaki, where I'd learned the Ducasse family has an apartment – and it's a hub for the pearl trade – but the specific location was in the sea, so I kept trying. I discovered that 'scans' followed by 'reports' followed by 'revalue' is in Chile…but that 'scans' followed by 'revalue' followed by 'reports' is a spot just outside Papeete. Three-square meters of land, a little way up a bank beside a narrow road that winds alongside a river. It's out past a big aggregate company's premises."

"I know this area. We used to live along that road," said Roimata quietly. "When Pai was still with us, we lived there – in a shack, on land that belonged to a farmer who was kind to us. It wasn't much, but we were…a family. Vaiarii was about seven back then…such a good little boy. It was at that time of his life that his father would take him to swim…maybe even here in the lagoon where he…died. He was so happy then, and carefree."

I said, "I suggest that's where you'll find Vaiarii's hidden pearls. And I'm going to guess that Vaiarii and Troy believed they'd be worth millions…of dollars, presumably. Again, because they were Vaiarii's, they'll be yours, now, Roimata."

Mahana whispered, "Oh, Roimata, I'm so pleased for you…in this, at least."

Everyone stared at Roimata. "These pearls would really be mine?" She sounded shocked. "They are…legal?"

We all turned to Charles, who shrugged. "No reason why not. Free diving for wild, natural pearls is…free diving for wild, natural pearls. There are some restrictions, but I think anyone would have a hard time preventing you from liquidating whatever pearls your son harvested from the sea, Roimata. You might be a very wealthy woman."

Roimata wailed, "I do not want money, I want my son. I want him to be alive. I want him to be healthy. And…and I want Troy to be alive, too."

I said, "I'm so sorry, Roimata – I know this isn't what you want…but think about this: what Vaiarii, and Troy, did for you could still do a great deal of good, for others. Why don't you have a chat with Annette; she can tell you about a support group she knows of for those facing the challenge of coming to terms with cancer in the family. I know that Henri always saw this resort as an investment; I dare say we'd all understand if maybe his appetite for it has dissolved, so – who knows – with a bit of persuasion, he might sell the entire place to you. You could run it as a retreat for locals who need it: a place of respite, or healing, or contemplation. You've got a background in accountancy, and I truly believe that Mahana has all the skills, and qualifications, needed to make a success of overseeing the place."

Mahana grabbed her friend's hand. "Yes, I would help. That would be a wonderful thing to do. I would feel as though, finally, I were doing something worthwhile."

Charles said, "For the memory of my beloved Francine, I could add some money to the pot, to help with running costs, especially if I knew that the operation was in your safe, caring hands, Mahana. Perhaps we could discuss it?"

Mahana smiled cautiously. "We shall see what we shall see, Charles." I noticed that Mahana's eyes were filling with tears as she spoke, whereas Charles seemed to be…considering something important. I wondered if it was a financial matter, or an emotional one.

Eloise's head popped up. "If you did that, I'd stay. And I'd take a cut in pay. It would be wonderful to have the chance to offer help to…people who are prepared to accept it."

Nadine grabbed her wife's hand, and the couple shared a tearful smile. Nadine turned her attention back to the group and stuck out her chin. "I'd stay too. I can offer so many more wellness treatments than Henri and Fleur thought would be appropriate for paying guests. It would be a great honor to play a part in such an undertaking."

Annette and Edouard exchanged a loving glance, and Edouard kissed his wife's hand. Annette said, "We'd stay, of course. If you'd have us. This could be a healing place for so many. And I know we both have some healing of our own left to do."

Mahana's voice had taken on a business-like edge when she added, "Maybe Roimata and I can discuss this, when the time is right. But, for now, Henri has put me in charge, so my responsibility is to operate this place as he and Fleur would have wanted…until he might decide otherwise. So, with that in mind, let's prepare for the delivery of all the potted plants. They said they'd be here before five; I'm going to check on that, and you should get going with dinner prep, Eloise."

Not for the first time, I was impressed by Mahana's ability to compartmentalize and get what needed to be done, done. But Roimata's earlier words about Mahana had burrowed into me, and I'd seen the way the no-nonsense manager had avoided looking at Charles when Roimata had been speaking about a passion that smolders over time; I wondered if Charles had ever had an inkling about how the young Mahana had felt about him, back in their college days, or about how she still yearned for him, all these years later. I took a moment to gauge how CeeCee's eyes were darting around the faces in the room, and I was pretty sure the young woman's significant astuteness would pick up on Mahana's feelings toward her father, now that there was at least a flicker of something out in the open, thanks to Roimata's rather pointed observations.

I said, "Look, it might not be for me to say, but I bet that, like me, Bud would be happy with something simple for dinner this evening. We're leaving in a few days – and I dare say that none of those days are going to feel 'normal' now. So, come on, it might be cathartic if we all shared a meal, don't you think? You and CeeCee, too, Charles."

There was general agreement voiced around the room, and everyone seemed to shake themselves. The energy shifted…and the grating gears of a large truck approaching reached our ears.

Mahana hugged her devastated friend with compassion, then bounced to her feet. "Incoming pot plants, everyone. Okay – all hands to the pumps: Annette, grab a housekeeping buggy, you too, Edouard. I'll get another, then we can unload and transport everything as quickly as possible. I'll do quality control as the plants come off the truck. Come along – there's no question that we've all got a great deal to process emotionally…but these plants won't wait for us. Let's get our work done, then we can all dine together. Roimata – you will be my guest tonight. Dinner for everyone, here in the restaurant, at seven – is that okay for the kitchen?"

"Indeed, it will be," replied Eloise. Nadine nodded too, then reached out to squeeze her wife's hand.

As everyone rose, and began to leave, Bud hugged me. He whispered, "Good job, Wife."

"You helped a great deal, Husband. As always." We kissed.

I said, "I think you'd better change out of those wet clothes, Bud. And I want to freshen up before dinner, too. As usual, my hair's a sweaty mess."

"As long as you promise to not sing that blessed song again in the shower when you're washing your hair."

I laughed. "Oi, I happen to have a lovely singing voice. To tell a Welshwoman anything else is close to heresy, you know." I winked. "But I don't think you'll be hearing that song again. I haven't the appetite for it that I've had for the past few weeks."

"Because of everything that's happened?" Bud held my hand as we headed toward our bungalow.

"Well, that…and I've been thinking about that musical in a different way this past couple of days. During the summer holidays when I was eight years old, a cinema in Swansea ran matinees celebrating the great cinematic musicals. Grandma Morgan took me to see *South Pacific* three times; I think she was secretly in love with Rossano Brazzi, because she constantly hummed 'Some Enchanted Evening' when she did the washing up. But the story's not what most people always seem to recall it as being: it's not all about happy talk, and there being nothing like a dame, and all that jollity…it's about war, of course, but it's also about how love, and hopes, can be challenged and dashed by the ugliness of racism, and death. It's a musical that appears shiny and bright on the outside, but there's a darkness at the heart of it. It's a sad story, rather like this one. Yes, there's a couple heading off into the sunset at the end of it…not a young couple, though – hopefully – a wise one, but there's a trail of bitterness and tears and broken dreams left behind. Like now."

Bud paused, and I turned to face him. He looked deep into my eyes. "You did what you had to do, Cait. We've both agreed, time and time again, that finding the truth – whatever that means – is what's important. There was nothing you could do but what you did. Fleur – Henri and Fleur – will have to face this. I believe they'll face it supporting each other. He loves her very much, you know. He's mentioned to me many times how he feels she rescued him from a life he felt was one where he was just going through the motions. Even admitted he'd only really opened up that bed and breakfast because it allowed him to meet people and enjoy their company."

I nodded. "And Fleur has told me how much she loves Henri. She, too, felt that he had helped her find a life she'd never have known without him by her side. I just wish this had all gone…differently for them both."

We walked on and finally entered our now-familiar room. I knew we'd be leaving soon, and – although I'd certainly miss some aspects of Tahiti – I was delighted that it wouldn't be too long before we'd get home.

"I might just put my feet up for a few minutes, Bud, and let you have the bathroom first. I just need to…stop thinking."

Bud hugged me. "Oh, Cait. I love you so very much. I can understand why people do things they'd never normally do to defend those they care deeply about. The law is the law, and you know I believe that upholding it is a worthwhile endeavor. And, let's be honest, we only even know each other because we both believe it's critical to do all we can to get justice for those who can no longer speak for themselves. But it must be…difficult to draw a line, in some circumstances."

I nodded. "I agree. But…let's hope we never have to find out just how hard it might be to not…go too far."

"You're not wrong, Wife."

"Now, go on, off you go, or I'll start singing something from the other film Grandma Morgan took me to see multiple times…a delightful confection about the rise of Naziism…*The Sound of Music*."

Bud chuckled. "That's my cue to leave. So long…farewell…"

Acknowledgements

This book began to wriggle about in my brain the first time I visited Tahiti: I was standing in a haberdashery store, trying to decide between two different patterns of fabric, when I overheard a group of women talking about their families, and the challenges they were facing. The women were sharing condolences for four deaths that had happened within the past few months. This conversation wasn't being whispered – though maybe the people speaking didn't imagine I could understand French, me looking so obviously like a tourist – so I didn't feel guilty for hearing what I did…but what they were talking about gave me pause. After that, I did a lot of "different" reading about Tahiti and its history, and that's influenced this book a great deal. In case you're one of those readers who come to this part of the book first, I won't say more, because I don't want to spoil the story for you…but if you've already finished the book, I dare say you can imagine what the women were talking about, as they selected their ribbons and curtain-headers that day in Papeete.

Having said that, it's taken several years for this tale to finally be woven into something that works as a whole; I always try to make each Cait Morgan Mystery a tale that could only take place exactly where it's set. Yes, that day I chose my fabric, I made the cushion covers upon my return home, and I've been fortunate to be able to return to Tahiti a few more times since that first visit, and to be able to view the place, and its wonderful people, with fresh eyes. Maybe, one day, I'll have the chance to go back again, and have another bottle of the thirst-quenching *Hinano* beer that I happily placed in Cait and Bud's hands.

Usually, an author's life is rather solitary…until it isn't, and it certainly takes more than just one person to allow a book to get out there, into the world. Thanks to my editor Anna Harrisson, and to my proof checker, Sue Vincent. When I tell you that we've all worked our hardest to make this the best possible version of this book I mean it sincerely – but, we're only human…so, if you spot anything that's managed to sneak past us (and things do…in every book I've ever written, or read) please let me know, and I'll do what I can to put it right. My email address is at my website.

I also want to thank Mum, who turned ninety just before this book was published; I was fortunate to be able to be with her and my wonderful sister in Wales so we could celebrate her milestone together. As always, my mother and sister are among my earliest readers, which is a wonderful feeling. And my love and thanks, as ever, to my husband, without whom I couldn't possibly keep working the way I do.

Then there are all the reviewers, bloggers, booksellers, and librarians – as well as all the readers who've written a review themselves – who might have helped you to discover this book. There are so many books available that finding the right one – with a story that transports and engages and entertains – sometimes feels like a miracle: I hope you enjoy/ed it, and thank you for taking the time to read it.

Cathy Ace, 2024

About the author

CATHY ACE was born and raised in Swansea, Wales, and migrated to British Columbia, Canada aged forty. She is the author of The Cait Morgan Mysteries, The WISE Enquiries Agency Mysteries, the standalone novel of psychological suspense, The Wrong Boy, and collections of short stories and novellas. As well as being passionate about writing crime fiction, she's also a keen gardener.

You can find out more about Cathy and all her works at her website: www.cathyace.com